DON PENDLETON'S
THE EXECUTIONER®
DEATH MERCHANTS

D0057813

A GOLD EAGLE BOOK FROM
WORLDWIDE®

TORONTO • NEW YORK • LONDON
AMSTERDAM • PARIS • SYDNEY • HAMBURG
STOCKHOLM • ATHENS • TOKYO • MILAN
MADRID • WARSAW • BUDAPEST • AUCKLAND

If you purchased this book without a cover you should be aware
that this book is stolen property. It was reported as "unsold and
destroyed" to the publisher, and neither the author nor the
publisher has received any payment for this "stripped book."

First edition April 2003
ISBN 0-373-64293-8

Special thanks and acknowledgment to
Tim Tresslar for his contribution to this work.

DEATH MERCHANTS

Copyright © 2003 by Worldwide Library.

All rights reserved. Except for use in any review, the
reproduction or utilization of this work in whole or in part
in any form by any electronic, mechanical or other means,
now known or hereafter invented, including xerography,
photocopying and recording, or in any information storage
or retrieval system, is forbidden without the written permission
of the publisher, Worldwide Library, 225 Duncan Mill Road,
Don Mills, Ontario, Canada M3B 3K9.

All characters in this book have no existence outside the
imagination of the author and have no relation whatsoever to
anyone bearing the same name or names. They are not even
distantly inspired by any individual known or unknown to the
author, and all incidents are pure invention.

® and TM are trademarks of the publisher. Trademarks indicated
with ® are registered in the United States Patent and Trademark
Office, the Canadian Trade Marks Office and in other countries.

Printed in U.S.A.

Let's make us medicines of our great revenge
To cure this deadly grief.

> —William Shakespeare,
> 1564–1616

We are all ready to be savage in some cause.
The difference between a good man and a bad one
is the choice of the cause.

> —William James,
> 1842–1910

My cause is just, as are my motives. I defend those
who can't defend themselves. I'll leave others to
judge whether I'm a good man.

> —Mack Bolan

To R.M.T., for everything.

Prologue

Orlando, Florida

"You think that chicken shit will show?"

"He'll show."

"What if he doesn't?"

"What if? We'll find another way in. We've got guns. Besides, he'll show."

"He damn well better."

With that, the squat man seated next to Hank Nickel turned and stared out the panel van's passenger window. He smoked a cigarette and tried to act relaxed, but fidgeted like a kid on the last day of school. Nickel smiled and shook his head, mystified by the guy's nervousness. If things went sour, it was Nickel's ass. The boss had told him as much. Having already screwed up once, this was his way back into good graces. The man planned to do it right.

Nickel threaded a customized sound suppressor onto the barrel of his SIG-Sauer pistol, jacked a 9 mm round into the chamber and waited for the delivery bay door to open. He was going to make this happen no matter what.

He had no other option.

SECURITY GUARD Dale Osbourne wheeled his Chevrolet Caprice around the parking lot of the Benjamin Davis Memorial Cancer Hospital, past the fountains and palm trees, and wished yet again that he were home rather than baby-sitting those on death's doorstep.

The hospital was a sterile, two-story oncology center in suburban Orlando. Medical journals lauded it as "pioneering," "cutting edge," "revolutionary." Osbourne and his fellow guards had dubbed it the "house of death." Patients came there for radical, last-ditch treatments meant to perform miracles. As often as not the miracles failed to materialize, or were too minor to make a difference, and cancer claimed another victim. Osbourne had seen it so many times he had started to joke about the constant stream of tragedies to anesthetize himself to their constant onslaught.

A mechanical hum filled the car as the guard rolled down his window and let the night surround him. He hoped the fresh air would revitalize him. He sucked down tepid coffee, turned the car down a driveway and mechanically followed it as it twisted behind the hospital.

Mindless doesn't begin to describe this gig, Osbourne thought. If this is what police work is all about, I need to go into plumbing.

He smiled as he imagined having that conversation with his wife. He had spent four semesters studying criminal justice at a local community college while working as an overnight security guard. Lisa was tolerant—barely—of sleeping alone five nights a week as long as she thought it was leading somewhere. If he quit college now, she might quit the marriage. He had vowed to make this career stick, land a good job that would allow her to stay home with their newborn baby.

He meant to keep the promise.

The Caprice rounded the corner and Osbourne saw a white panel van pull up, then back into the loading dock. Probably a laundry truck, but no one had told him about it. He grabbed the microphone from the security radio, raised it to his lips and depressed the call button.

"Two Nora One to base," he said. Osbourne was patrolling the sprawling campus as the north-sector unit.

"Two Nora One, go." It was Aaron Jackson, the shift supervisor.

"Aaron, are we expecting a delivery? Please say yes."

A pause. "No, Dale. You got something?"

"A van. Looks okay. Probably a last-minute delivery and someone forgot to tell us."

"They never tell us anything. You need me there?"

Osbourne detected a slight crack in Jackson's voice. He ignored it. The guy was always too high-strung for his own good.

"Negative. My guess is the administrative people decided we didn't need to know. Besides, the bay door's open. Someone let them in."

"Call if you need me."

"Clear," Osbourne said.

He hooked the hand microphone back to the radio. His breathing quickened and fear tickled inside his stomach as he approached the van. Osbourne assumed it was nothing, but he had learned enough in school to know every situation held at least an outside risk of danger. Despite his fear, though, Osbourne refused to ask for backup. He felt too silly doing that, knowing that odds were the late-night visitors were dropping off fresh sheets, medicines or food.

He pulled the Caprice parallel and ten feet away from the panel van, aimed his spotlight at the vehicle and flicked it on. The driver covered his eyes, but waved at Osbourne and smiled. The driver wore a gray uniform, the kind one would expect a delivery driver to wear.

"Hey," the driver said, "how 'bout killing the light?"

"Sorry," Osbourne said.

He didn't extinguish the light, but instead shifted its glare to the right to get it out of the driver's face. Osbourne opened the patrol car door, stepped onto the asphalt, shut the car door behind him and started toward the van. The driver's smile re-assured him somewhat. The 9 mm autoloader strapped to his side bolstered his sense of well-being even more.

A second man, also dressed in coveralls, sat in the passenger seat, smoking a cigarette and staring absently out his window. Osbourne greeted him, too, but the short man only grunted back and continued staring at nothing through the window.

"You guys making a delivery?"

"Pickup."

"Pickup? What are you picking up at this hour?"

"Got some controlled substances to get."

"You on the schedule?"

"Should be," the driver said. "I don't do schedules. I just drive a van. Pick up boxes. You know what I'm saying?"

"Sure," Osbourne said. "But I got a boss, too. Let me call him real quick. You know, double-check."

"Fine with me. I'll just smoke a cigarette with my buddy here."

The security guard smiled, turned on his heel and started back toward his car. The silenced SIG-Sauer coughed three times. The first Parabellum slug slammed into Osbourne's neck, ripped through his spinal cord and pitched him forward before exploding from the front of his throat. The second and third shots drilled into his back, hastening his fall to the ground.

The last two shots were window dressing. The first slug had snuffed out Dale Osbourne's life before he hit the ground.

"JESUS, HANK, you never said you were going to kill anyone," Aaron Jackson said.

Nickel had stepped from the van and stared at Jackson. The security chief had bypassed the alarms and cameras and opened the delivery bay door for Nickel and his crew. Nickel clutched the SIG-Sauer pistol in his right hand and pressed it tightly against his thigh. He put his face into that of the sweating guard.

"Why do you think we brought guns if we weren't going to kill anybody? You were supposed to make sure no one saw us. You didn't do it. Because you didn't do what you were supposed to, this guy saw my face. That means his death is on your head."

Jackson looked at the ground.

"I didn't know," he said, as if trying to convince himself.

Nickel shoved the mumbling guard out of the way. Judging by Jackson's reaction, Nickel figured he'd probably have to shoot him, too, before the night ended. It didn't matter. Once they got what they came for, Nickel and his men would never return, never be found out. Within six months, they would never have to hit another cancer hospital again. This was just a means to an end.

And it was going to be a damn profitable end; the boss had assured him that much.

Nickel walked to the back of the panel van and opened the door. Eight men dressed in black and armed with pistols and submachine guns sat inside.

"C'mon, get the hell out of there," he said, his voice just above a whisper. "Let's move. Someone get rid of that body. Everyone else come with me."

One of the black-suited men rolled the dead security guard onto his back, looped his arms underneath the man's arms and dragged him to his patrol car. Nickel knew he would drive the body somewhere on the grounds, dump it and be back in time for them to leave. He didn't care what they did with the corpse specifically. He just wanted it out of plain sight.

He stripped away his gray coveralls to reveal a black bodysuit similar to those worn by the other men. Grabbing his submachine gun, he motioned for the others to enter the delivery bay with him.

Nickel and the others had spent the past week memorizing the hospital's layout and drilling themselves on the mission. That greedy bastard Jackson had been only too happy to get hospital floor plans for them to study. Nickel knew the prize lay on the second floor.

He also knew he had to get it; there was no other option.

AT THAT HOUR, the service stairwell was empty and allowed the intruders to ascend undetected to the second floor. Poised on the landing next to the second-floor door, Nickel shut his eyes to recall the floor plan. Getting to the pharmacy from there would require walking down a ten-foot corridor, turning left onto the main hallway, then passing several rooms. They should be able to do that easily. Two other teams had pulled off similar ops in two other states within the past week without incident.

Hank Nickel's team wasn't going to be the one to screw up.

He opened his eyes, pushed open the door and stepped into the hallway. The small corridor housed a couple of offices, both empty. The men moved quietly down the corridor, weapons pointing forward. The next phase was the biggest challenge. They could expect to encounter people, which Nickel knew always put more variables into the mix. He shoved his worries into the back of his mind and kept going.

No excuses. This was going to go off flawlessly. Success was more than a point of pride with Nickel; it was a matter of life and death. The boss was still angry about a cocaine shipment seized by U.S. Customs agents the previous month. Nickel had been ten minutes late stopping at the locker at Orlando International Airport. Tardiness caused by a last-minute trip to a prostitute had cost the boss millions, which in turn nearly cost Nickel his life.

Nickel was living on borrowed time.

He hoped the ten boxes of Vitalife stolen this night would buy his way back into the boss's good graces.

With a series of hand signals, he indicated to his men that he would go first, flanked by two, then three more, then three more. The last man would stay behind. If by some chance everything went to hell, the guy would run to the van, kill Jackson and get out of there.

Nickel turned the corner, followed by the others. He wasn't surprised when he heard the first scream. It rose above the murmur of nurses' voices and in-room televisions. Nickel wasn't sure where it came from. By the time he looked at the nurses' station, two more of the women in blue scrubs were screaming at the armed men.

"Shut the fuck up," he ordered, pointing his weapon at the nurses, "and get on the floor."

An East Indian man in a white coat had stepped forward, holding up both hands to stop Nickel. His eyes were pleading.

"What do you want? These are sick people. Dying people. Why are you doing this?"

Nickel admired the doctor's bravery; he doubted whether he would react the same way were the roles reversed. He also knew he had to quell any grandstanding quick, before someone else got crazy, too. He shoved the sound suppressor into the guy's stomach.

"You're going to join the sick and dying if you don't get your ass on the floor," he snapped. "Understand?"

The doctor's eyes bulged and his lips moved wordlessly. He nodded, stepped back, dropped to his knees and did as he was told.

Nickel signaled four of the men to stay with the hostages. He headed toward the pharmacy with a couple more men in tow.

WHEN HIS WIFE had been diagnosed with ovarian cancer, Orlando police Detective Jon Sanchez figured life couldn't get worse. But, as the cancer continued to spread throughout Liz's body, and death neared, he knew his initial hopes were little more than a pipe dream.

Lying on the cancer ward floor, he wondered if he would live long enough to see things get better. Not that living was a great prize now that his wife was days from dying. But he wouldn't do anyone here any good dead.

He tried to snatch glimpses of the men whenever possible, gathering vague senses of height and build. All wore masks and carried weapons. Gloved hands would leave behind no fingerprints for his co-workers to pick up. He tried to notice mannerisms, accents, anything that might help later.

For an instant, he thought of the off-duty 9 mm pistol in his ankle holster, but nixed any notion of trying to take down these guys in a firefight. They would kill him and everyone around him before he cleared leather.

The best he could do was hang tight, let these guys do their business and pray things didn't get even more out of hand. Considering his track record the past six months, he didn't feel optimistic.

NICKEL TURNED the corner and in long strides covered the distance between himself and the pharmacy. A pretty blond nurse screamed and backed against the wall. He moved to her, grabbed her by the head and shoved her toward the floor. She went limp and let him put her down.

He pivoted toward the glass window of the pharmacy and spotted a man and a woman inside. Nickel held up the machine pistol.

"Open the door," he demanded.

The woman pressed a buzzer under the counter, and Nickel pulled the door open. He stormed into the pharmacy first, his men in tow. The room was filled with white shelves, dispensing tables and computers. Nickel threw a canvas bag on the floor.

"Morphine and Vitalife. Give them to me. Now."

Both pharmacists began unlocking cabinets, grabbing boxes and vials and stuffing them into the bag. Nickel counted six boxes of Vitalife. He looked at the man, whose bald scalp broke into a sweat when their eyes met.

"The Vitalife. Where's the rest?" Nickel asked.

"That's all we have. We get more tomorrow."

Nickel felt a pang of fear pass through his stomach, which turned to rage. The only way to get the medication was through a hospital. Or buy it on the streets, which didn't help his boss's plans at all.

"What the fuck do you mean tomorrow?" Nickel shouted. "That does me no good. What are you trying to pull?"

"Really, that's all we have."

Nickel swung the machine pistol in a tight arc, using the barrel to knock vials and boxes from a dispensing table onto the floor. The pharmacists started under the sudden movement.

"Bullshit. Where's the rest? There's got to be more. You holding out on me?"

The pitch of the male pharmacist's voice rose a notch.

"Honest to God, we don't have any more. That's it."

"He's telling the truth," the woman said. "We've got more morphine if you want that instead."

"I don't want the stinking morphine," he said. "I want Vitalife."

One of the other raiders spoke up. "Let it go. We've got to get out of here. We're wasting time."

Easy for you to say, Nickel thought. *Not your ass on the line when you come up short on the painkiller. If I go back with six boxes rather than ten, I'm dead.*

"C'mon man," another of the intruders prodded. "Let's go."

"Fuck," Nickel said. He pulled the trigger, slamming a volley of 9 mm slugs into the male pharmacist's ample midsection, causing him to jerk wildly as he fell back against the wall, crimson blossoming from his chest as the slugs punched through him. When Nickel let off the trigger, the man dropped to the floor, dead.

The woman screamed and began sucking for air as terror clutched her chest tightly. "Oh, my God. Oh, my God."

"Shut up, lady," Nickel said. "Just shut up."

She continued gasping and yelling. Nickel thought about shooting her, too, but a firm hand on his arm stopped him. The voice sounded as though it were coming at him through a long tunnel.

"This mission's screwed. We need to get out of here. Grab the bag and go."

Nickel reached down, snatched up the canvas bag and considered again whether to shoot the woman. He emerged from his panic-induced trance long enough to realize that the mission was blown and he needed to leave. "C'mon," he said. "Let's go."

JON SANCHEZ JERKED when he heard the submachine gun chatter. Other hostages screamed and sobbed at the sound of the gunfire. Sanchez sucked in a deep breath and started running options in his head. No way could he take down all these guys with his pistol. They probably would shoot him the moment he reached for it.

He also couldn't sit back and let these guys slaughter innocent people. If this went far enough, Liz, who lay in a nearby room nearly unconscious with painkillers, could get caught in a cross fire and killed. Sanchez knew he didn't want that on his conscience, even if cancer was ravaging her body and killing her anyway. In her pain and delirium, she had begged Jon to shoot her or inject her with something that would take her life more quickly than the cancer. Neither his marital vows nor his lifetime as a practicing Catholic would allow him to do that.

As Sanchez mulled his options, he noticed someone else preparing to pluck the decision from his hands.

A young woman, eyes wide with terror, stared at the off-duty cop from across the floor. He couldn't recall her name, but remembered that she had cared for his wife and knew Sanchez was a police officer.

He recognized the look she was giving him. She wanted him to do something, anything to make this whole thing stop. She didn't understand that this wasn't a television show where the cop single-handedly took down a bunch of armed men in a slow-motion shoot-out.

Sanchez knew real life didn't work that way. Grandstanding would create a massacre.

The young woman propped her upper torso up on her left forearm and pointed at Sanchez.

"You people better back off," she said. "He's a police officer."

In unison, raiders and hostages alike turned to look at Sanchez. As more than a dozen faces focused on him, Sanchez wondered whether the young woman's pronouncement would cost only his life or that of all the hostages.

THEY WERE LOSING control of the situation, and Nickel knew it. Killing the pharmacist had been a reaction to his own panic and a stupid move. Slaughtering innocents always raised the ire of the public and the police. So not only had Nickel failed to get enough of the valuable painkiller, but he had also turned up the heat on his boss.

That made him a dead man walking and he knew it. It was time to do whatever he deemed necessary and to hell with the consequences.

As Nickel entered the main area, a couple of his guys stood there looking at a big Hispanic guy in jeans and a short-sleeved shirt. Two others held the guy's arms behind him.

"What's the problem?" Nickel asked.

"Cop," one of the men said.

Nickel exhaled. That was all he needed. He knew one cop couldn't stop them. But he probably had been using his eyes and ears to gather evidence ever since they first raided the hospital ward. Sure, the others probably were, too. But regular folks made nightmarish witnesses. Conflicting stories. Bad memories. Faulty information. Even though the cop looked scared, Nickel imagined he wasn't too panicked to memorize things that might take them down later.

"Move," Nickel said to the men holding Sanchez. The men released the cop's arms. He rubbed his right biceps with his left hand and smiled at Nickel.

"Look, man, this doesn't have to go down bad," the cop stated.

"Yes," Nickel said, "it does."

He raised the machine pistol's muzzle, aimed it at the cop and shot him with a quick 3-round burst. The slugs slammed into Sanchez's chest, killing him before he hit the floor.

"Let's get the fuck out of here," Nickel said, "before I have to kill someone else."

Mack Bolan watched the pretty redhead, appreciatively noting her smooth curves as she and her thug escort exited his silver Volvo, walked the circular driveway in front of Emilio Vega's stucco home and approached the door.

Bolan recognized neither of them.

Despite her hard-looking escort, the woman seemed to be entering under her own power. The two talked and laughed as they sauntered up the driveway. An exterior guard stopped the hardman, a tall Latino with his head shaved, motioned for the lady to proceed inside the house. The two talked for a moment. Her escort's expression turned somber as the two men spoke. The change in the hardman's mood triggered Bolan's alarm bells, but he decided to let it go for the moment. The hardman's sour expression could be in response to anything.

Bolan wanted something specific.

He had come to kill Emilio Vega. His mission was a government sanctioned preemptive strike against a drug dealer ready to unleash a potential plague upon America—a plague that had already claimed its first victims.

Half an hour later, a spotless 1978 Pontiac Trans Am rolled up to the curb. A burly guy, bald with freckled scalp, stepped from the car, swaggered past the exterior guard. He made a gun with the forefinger and thumb of his right hand, shot the guy as he passed. Both men laughed. Bolan removed his war book from the pocket of his black suit, recorded the license plates of the Pontiac and Volvo, then returned the book to his pocket.

Several more minutes passed, and still no Vega.

Armed with a pair of binoculars, Bolan continued to monitor the comings and goings at the estate of one of Florida's biggest drug dealers, waiting for the main man to arrive. As he recorded small facts about the house's layout, his mind drifted back to earlier in the day when Stony Man chief Hal Brognola had dropped the mission in his lap.

Stony Man Farm, Virginia, earlier that morning

BOLAN SIPPED some coffee to ease the ache in his head as he sat with Brognola in a conference room. The big Fed looked as tired as Bolan felt. A half-empty foam cup of coffee and two folders sat at the Justice man's right hand. His tie hung loose from his neck as if it were the end of the workday rather than the beginning. Sometimes for Brognola the two ran together.

"Sorry I can't give you more time between missions, Striker. Something's come up."

Bolan nodded. The soldier took the folder and opened it in his lap. A picture of a man Bolan assumed was Hispanic stared back at him. The guy was in his midfifties, with black hair and deep brown eyes that smoldered defiantly.

"Know him?" Brognola asked.

"Emilio Vega," Bolan said. "He oversees a drug conduit between Colombia and Florida. He buys cocaine from Colombia, marijuana and heroin from Mexico and sells them to major drug kingpins between Miami and Detroit. He's pretty far removed from street-level sales, from what I know."

"Probably hasn't seen a street dealer or a junkie in years,"

Brognola said. "It helps to sleep at night when he doesn't have to see his junk kill other people."

Clutching his mug, Brognola stood and walked to the coffeemaker for a refill.

As he filled his cup, he continued. "His son Ernesto was killed last year during a multiagency drug bust called Operation Thunderbolt."

"I remember," Bolan said. "Three DEA agents died during that operation. The Feds seized millions in cash, cocaine and marijuana."

"Along with hundreds of thousands more dollars in boats, houses, guns and cars," Brognola said. "We seized at least one-fourth of the assets that comprise the Vega empire. We hobbled his drug operation, too. But I think Emilio's more pissed off that junior and a couple of other guys took a bullet during the whole thing."

"So did three federal agents, Hal."

"Preaching to the choir, Striker," Brognola said, returning to his seat. "But I don't think Vega looks at it that way."

"I would expect not," Bolan said. "So where do I come in?"

Brognola leaned back in his chair and clasped his hands behind his head. His forehead wrinkled as he gathered his thoughts.

"Seems Emilio has found a new product line—Vitalife. It's an experimental painkiller used on terminal cancer patients. It's six times as powerful as injected morphine and ten times as addictive. On a healthy person, it has a tranquilizing effect, slows people way down. Also tends to create an overarching sense of well-being that lasts for hours. Problem is, it's started to trickle onto the streets. Addicts can ingest it or burn it down and inject it and make the world go away for a while."

"I've heard about that," Bolan said. "Stuff's big in Kentucky, Ohio and Pennsylvania. Problem is, it relaxes people so much they stop breathing."

Brognola nodded. "Without a doctor to administer it, the 160-milligram tablet turns from a wonder drug to a killer in short order. The only saving grace right now is that it's extremely rare. Not even widely distributed enough to get through regular channels such as prescription fraud. The demand's insane. Stuff fetches two dollars per milligram on the street. That means a 160-milligram tablet sells for more than three hundred dollars. The sales potential is staggering."

"So how does Vega fit into this?"

Brognola pulled his arms from behind his head, sat upright and rested his forearms on the table. He put his big hand on another folder but didn't slide it over to Bolan.

"Within the past two weeks, three cancer hospitals have been hit by teams of armed men. The modus operandi is always the same. Hit late at night, steal morphine and Vitalife and get out. Sources have told the DEA that Vega is the brains and bankroll behind these operations. We have no reason to believe otherwise."

"Why steal the morphine? That hardly seems worth the risk when it can be easily bought on the streets."

"It's a blind," Brognola said. "Initially we thought they wanted both. But when the hospital they hit last night came up short on Vitalife, one of the raiders got jerked out of shape. The woman offered to give him more morphine, but he told her he didn't want it. Then he shot her co-worker. Guy was a father of four. Scared out of his mind and understandably so."

Brognola slid the other folder across the table to Bolan. He opened it and, along with some papers, saw a photo of a middle-aged man crumpled in the corner, white coat soaked with blood. He set the photo aside and found a second with a casually dressed Hispanic man lying on the floor, also apparently dead of gunshot wounds. Bolan looked up at Brognola.

"Jon Sanchez," Brognola said. "Orlando police detective. He was staying with his wife, who's on her deathbed with cancer. One of the hostages identified Sanchez as a cop, and the same guy who killed the pharmacist, killed Sanchez. They also killed a security guard, but burned his remains in his patrol car. You don't want to see those pictures. The security supervisor disappeared."

"Were the other raids this bloody?"

Brognola shook his head. "No one ever fired a shot until last night. Otherwise we may have involved ourselves sooner. This had been the DEA's case, but now that three people have died, the Man wants our help. We can't have commando teams shooting up hospitals."

"So what do you need from me?"

"The DEA is looking into the Vega connection. But that could take too long. They're hampered by certain rules—gathering evidence, building a case. You're not."

"You want me to kill Vega," Bolan said.

Brognola nodded. "And whoever else you deem necessary. The second folder includes a dossier on Vega and whatever intelligence we have on the case. Jack can fly you to Florida when you're ready to go. We'll have a car waiting for you when you get there."

"Don't get me wrong, Hal, what these guys did at the hospital was horrible," Bolan said. "But why involve me in this? Seems odd for the President to bring me in on what seems like a glorified armed robbery."

"The concern is less about the hospital raids, and more about whether Vega might succeed with the grander plan," Brognola said. "The problem with Vitalife isn't its narcotic effect. It's the addiction-withdrawal process it creates. The detox from this stuff is extremely tough. Physically, people vomit for days, tremor, hallucinate. Without a doctor's help some don't survive. Emotionally, the pain is so great they'll do anything to get another fix."

"What do you mean anything?"

"Kill people—including their own family—for money to buy more. Beat up, even kill, doctors and nurses in a detox ward. The Man's worried about the bigger picture. He doesn't want a repeat of the crack-cocaine epidemic with all its associated violence. The country doesn't need that."

Bolan knew his old friend was right. "Tell Jack to warm up the plane," he said. "I'll get my gear together and head for Florida."

BOLAN WORKED the action on his Beretta 93-R while Stony Man pilot Jack Grimaldi ferried him to Florida. The soldier already had performed final checks with other weapons in his cache: a Colt Commando, an Uzi and his .44 Magnum Desert Eagle. He stuffed the weapons into a canvas duffel bag that also contained his combat blacksuit, spare ammunition, knives, garrotes, grenades and other tools of his lethal trade.

"Don't you ever travel with just a toothbrush?" Grimaldi asked.

"It's hard to kill someone with a toothbrush."

"Bet you could."

"Let's hope I never have to try," Bolan said, grinning. "How long until we reach Orlando?"

"Another forty-five minutes tops. What do you think this guy's angle is, Sarge?"

"Vega sounds like he's trying to rebuild what he lost. Put himself back on the top of the heap."

Grimaldi shook his head. "The slime heap. He has to be worth millions. When you come within inches of getting busted and your own son ends up dead, you'd think you'd quit crime and take up golf or something."

"Greed makes people crazy, Jack," Bolan said. "You know that as well as I do. Hell, maybe this is a point of pride with Vega. Maybe he just can't stomach losing."

"How long should I wait?" Grimaldi asked.

"We should land at 1100 hours. Give me until the same time tomorrow. I'd like some recon time before I go into Vega's territory. I'll hit him overnight. First I'm going to visit Orlando PD, see what they know."

Orlando, Florida

FORTY-FIVE MINUTES later, Grimaldi landed the plane. Dressed in a dark blue suit, white shirt and red tie, Bolan slung his duffel bag over his right shoulder and carried a suitcase in his left hand. He bid Grimaldi goodbye and headed across the airfield toward the terminal.

Although it was late October, the temperature hovered well into the eighties and the sun warmed the skin of Bolan's face, neck and hands. By the time he reached the building, perspiration had broken out on his back. He wished for a moment he had come for pleasure rather than business, then purged the thought. He needed to focus on the job at hand.

Within minutes, he was driving a rented Dodge toward downtown Orlando. Brognola had used his FBI contacts to have an agent rent the car under a pseudonym and deposit it at the small suburban airport. Shortly thereafter, Bolan found Orlando police headquarters at 100 South Hughey Avenue, parked the Dodge and made his way inside the police complex. Soon he sat in the office of Captain Michael Waters, a homicide detective in his midthirties. Scattered around Waters's office were several pictures of a pretty blonde, whom Bolan assumed was the detective's wife or girlfriend, and of two small boys. Stacks of papers and file folders topped the detective's desk.

Bolan had introduced himself to Waters as Michael Belasko, a Justice Department agent investigating the hospital raids. Brognola had called ahead, personally asking the police chief for help and greasing the wheels for Bolan to get local cooperation. Stocky and balding, Waters had greeted Bolan with a scowl and a grunt that told the soldier he had better things to do.

"So why is Justice interested in this case?" Waters asked.

The detective tipped back in his chair, sipped coffee and waited for an answer. He didn't bother to offer Bolan a cup.

"There have been two similar raids at other cancer hospitals during the past week, one in Georgia, the other in Kentucky," Bolan said. "In each case they took other drugs, but focused on Vitalife. In each case, they seemed to have inside help. They knew exactly where to find the pharmacies, how to sneak into the hospitals largely undetected. Then they made a big noise while they stole the stuff. Sounds like a pattern to me."

"Yeah, except in those other cities no one died," Waters said. "Now someone's dead, we've got reporters from CNN, *USA*

Today and the *New York Times* crawling around Orlando, interviewing victims' families, combing through our reports. Suddenly the federal government wants to help us."

"We were interested before," Bolan said. He could appreciate the cop's frustration. But he also had no intention of participating in a full-blown pissing match over territorial issues.

Waters dismissed Bolan's last remark with a wave of his hand. "Whatever, Belasko. You know who got killed at Davis Memorial, don't you?"

Bolan nodded. "One of your guys. Jon Sanchez. He was supposed to be a good cop."

"Jon was a friend of mine. A good friend. His wife, Liz, still is, though I don't look for her to be around much longer. She's got ovarian cancer that turned into cancer of the stomach and esophagus. The pharmacist and security guard who got killed, those are a damn shame, for sure. But Jon's death I take personally. We all do. So don't think you're going to breeze into town, thank us for our diligent work and steal our investigation."

Bolan nodded again. "I just want to solve the case, Waters. I've taken down more cop killers in my career than I care to count. If I can nail more, that's what I want to do. I don't worry about who gets credit. I don't need the PR."

Waters searched Bolan's face, apparently trying to determine whether the big man was sincere. After a few moments of scrutiny, his face relaxed.

"I don't care, either, Belasko. All I want is to make an arrest. If I got fired tomorrow, I'd still track these bastards. I plan on finding them as soon as possible. I'd appreciate it if you would do the same."

"Consider it done," Bolan said.

"You want a cup of coffee?" Waters asked.

"Yeah."

Waters refilled his own cup, filled one for Bolan and handed it to him. The soldier took the coffee and Waters returned to his seat.

"I know about these other raids, Belasko," Waters said. "I

just don't understand why these folks suddenly decided to draw blood. They never killed anyone before. Why this time?"

Bolan shrugged. "You know what the witnesses said—the leader got agitated when he found out how little Vitalife the hospital had on hand. He panicked and lost his head. That's when he started shooting."

"I know that. Still, why get so bent out of shape over the Vitalife? The place was full of other painkillers—morphine, for example. Hell, the lady offered them plenty of other stuff to take and sell."

"Maybe these guys thought it had the best resale value," Bolan offered.

He debated whether to mention the Vega connection. Waters seemed trustworthy, but Bolan knew better than to dump his guts to every potential ally crossing his path. For sure, the two were on the same side, but their goals conflicted. Bolan was here to kill Vega and prevent the shedding of more innocent blood; Waters also wanted to prevent more killings, but he understandably would want to handle the situation like a cop. The Executioner didn't plan to have Vega endure a lengthy trial. His solution was more immediate. The last thing Bolan needed was a pissed-off cop rousting Vega before Bolan could visit him.

"You could be right," Waters said, breaking into the Executioner's thoughts.

"What's that?"

"Maybe the Vitalife was all they really wanted."

"You guys have much of a problem with its abuse here in Orlando?"

Waters shook his head. "Not yet, thank God. With all the crack, grass, heroin, ecstasy and coke moving through Florida, the last thing we need is one more drug to contend with. You know what I think?"

"What's that?"

"I think these shitheads work for someone else. Someone's got to be orchestrating this whole thing. It's just a gut feeling, but that's what I believe. Maybe the guy panicked because he knew someone else was going to be pissed off when he went back with a smaller-than-expected load."

"Makes sense. Who do you think he's working for?" Bolan asked, trying to get a line on how much Waters really knew.

"Hell, take your pick," the detective said. "We've got more than a couple of drug dealers in Florida. And these guys are working in several states, so it could be anyone. You're the Fed. You tell me."

Bolan smiled and decided to act dumb. "If I knew that, I wouldn't be here talking with you."

Waters gave Bolan a tight smile. "We both know more than we're telling, bud. You earn my trust and I'll tell you more. I assume it's vice versa."

"Yeah," Bolan said. He grabbed one of Waters's business cards from a clear plastic holder on the detective's desk and scrawled a number on the back with a borrowed pen. "Here's my cell number and the motel I am staying at." He handed the card to Waters, who took it and studied it for a moment.

"Not exactly high-class lodging, Belasko."

The Executioner shrugged. "I don't plan on staying long. Speaking of which, I'd better get going. I've got another meeting to prepare for."

Waters stood and extended a hand across his desk. Bolan took it.

"You need anything, give me a holler, Belasko. And if you get a line on who this is, you definitely call me. You seem like a guy who can handle himself, but these guys are carrying Uzis and all the government gives us is these." Waters patted the Glock holstered on his belt next to his badge. "No need to be a cowboy here when there's strength in numbers."

Bolan thanked him and left. He appreciated Waters's concern, and the guy seemed decent enough. But the fretting was unnecessary. Bolan played by a different set of rules entirely. They were rules he developed while stomping on the Mafia years ago, and continued to refine as the years brought him more and different enemies. His rules were to have as few rules as possible. He compensated for lack of numbers with brains, brawn, firepower and sheer will of spirit. When Vega's men met Bolan this night, they would know they had encountered an army. A one-man army called the Executioner.

2

Even as Mack Bolan waited for Emilio Vega to return home, the drug lord sat in Victor Sampson's study and seethed as Sampson kept him cooling his heels. Surrounded by hand-carved antique cabinets, Tang horse statues and hand-woven rugs, Vega realized that he admired Sampson's tastes much more than the man himself.

Sampson epitomized everything the drug runner hated. Sampson came from old money, had never gone hungry or grown up in the slums of Miami as had Vega. Sampson had walked right into leadership of a multinational medical supply and pharmaceutical business. He had grown up with enough food, clothes, cars and education. He had grown up without the shame of poverty, a constant companion of Vega still, even though he was worth hundreds of millions of dollars.

As a child, Vega only dreamed of such prosperity. When he was old enough, he decided to grab wealth for himself. The son of a Colombian father and American mother, he now had a fortune of his own. But he had sweated blood to get it. He had used people of money and their children to buy his drugs and build his business; he gladly took cash from those who could afford it, when they needed to buy his drugs. He viewed drug addiction—and the people who bought his drugs—as weak and stupid.

He had no sympathy for the weak and stupid.

As his business grew, Vega began selling cocaine, marijuana, crack and heroin to other pushers, then to their bosses, eventually growing his trade until he no longer dealt with street-level sales at all. He distributed to the big boys, and gained control of a good portion of Orlando's drug trade in the process.

It was the ultimate pyramid scheme, and Vega was the top of the pyramid.

"Emilio, how good to see you," a voice behind him said.

Vega grimaced at the voice, replaced the scowl with a smile, stood and turned to greet the speaker.

A man in his late fifties, Sampson stood several inches taller than Vega's own five feet ten inches. His hair was white, trimmed neatly and he had the athletic build of someone who played tennis or jogged several times a week. A young man with slicked-back hair and a gray suit stood next to Sampson. The man was Richard Ahern, Sampson's personal assistant and shadow. Vega considered him a toady and all but ignored him.

"Victor, you look well."

"Please, Emilio, sit. Richard, refill his drink. I assume it's the usual?"

Vega nodded. Sampson gave him a knowing look, as though to indicate that this small gesture of familiarity bonded them, made them family. Vega knew better. He had lost the family that mattered most to him, a young man of honor and strength. His own son.

That death was the one thing that bonded him to Sampson. It was a tie he gladly would sever.

The two men sat across from each other. Ahern brought Vega a fresh drink. The drug runner ignored him, but took the drink, swirled the glass in lazy circles to melt the ice and dilute the alcohol. Sampson leaned forward. He looked serious.

"The raid in Orlando went very badly, Emilio. Three people died, including a police officer. That can only hurt us. We have to expect some sort of aggressive investigation to occur after that."

"I realize that," Vega said. "My guy lost his head. He neither brought back enough of the Vitalife nor did he handle the job properly. I'll deal with him soon enough. Don't worry."

"We don't need the attention. We have a lot at stake here."

"Don't tell me about the stakes, Victor," Vega said, his voice hardening. "I understand your position. I'm sure you're worried about being tied with me, a known drug dealer. What with the *New York Times* and the *Wall Street Journal* articles, and all. Hanging out with me can't help your reputation."

Sampson sat back, stung. When, like Vega, his son had been shot by DEA agents during Operation Thunderbolt, it had created a national scandal. Several national newspapers and television news magazines carried stories ranging from poignant to salacious about the drug-running son of a corporate chief. Vega's own son had been a side note, a few paragraphs in a larger story. When a drug runner's son died, it was certainly no shock. Vega knew most people probably took some sort of false comfort from it, as though one person's death magically solved the nation's drug problem. A blow for justice and all that bullshit. But when a blue blood got mixed up in drugs and died as a result, that was news.

Sampson's plight had simultaneously amused and angered the drug runner. He had enjoyed seeing Sampson squirm and hide behind a wall of public relations people. But it also pointed out in no uncertain terms Vega's own standing in society. Money had bought him everything except respectability. Finally he decided he could live with it.

"It's not my own image I'm worried about," Sampson said. "It's the operation. We need discretion for this to work."

"I've been running drugs for years, Victor. It's too bad the shootings happened. But it wasn't a complete surprise. When you storm places with guns, you run the risk of people dying. It's just the way it works. You let me handle this."

He let the words sink in for a moment, then asked, "How's the laboratory prototype coming?"

Sampson brightened. "It's going well. Soon we can set up laboratories in Cincinnati, Pittsburgh and Louisville to make our own version of Vitalife. We already had been working on a similar drug to compete with Genesis Laboratories when its Vitalife patent ran out. So duplication hasn't been a problem. Full production isn't far away."

"You trust your people?"

Sampson's eyes turned hard. "Implicitly. As much as you trust yours. And so far, mine have created fewer problems."

Vega let the remark slide.

"And the pill. You can copy it?"

"My people have done so with great success, Emilio. There are still a few bugs to be worked out, but it's nearly as good as real medication."

"What's the problem?"

"Proprietary technology," Sampson said. "There are some elements the real manufacturer has included that we haven't isolated. But we are close to doing so."

"How close?"

"Close enough to test on humans. We found some willing subjects that agreed to use the medication. They're popping the 160-milligram pills and usually having no problems."

"You said 'usually.'"

"That's a strong dose, Emilio. Enough to dull pain for someone whose internal organs are being eaten alive by cancer. Administered without a doctor's supervision, it can kill someone. If the medicine doesn't kill them, the withdrawal does."

Emilio drained his glass and set it on a coaster. Sampson looked at Ahern, who immediately went to the table, scooped up the glass and went to the wet bar to get Vega a refill.

"How often does it kill someone?"

"About twenty-five percent of the time," Sampson said. "We're hoping to isolate the problems and whittle that down a little more."

"How long will that take?"

"Three months. Certainly no longer."

Ahern set a fresh drink in front of Vega. The little kiss-ass even had wiped the condensation from it. The drug kingpin grasped the glass but didn't drink. He squelched an urge to stand up, reach across the table and smack Sampson across the mouth. Instead, he stared into the man's eyes.

"Three months? That's too damn long."

"We can't put it out there with those kinds of death rates, Emilio."

Vega purposely slowed his voice, stretched his words, as if lecturing a child.

"Victor, this isn't a legal drug. We're counterfeiting a drug and selling it on the street. We don't need FDA approval. People want this stuff. It goes for two dollars per milligram on the street. We need to mass-produce and mass-market this shit before some-one else gets the bright idea. It's business, pure and simple."

"I do worry about the ramifications if we get caught. Should someone die, I mean."

Vega, who had just sipped his drink, damn near spit it right back out. Suppressing a guffaw, he swallowed hard and stared at Victor. "If we get caught for this, a handful of dead junkies will be the least of your worries."

"It could be hundreds, thousands of dead users," Sampson replied.

"I said don't worry about it, Victor."

Sampson's eyes narrowed, but he smiled at the drug lord. "Of course you're right, Emilio. Forgive me. I'm a little new to this side of the business."

Vega swallowed another laugh. As far as he was concerned, corporate tycoons such as Sampson ranked as the world's biggest criminals, leagues ahead of him on the crime contin-uum. Vega ran a business, albeit an illegal one, but a business nonetheless. He made lots of money. Donated some to churches or charities. Raised a family. But society regarded him as a pariah while it adored people like Sampson, who skirted the law, made billions and trampled people along the way.

Enough of this, Vega decided. "When do I get to see the drug laboratory?"

Sampson smiled and spread his hands. "Anytime you would like, my friend. Anytime."

"Wonderful," the drug runner said. "I'll be looking forward to it."

Sampson flashed his best boardroom smile. "You name the time and I personally will walk you through it. I think you will be pleased with what our partnership is creating."

"I have no doubt."

SHORTLY AFTER THE DRUG lord and his men left, Victor Sampson had Ahern pour him a bourbon and water. With a grunt, he dismissed his assistant and stared out the window, watching Vega and his crew pile into an armored Mercedes and leave the grounds. He smiled at the drug runner's confidence, thinking he commanded Sampson.

No one commanded Victor Sampson.

Sampson could act compliant, act cowed by the drug runner. But it was just that—an *act*. The reality was that every meeting between the two was monitored by a security team comprised of former military soldiers and mercenaries. For generations, the Sampsons employed the best security money could buy, men of unflinching loyalty who kept their mouths shut and jumped in the path of bullets willingly. Even Ahern, whom Vega treated with outright disdain, was a former Green Beret, a veteran of several black ops before criminal prosecution forced him from the U.S. Army. The seemingly tame assistant could snap Vega's neck before he knew what was happening.

Sampson always held meetings in the study because of the security it afforded. His team could watch every movement, hear every word. Gun ports and secret entrances would allow them to storm the room or put a bullet into whoever might pose a threat to the executive's well-being. Sampson allowed the drug boss to live because it suited his needs, not the other way around.

Vega would be smart to learn that. No matter if he didn't, though. Sampson was more than willing to let him wallow in ignorance, let him continue to believe he had the upper hand.

Until he decided to teach him otherwise.

When the DEA killed his son, Stephen, in a shoot-out, it had crushed Sampson. For months, it kept him awake, affected his concentration at work, caused him to lose weight. Sampson had damn near died right along with his son. Eventually he decided he was too strong to do that. He would miss Stephen, of course, but he also had to get on with his life. He would continue to run his family's business, socialize—live as he had before.

Nevertheless, he also would have revenge. He would get even with the DEA for killing his child. And he would have revenge on Vega in ways the drug runner couldn't fathom.

He smiled at the thought. Indeed, more Vega and DEA blood would be spilled before this ended. And Sampson would enjoy every goddamn last minute of it.

3

Another two hours of visual recon told Bolan what he needed to know about Vega's estate. Four guards walked the grounds, with more gunners inside. An eight-foot high fence with a single gate surrounded most of the property. The two guards inside the fence carried shotguns; the two patrolling the front of the house had telltale bulges in their armpits but kept their weapons hidden.

During the past fifteen minutes of Bolan's surveillance, the drug lord arrived, traveling in a Mercedes and surrounded by guards. Situated in a nearby house, the Executioner had watched the luxury car pull into the crescent-shaped driveway and stop directly at the front door to deposit Vega. Two bulky men stepped from the car first, each scanning the street, the bushes and tops of the walls surrounding the big estate, but never looking high enough to see Bolan. Satisfied of Vega's safety, one of the men opened the Mercedes's back door and Vega stepped from the car. He walked into the house, with two of the big men immediately covering his back as he moved toward the house.

Bolan could imagine Vega in his luxurious surroundings, probably congratulating himself on again making it home safe. The master of the universe in his natural habitat. Bolan knew little of the drug lord's personality, but he was familiar with the arrogance it took to enrich one's self off the suffering of others. Bolan had seen it more times during his career than he cared to remember.

Within three minutes, Vega appeared in a window, flanked by two of his guards. His arms swung wildly and his face looked animated. Bolan put the binoculars to his face and focused in Vega. Anger flushed the drug lord's cheeks, and he shouted at someone Bolan couldn't see. Someone was getting a royal ass chewing courtesy of the boss. For a moment, Bolan wondered who and why, then decided it didn't really matter.

Bottom line—Vega would be dead within an hour. The Executioner would see to that.

The house Bolan occupied was empty. Stony Man computer whiz Aaron Kurtzman had checked Orlando PD's dispatch computers and found the owners had asked police to make extra checks of the home while they vacationed. Three days' worth of unread newspapers and a stack of unopened mail overflowing on the dining-room table verified that no one was home.

The empty house had given Bolan the space he needed to get acquainted with Vega before killing him. Now it was time to meet his quarry head-on.

He opened the sliding glass door on the balcony, quickly made his way through the house and exited through the back door. He entered the front yard through a wrought-iron gate and crept along the side of the house, taking it slow and allowing night to swallow the last vestiges of daylight.

Fortunately the only signs of life in the neighborhood were Vega's two guards and the sputter of several yard sprinklers. This was the kind of high-dollar neighborhood where the residents likely were up-and-comers, more apt to be in the boardroom than hanging out in the front yard sipping margaritas and socializing with neighbors. During his two hours perched in the empty house, Bolan watched Vega's home. He also took the neighborhood's pulse, and found it nearly flat lining. During four hours, a couple of joggers, a few soccer moms in BMWs and a woman walking a lumbering golden retriever had crossed his radar screen. Otherwise, the streets had been quiet.

That suited Bolan fine.

He crossed the street to Vega's home and sidled against the house. A hushed conversation to the rear of the home between two men stopped Bolan in his tracks.

"Jesus, Nickel is as good as dead," a deep baritone said. "I'm glad it's his ass on the line and not mine."

"Guy screwed up," a gravelly voice said. "Lost his head when he was stealing the drugs in Orlando. He killed a cop, for God's sake, without even giving it a second thought. Vega hates cops, but he knows better than to shoot one for no reason. It just brings attention."

"And Nickel got us that, for sure," the other voice agreed. "I heard him getting yelled at. It was brutal, man. Bet he won't last the night."

"I don't think the lady cop is going to do much better."

"Yeah. At this point, Vega is acting as crazy as Nickel. He's so screwed up over this whole operation he ain't thinking straight. He's liable to kill her just like Nickel killed that other cop. Everyone's going crazy, if you ask me."

"He could give her to me," Scratchy said.

The baritone laughed. "No shit. She could slap the cuffs on me anytime."

Both men laughed.

Bolan's blood ran cold. He had happened upon a hostage situation. A police officer might die unless he intervened. That changed the warrior's plans, but he could live with that. A good soldier stayed flexible and focused during combat. Those qualities held the keys to both his survival and that of his new, unknown ally.

Bolan started for the men, but froze when a third voice, also male, rang out.

"You two get your asses in here," it said. "We need you to take care of something."

The men grumbled, their conversation growing softer as they headed toward the house. Bolan took a few steps back and with a running start scaled the white concrete fence that surrounded much of the property. He dropped into the backyard and hugged the shadows as he headed for the house. He pulled the silenced Beretta from its shoulder rig, figuring his entry might call for precise but silent work. He let the Colt and the Uzi hang on either side of him, the straps forming an X across his chest.

A guy in tan khakis and a red polo shirt stood on the patio, smoking a cigarette. A pistol rested on his left hip, the butt facing forward, ready for a cross draw. He stared into the night, humming. Bolan aimed the 93-R and squeezed the trigger, a trio of 9 mm Parabellum rounds drilling into the careless guard. He was dead before he hit the brick patio.

Bolan grabbed the corpse's feet, dragged it into the darkness and shoved it against the house. The soldier moved to the sliding glass door and peered inside. The room was furnished with a big-screen television, DVD players, CD players and other electronics and fat couches and chairs. But he saw no people milling about the room. He eased back the glass door and moved into the home, Beretta leading the way.

The soldier crossed the room in a few steps and pressed against the wall next to the doorway. He heard the crinkling of plastic. The two voices he had heard in the backyard emanated from the room, complaining.

"They couldn't put the plastic down themselves," the baritone said. "Lazy bastards. Call us back in the house to do the shit work."

"Would you rather be the one to pull the trigger on Nickel?" the smoker shot back. "Guy's a jerk, but he's one of us. Don't like to shoot my own people. It's bad karma."

"Karma? Jesus Christ, what are you talking about?"

"You know, karma. It's—"

"Whatever. I could pull the trigger on Nickel. He's a psycho. World's better off without him."

"Just get on the floor and help me spread this tarp."

"Why? You're doing fine."

Bolan stepped into the hall and approached the room where the two men were discussing spiritual beliefs as they set down plastic to protect the carpet from blood splatters. Bolan looked around the doorjamb and saw a big man kneeling on the tarp, smoothing it down. A second guy—Bolan assumed the one with the booming voice—stood over the first and continued to extol the virtues of killing Nickel.

The Executioner filled the doorway and raised his pistol. He squeezed off a 3-round burst into the standing guy's chest. The man jerked and convulsed as blood sprayed from his torso. Without looking over his shoulder, the second man rolled away, his hand clawing inside his jacket for hardware. A second burst from the 93-R stopped him cold.

The Executioner turned on his heel and started down the hallway. He could hear Vega yelling again and headed toward the sound.

"I got something else for you, Nickel, you dumb son of a bitch. Here's your goddamn lady friend."

"Madeline, what the hell are you doing here?" asked a voice that Bolan assumed belonged to Nickel.

"She's DEA, Hank. You brought a DEA agent into the organization."

"Hey, man, I just sponsored her. You took her in, Emilio. You made the decision, not me."

"So what's up, lady? You give Hank some nookie to let you in? Flop on your back for him?"

"It wasn't like that, Emilio," Nickel said. "She had contacts. She led me to suppliers. She seemed legitimate. She knew people."

"Of course she knew people, you moron," Vega said. "She's a goddamn narc. First you lose my cocaine. Then you screw me on the Vitalife. You kill a bunch of people and get our operation plastered all over CNN. Then you invite the DEA to join our organization. You're a goddamn liability. I can't have that. This is no way to run a business. You're killing me."

"Emilio, I'm sorry, man," Nickel said, his tone pleading. "I didn't mean to screw things up."

"But you did, Hank. And we're going to use the lady as a visual aid of what's going to happen to you next."

Bolan stood outside the living room where the discussion was occurring. He had wanted to make killing Vega his first priority, but the DEA agent's plight changed all that. He turned the corner and took a mental snapshot of the scene: the redhead, emerald eyes registering fear; a big guy holding her from behind with an arm around her neck, hand clenched in a fist; the opposite hand clutching a clump of her hair, pulling her head away at an uncomfortable angle; two guys to the left, arms crossed over their chests, their expressions amused; Vega standing before a scared-looking guy seated on the couch; two more guys standing at a wet bar, engrossed in the exchange as they nursed drinks.

Bolan planned to change the composition more to his liking. He slid the Beretta into the shoulder rig and filled his hands with the Colt Commando, which was loaded with soft-nosed tactical bullets. Pulling it to his shoulder and sighting down the barrel, he squeezed off a single round. The slug screamed across the room and drove into the nose of the guy holding the DEA agent. The lady screamed as blood splattered over her hair and shoulders. As the thug's grip loosened, she freed herself and dived to the floor.

Bolan switched the weapon to full-auto as he swung it toward the two guys to his right. One was pulling a pistol from his jacket and trying to bolt toward the woman. The assault rifle chattered and sent a burst of 5.56 mm manglers ripping into his center. Before the guy hit the floor, Bolan was tracking his neighbor, who was bringing an autoloading pistol to bear on the man in black. The thug squeezed off two shots that went wild, zinging past Bolan. The Executioner returned the favor, slamming a volley of slugs into the man's center mass.

Even as the dead hardman was hitting the floor, Bolan was on the move. The next pair of guards had split up. One was ushering Vega from the room while the second aimed and fired in Bolan's direction. The guy's Uzi stuttered in the soldier's direction, the fusillade of slugs forcing him to the floor. He rolled behind an overstuffed couch, came up in a crouch and squeezed off a burst at the hardman with the Uzi. The burst of 5.56 mm slugs pounded into the guy. Plumes of blood exploded from his chest and abdomen.

The guy Vega had called Nickel was stooped over one of the corpses, prying a gun from his hand. Bolan, almost as a second thought, fired a volley into Nickel, returning the same treatment he had shown Jon Sanchez and the other two men killed at the cancer hospital.

Bolan looked at the woman. She had collected herself and was digging into the jacket of the man who only seconds before had held her captive. She had freed his pistol from a shoulder rig as Bolan approached her. She regarded the Executioner warily, and he couldn't blame her. Even though he had saved her life, she had no way of knowing whether he was legitimate or from another drug organization.

"I'm Justice Department," he said. "Are you okay?"

She nodded, rose to her feet.

"We need to get Vega," he said, as he took off across the room, the woman following. They traversed a long hallway that eventually opened into a large kitchen outfitted with patterned ceramic tile floors and big stainless-steel refrigerators. A doorway connected the kitchen and living room. The front door to the house hung open. Bolan headed toward it, already knowing what to expect as he looked outside.

The Mercedes was gone and so was Vega. Even if he could get to his rental fast enough to give chase, Bolan had no idea where the guy was. He turned and found himself staring down the barrel of a captured pistol.

"I need to see some ID, Mr. Justice Department," the DEA agent said.

"I don't have any," Bolan said. "Why do you think I would be carrying ID while I'm undercover?"

"I've got my badge on me. I always carry it. How do I know you're with Justice?"

Bolan exhaled. He heard sirens in the distance and knew there was no time for this exchange. "If I was a drug dealer, I would have killed you already. Make sense?"

"Yeah, that makes sense," she said, neither looking nor sounding convinced.

"Good," Bolan said. "Do you mind lowering the pistol?"

She hesitated for a moment, then lowered the weapon. Bolan felt relieved, knowing it was the first thing to go right with the mission. He had already moved his finger outside the trigger guard of the Colt Commando and planned to comply with the lady if she didn't back off. He had sworn long ago never to shoot a law-enforcement officer, even a corrupt one. That vow would remain intact tonight.

The sirens sounded as though they were just blocks from the house. Bolan slung the Colt and weighed his options. He imagined the neighborhood either was sealed off or would be by the time he got to his car. To continue the mission, he would have to ditch the rental car and leave on foot, try to sneak past a bunch of nervous police officers responding to a shots-fired call at the home of a known drug dealer and perhaps cross paths with an officer and risk a confrontation with them—all on the outside chance that he could catch up with Vega. As he mulled his situation, tires squealed on the pavement in front of the house and sirens blared. The rotor wash of a helicopter beat down on the house. Bolan saw a searchlight scouring the backyard.

He sighed, walked to the kitchen table and sat down. He would need to find Vega and finish what they started here. But he wasn't going to rip through a wall of police to do it.

4

"Just what the hell were you doing out there, Belasko?" Waters said.

Bolan had surrendered to the officers at the scene, identifying himself as Mike Belasko. Madeline Glynn, the DEA agent, had vouched for his story. They confiscated Bolan's weapons and transported the pair to police headquarters, where Glynn had showered and changed into a borrowed sweat suit with an Orlando PD logo emblazoned across the front. Within an hour, Waters had arrived wearing a pair of jeans, a white T-shirt and light jacket.

"You come into my town, tell me you have no suspects, say you're going to assist us in the investigation," Waters said, ticking off each point with the fingers of his right hand. "Then you go to the home of a known drug dealer and shoot more than a half-dozen people. I ask again, Belasko, what the hell were you doing?"

"A source dropped Vega's name," Bolan said. "I was checking him out. I discovered he had a hostage and entered the house to assist."

"Thanks for boiling it down to three sentences," Waters said.

"Now, fill in the gaps. You went there carrying an assault rifle, a submachine gun and two pistols. You're wearing some kind of combat suit. And you expect me to believe you went there looking to interview someone? You were looking for trouble."

"I need to talk with my boss before I say any more," Bolan said.

Waters seemed like a good cop and a good man. Bolan hated like hell to play automaton with him, but he also knew he wasn't going to dump his guts to this guy.

"Captain," Glynn said, "Agent Belasko saved my life. My cover was blown. Vega was going to have me killed and threatened as much. He already had imprisoned and assaulted me. That's enough federal offenses right there to swear out a warrant on the man. He also planned to kill Hank Nickel, the man who murdered three people at the cancer hospital, including Jon Sanchez, one of your fellow officers."

Leaning back in his chair, Waters cupped his chin with his right hand. He bolstered his right elbow with his left hand and looked at his feet, contemplating the DEA agent's words.

"I know who Jon Sanchez is, Agent Glynn."

He looked up at Bolan. "This creates all kinds of problems for me, Belasko. You know that, don't you?"

Bolan nodded. "I am sorry for that," he said. And he was.

Waters let out a big sigh and looked deflated.

"Look, Belasko, I know those guys deserved what they got," he said. "Off the record, my only real regret is that I wasn't there to see Nickel take a bullet. But the bottom line is you sat in my office and acted like you knew nothing. Then, hours later, you're shooting up a known drug dealer's house. Makes it hard for us to work together if we can't have some kind of trust."

"You're right. I guess that means you people had no idea Vega was involved in this. No one on your drug-interdiction team had any inkling of this going down."

"Shit, Belasko."

"That's what I thought," Bolan said.

"Hey, look, I hardly know you," Waters stated. "You can't expect me to tell all just because you have Washington credentials."

"My point exactly."

Waters grinned. "You bastard. Yeah, I guess we both held out on each other. Least you saved me the trouble of finding and prosecuting Nickel. I probably would have enjoyed it. But this saves me the hassle, nonetheless. What do you think Vega will do next?"

Bolan shrugged. "My guess is hit another hospital, probably keep doing the same thing until he's got enough drugs. 'Where' is the real question. He's already shown there's no real rhyme or reason to where they hit. It could be anywhere in several states. He probably will go underground in the meantime."

He turned to Glynn. "You know anything?"

The DEA agent looked at Bolan as she collected her thoughts. Her green eyes bore into Bolan's, and he caught himself thinking of things other than the mission at hand.

"I don't know a specific location," she said. "But the scope of this goes far beyond stealing drugs. Vega's plans are much bigger."

"How so?" Bolan asked.

"Nickel told me Vega plans to make his own Vitalife. He's going to sell the stolen drugs on the street, use the money to open a series of labs across the country to produce a counterfeit form of the drug. He may even go for worldwide distribution."

"Create a new drug epidemic, like crack cocaine or crystal meth," Bolan said.

Glynn nodded. "That's the idea. He has a partner. Obviously someone with some money, but Nickel had no idea who it was. Nickel was on Vega's shit list so he was out of the loop. It's a miracle Vega allowed him to lead the raid on Davis Memorial."

"An unhappy miracle," Bolan said.

"Nickel saw it as a chance for redemption," Glynn said. "That's why he freaked when the operation turned bad on him."

"How long had you been undercover?" Bolan asked.

"Just a couple of weeks," she said. "I had hoped to work my way up. Maybe find out who the partner was, find out which hospitals were in danger. Nickel told me a lot of stuff because he wanted to have sex with me." Her face flushed and she looked at Bolan and Waters. "I never did. We don't do that Mata Hari bullshit like they show in the movies. At least I don't. But I did play along a little. Flirted, intimated that the potential was there."

Bolan just nodded when her eyes searched his face for a reaction. He wouldn't judge her either way.

The agent continued. "Anyway, one of Vega's newest hires was a guy whom I had busted two years ago as part of a smuggling operation. He recognized me, reported me to one of Vega's lieutenants and I've been a prisoner since this morning."

"That would explain why Vega looked so angry when he got home this evening."

She nodded and shivered as a chill passed through her. "Exactly. He called me out there and knew I'd be waiting when he showed up. That's when they took me prisoner. He said the last undercover agent he caught had died a lingering death. They used an acetylene torch to burn off body parts. Slashed him open in several places with razors and knives. Told me they would do the same thing with me and mail my remains back to Washington. That was when you came in."

Glynn looked down at her hands and drew in a deep breath. She seemed shaken, as though the enormity of her situation suddenly had crashed on her shoulders. Bolan knew in the heat of battle, fueled by adrenaline and purpose, it was easy to forge ahead. It was usually afterward that physical symptoms of an overloaded nervous system—jumpiness, fatigue, shaking hands and the like—settled in.

He also was familiar with the practice of which she spoke. He had seen several dismembered, mutilated bodies left during his battles with the Mafia. Some had been close friends, people he had allowed to become allies in his never-ending war on criminals and terrorists. The Mafia called the victims, or at least their remains, "turkeys." He had seen other forms of torture, each more disgustingly creative and inhuman than the last, as he had dedicated his life to fighting criminals and terrorists.

The Executioner had shown many of these sadistic bastards

the error of their ways. Usually it was the last lesson any of them learned. He was anxious to teach Vega and his mysterious partner the same thing.

Glynn looked up from her lap, her eyes tired. "I think I'm going to need a few hours of sleep before I do anything else," she said. "Captain, I'd be happy to provide more information in the morning."

"Go rest, lady, you've had a hell of a night," Waters said. "We can find a motel for you, if you need. Let the Feds pick up the tab."

"You can stay at my motel," Bolan said.

The woman eyed him warily for a moment. Bolan knew what she was thinking and he held up a hand to put her at ease. He was attracted to her, sure. But he also wasn't the type to play games. If sex had been his motive, he would have said as much. Bolan wasn't about to take advantage of a weary soldier recovering from a near death experience. He had a job to focus on.

"Nothing funny," he said. "It would be more convenient if we were in the same place. Not the same room, but the same building. I'm not convinced Emilio is going to let us slide so easily."

Glynn nodded. "You're probably right. Though I wouldn't call what we went through at his house easy."

"Point taken," Bolan said.

"I can send over some uniforms to keep an eye on things," Waters suggested.

Bolan shook his head. "I appreciate the concern, but I don't need a shadow. I come and go as I please."

"No one wants to stand in your way, Belasko," Waters told him. "Just want to watch your back for you. How 'bout we keep a few near the motel. If something goes down, you say the word and we swarm. That sound okay?"

Bolan nodded. "That works."

"My guys brought your car here. You talk to the desk sergeant, he'll get you the keys and send you on your way. You'll probably have to fill out some forms."

"In triplicate, I suppose," Bolan said. He smiled at Waters.

"Just try not to shoot anybody between here and the front desk."

MADELINE GLYNN STUDIED herself in a small mirror on the back of a sun visor on the passenger side of the car. Bolan navigated the rented vehicle back toward his motel, allowing Glynn a few minutes to collect herself before the questioning began. With Vega underground, Bolan would need another starting point.

"Who would know the location of the next hospital raid?" he asked finally.

Glynn thought for a moment.

"Harry Van Zant. He's Emilio's top lieutenant. He does the heavy lifting, makes sure things happen."

"He's an enforcer."

"Right. He makes sure the day-to-day stuff goes okay. The less Emilio worries, the better a job Van Zant is doing."

Bolan nodded. He didn't know Van Zant, but he knew the type.

"Where's the guy live?"

Glynn told him. Bolan memorized the address. He tried to pinpoint it in his mind's eye on the maps he studied during the plane trip. He guessed it was a good twenty-minute drive from the motel.

"You're going to see Van Zant."

"Yeah, I am. I plan on doing it alone. This hopefully is going to be a softer probe than the last one."

"That wouldn't be difficult," she said, a wry smile crossing her lips.

Bolan returned the smile. He admired the woman's sense of humor, her toughness. She had been through hell during the past couple of hours and seemed okay. Tired and rumpled, but okay.

"That was pretty ugly back there," she said. "That's the closest I've come to dying. You always keep it at the back of your mind, you know? But you don't dwell on it. Otherwise, you couldn't do the job. Usually it's kind of an abstract concept. Tonight it became very concrete."

"Are you okay?"

Death Merchants

"Not bad," she said. "I could go forever without washing blood from my hair again. I feel like I screwed things up. We had Vega dead to rights."

"You did fine," Bolan said. "You kept a level head in some bad circumstances. That's all anyone could ask. Sometimes we have to make judgment calls when we're on the front line."

"I did cause us to lose Vega. I'm sorry I pointed the gun at you."

"You did the right thing," Bolan said. "You needed to know I was legitimate. You're a federal agent. I was killing people. You had every right to check me out."

"I appreciate what you did for me. I was as good as dead back there. I never got a chance to say thank you."

"You're welcome," Bolan said. "You might get a chance to return the favor before this is all over."

"Which division of Justice are you with, Mike Belasko?"

"One you don't talk about," Bolan said. He turned into the motel, pulled up to the office and looked at the DEA agent. "No offense."

"None taken, Mr. Cloak and Dagger," she said. "You think they have extra rooms? There must be three cars in the parking lot, including ours."

"They might squeeze you in. I'm staying in room 4. Try to get them to put you into three or five. I think five has a doorway into my room."

"In case I need someone with an Uzi."

She smiled at Bolan, opened the door and walked toward the office. He watched the sway of her hips as she moved away. Her T-shirt clung to a slim waist, the lustrous red hair spilling around her shoulders. One tough lady, indeed.

5

"Don't worry, Emilio," Harry Van Zant said into the phone, "that son of a bitch is as good as ours. I don't let people take shots at you and get away with it."

"Fuck you, Harry," Vega said. "Where the hell were you when this guy was murdering our men. Huh? You want to talk tough? You back it up with action. Otherwise shut up. I don't have time for your mouth."

"I understand, Emilio," Van Zant said.

"You don't understand shit, Harry. Listen, this guy took down your best all by himself. Shot them dead. He wasn't a cop like the woman, he was a soldier. I barely got out of the house alive. If he hadn't been so worried about the DEA bitch, I'd be dead, too."

"Sure, Emilio," Van Zant said.

The enforcer's stomach tightened as he uttered the words. Vega was busting his balls good, and Van Zant hated it. But he wasn't about to give his boss attitude. Vega had just had a near death experience and Van Zant handled security. That made it his fault. If he got off with just a tongue-lashing, he was damn lucky.

"Where you at, Emilio?"

"I'm hiding, stupid."

"I know. Where?"

"I'm not saying over the phone. I'll tell you later. In the meantime, you keep doing what you're supposed to be doing."

"This doesn't change anything?"

"This doesn't change a damn thing."

"You got it, Emilio."

Vega hung up the phone without saying goodbye. Van Zant smiled grimly, clicked off the handset of his phone and returned it to the recharging unit. Vega was a loudmouthed prick, a bully, but he never stayed mad long. The way Van Zant figured it, the best thing he could do was to put his head down, do as he was told and let the storm pass. If indeed it passed. No one had ever gotten that close to Vega. That someone did pointed to a security problem. Having someone that capable gunning for Vega was a big problem. That a DEA agent with intimate information about the man's operations was on the loose was another big problem.

Vega despised big problems. They pissed him off and when he got angry, the shit always rolled downhill until it struck Harry Van Zant square in the chest.

It was still early. He lit a cigarette, stuck it in his mouth and rubbed his temples. He craved a cup of coffee to go with his cigarette. He stood, slipped a robe over his T-shirt and shorts and started out the door of his bedroom. He could smell the coffee already brewing and thought longingly of the bottle of whiskey in the kitchen cabinet. The two would make for a good morning pick-me-up.

LIKE A SHADOW, Bolan fell in behind Van Zant as he started down the hall. The Man from Blood already had taken down Van Zant's four guards with deadly precision.

Van Zant stopped for a moment, dragged on his cigarette and scratched himself. Bolan decided it was a good time to make introductions.

"You and I need to talk, Harry," the Executioner said.

The enforcer spun, his face at first angry, then slipped into surprise as he saw the man behind him. Bolan carried the Beretta, the Desert Eagle and an Uzi. Stun grenades and garrotes hung within easy reach on his combat harness. An Applegate-Fairbairn commando dagger hung in a point-up sheath opposite the Beretta's shoulder holster. The Executioner gripped the Beretta, charged with a fresh clip, in his right hand, the snout pointed at Van Zant's chest.

Van Zant let the surprise drain from his face. He donned his best tough-guy mask, his eyes stabbing into Bolan's own. The Executioner suppressed a weary smile. Resistance and bravado usually made up the interrogation drama's opening scene. But the final act would find Van Zant spilling his guts, figuratively, literally or both.

"Who the hell are you?" the enforcer demanded, straightening and pulling his robe.

"A friend of your boss," Bolan said. "I visited him earlier. I'm sure he mentioned me."

"Yeah, he mentioned you."

"So, where is he, Harry?"

"Screw yourself. I wouldn't say if I knew. And I don't know."

"You talked to him," Bolan said. "I overheard you through the door."

"Yeah, I talked to him," Van Zant said, his voice rising slightly. Bolan saw the guy's eyes ease to his left, as though he expected someone to appear.

Bolan shook his head. "Forget it, Harry. Your people are gone. I gave them the night off."

"Shit. Where are they?"

"Dead. Just like the ones at Vega's house. The same thing can happen to you, too."

"What do you want?"

"Vega. Where is he?"

"Honest to God, man, I don't know," Van Zant said. "He just called me. Said he didn't want to tell me his location over the phone. That's the truth. You've got to believe that."

Bolan did. During his War Everlasting, he had developed keen intuition, combat sense, whatever. He could tell by the quaver of someone's voice, the look in their eyes whether he was lying. He had a 99.9 percent accuracy rate, better, he was sure, than a polygraph.

He believed Van Zant, but he wasn't ready to tell him so. He straightened his arm and pointed the gun at Van Zant's head.

"You're starting to piss me off, Harry. You're Emilio's top lieutenant. You expect me to believe you don't know where he is?"

Panic entered into Van Zant's eyes. His lips moved silently for a moment, until words finally exploded from them, like a muted television that suddenly regained its sound.

"I'm telling the truth. Vega's pissed at me. He's not saying anything to me until I regain his trust. That's how he gets when he's mad. He'll call me again after he cools off, ask me to send some guys his way to watch his ass."

"What are you doing in the meantime?"

Van Zant spread his hands, palms exposed, fingers splayed open and pointing toward the floor. He flashed Bolan an unconvincing smile.

"Sitting around here and waiting for the boss to tell me my next move."

Bolan took a step closer, the Beretta's muzzle steady.

"That's bullshit, Harry. I know about the hospitals. Where and when is the next one slated to go down?"

The flapping, soundless mouth again, then the verbal explosion.

"Georgia. We're hitting a cancer hospital in Georgia. It's going down tonight."

"Which hospital?"

"Masters Cancer Center. It's in Buckhead. Supposed to be an upscale suburb of Atlanta. We hit after midnight, just like the others."

"No, you don't," Bolan said. "This hit will not go down. How many raiders this time?"

"Ten."

"As bloody as Davis Memorial?"

Van Zant again raised his hands defensively.

"Hey, man, that was Nickel's mistake. Guy was shit-deep in

trouble with Emilio. Hank lost his head and did something stupid. Emilio never wanted anyone to die during one of these. Creates a lot of unwanted problems for us."

"Not to mention it leaves a bunch of innocent people dead," Bolan said. "I guess that never crossed your mind."

Van Zant stared at his bare feet, like a chastened child. "Don't lecture me, man. It wasn't supposed to happen the way it did."

"This one in Georgia won't go down at all," Bolan said. "You tell Vega that. Make sure he knows the guy who shot up his house is gunning for him and won't stop until he's dead. Tell him the cancer-hospital raids are over."

Van Zant shook his head. "I can do that."

Bolan guessed he would, too. Harry Van Zant struck Bolan as a survivor.

"Are we cool, man?" Van Zant asked.

"Not yet, Harry," Bolan said. "You tell Emilio I know about the labs, too. Those won't happen, either."

"Damn, man," Van Zant said. He smoothed back his hair with his left hand, let the fingers linger over the long ponytail that hung in back. "Emilio is going to kill me if I say that. No one's supposed to know about the labs."

"I know about them. So does the DEA. Now, tell me— where's the prototype lab going up?"

"I have no idea," Van Zant said. The steadiness of his voice indicated to Bolan he was telling the truth.

"Why don't you know, Harry?"

"Emilio's got a partner. The guy's setting the whole thing up. We're supposed to go out at the end of the week, see the damn thing. Until then, Emilio was keeping the details to himself. He said the fewer people he has in the loop, the better. Probably won't tell anyone until he gets there."

Bolan detected a note of bitterness. "Who's the partner?"

"Victor Sampson," Van Zant said. "Sampson's kid got burned in the same operation that took Emilio's son. Emilio hates the blue-blood son of a bitch, but Sampson has deep pockets and an army of chemists. He's also got as big a hard-on for the DEA as Emilio."

He looked self-consciously at Bolan, as if realizing for the first time whom he was talking to. "Hey, I didn't tell you any of this stuff, right?"

"Tell Emilio I'm in his rearview mirror. For now, lie down on the floor and put your hands behind your head."

Van Zant sank first to his knees, then onto his palms and knees and finally lowered himself to the floor. Fingers laced together, he rested his hands on his head.

"You're not going to kill me, are you? I helped you and all."

"Hard to deliver the message if I kill you," Bolan said. "Now shut your eyes and count to ten out loud."

Van Zant began counting. When he hit "five," he cracked an eyelid, peered around the room. The man in black seemingly had disappeared, just like a ghost. Just to be safe, Van Zant finished the count. He pulled himself from the floor and finished his trip to the kitchen. Along the way, he readjusted the coffee-to-whiskey ratio in favor of the liquor.

MINUTES LATER, the Executioner sat in his rental just outside Van Zant's home. Bolan had slipped a pair of baggy gray coveralls over the black suit and hid the Uzi under the driver's seat. He had plucked the grenades from the combat harness and placed them under the seat, too. The coveralls were unzipped to his waist, allowing him easy access to the Beretta should he need it.

He set a small device that resembled a radio on the passenger seat, uncoiled a thin white cord and stuck an earpiece attached to one end into his ear. Stony Man's technical wizard, Gadgets Schwarz, had worked up the handheld device to allow those in the field to listen to bugged telephones. The device was small enough to fit in a pocket and looked innocent enough to escape notice. Bolan had tapped Van Zant's phone before confronting him.

The warrior knew Vega would call his top man when he cooled down. Bolan wanted to hear what he had to say about Van Zant's early-morning visitor. He also hoped to get a location for the drug lab.

While he waited for Van Zant to get another call, Bolan picked up his digital phone and dialed up the cutout number that eventually would patch him through to Stony Man Farm.

It was too early to reach Aaron Kurtzman directly, but Bolan knew the installation had a voice-mail system that would allow him to leave a message. He waited through several beeps and clicks as the phone system verified the codes he had entered. He entered a few more numbers and Kurtzman's recorded voice said, "Kurtzman," followed by a beep.

"This is Striker," Bolan said. "Gather intel on Victor Sampson. Especially as it relates to commodities. I'll call."

He clicked off the phone with his thumb and pocketed it. If Kurtzman had been available, he might have asked him to tap into the National Security Agency's satellite system, track the phone call and find Vega's hiding place.

As it was, Bolan would use shoe leather to find what he needed. He considered calling Glynn, too, to make sure she was all right, that Vega hadn't sent visitors, but dismissed the idea. At last check, she hadn't requested a baby-sitter.

A beep from the receiver alerted Bolan to an incoming call. He pushed a button and waited to cut into the conversation. Van Zant's taut voice boomed into the ear piece.

"...guy said he knows we're behind the hospital raids. He also knows about the drug laboratories, Emilio."

Vega swore then said, "How does he know that?"

"Probably the chick Nickel brought into the operation. Goddamn Nickel destroyed everything. We're better off with him dead."

"Nickel destroyed nothing, Harry. You got that? He destroyed nothing. This all goes ahead as planned."

"Even Buckhead?"

"It goes."

A barely perceptible pause, then, "You sure, Emilio? What if he knows about the location?"

"How would he know, Harry? Did you tell him?"

"No, man," Van Zant said, his voice strained as he lied. "But what if the DEA agent said something? Maybe Nickel told her."

Bolan had pegged the guy right—a survivor.

"Nickel didn't know locations," Vega said. "None of the team members were told anything about other raids in case they got arrested. You know that, Harry. That was your idea. What the hell's the matter with you?"

"Nothing, Emilio," Van Zant said. "Just nervous is all. I got a house full of dead bodies. I almost got a bullet put in my head. Makes a guy edgy."

The drug lord's voice hardened. "Pull it together. Remember what happened to the last guy who panicked and brought me trouble."

"I'm cool, Emilio. You need some guys?"

"Hell, yes, I need some guys. I got a crazy man trying to kill me. Call our people in Georgia, tell them Emilio wants help. Now. You send some up here from Orlando, too, for God's sake."

"Where do I send them once they get there?"

"Get them to Georgia. We'll make sure they get to the lab. Tell them to bring something besides pistols. That lunatic had grenades pinned to his chest and was killing us with an assault rifle."

"You going to the lab, Emilio?"

"Catching the plane in a few minutes. You stay there. I'll need someone to ride herd while I'm gone. Can you do that?"

"Of course."

Bolan cursed. The men were playing it close to the vest, giving him few details to go on. Obviously they lived with the threat of surveillance on a daily basis and fought it by divulging as little information as possible. Bolan wondered whether he had underestimated Vega's shrewdness. He hoped not. Underestimating the enemy had spelled the end for more than one soldier.

He made a note to have Kurtzman and his cybernetics team begin tracking flights out of area airports. With his massive intelligence-gathering network, Kurtzman easily could widen the search to include both metropolitan and suburban airports. Bolan also decided it was time to page Grimaldi, put him on standby in case he needed to fly. It was several hours from their appointed rendezvous time, but Bolan knew the Stony Man pilot could be ready on short notice.

Van Zant's voice brought Bolan back into the moment.

"Is the cook in town?"

"Yeah. He's meeting with me. Guess the timing was good for him to leave home. Couple of his guys blew up a motel room trying to mix some methamphetamine."

"That son of a bitch is trouble, Emilio. Mark my words."

"Drop it, Harry."

"Sure, man," Van Zant said, his voice softening. "What do you want me to do about this Fed?"

"Kill the bastard. Find him, find the woman and kill them. Can you handle that much on your own, for God's sake?"

"Yeah, I can do that," Van Zant said. His voice tightened, the pace of his words quickened. "But if this guy knows about your connection to Davis Memorial, Orlando PD probably knows, too. Cops swarmed your place after the shooting. Plus the woman probably told them what's up."

"So what if they know? I'm gone. They'll never find me. If you get rousted, tell the cops to kiss your ass, call the lawyers, shut up and wait. You know the drill. As long as they don't know about tonight's raid, we're golden. What's eating you, Van Zant? That guy steal your brains and balls while he was in your house?"

A quick pause, then Van Zant spoke. Bolan guessed the enforcer used the silence to swallow his true words, and instead inserted in their place the ones the drug lord wanted to hear.

"No, Emilio," Van Zant said. "Just want to make sure we're on the same wavelength. Don't worry about me. I'll take care of stuff here."

"Make damn sure you do. I like you, man. You help me make this happen and I'll cut you in on stuff. When all this blows over, we'll fly to Tahiti, chase women, get drunk. Just like old times. How's that sound?"

"Sounds great, Emilio."

"So you're going to relax, take care of stuff for me in Florida?"

"Consider me relaxed, Emilio," Van Zant said, his voice unconvincing. "Orlando is in good hands."

"That's better. We'll talk later."

Vega clicked off, followed by Van Zant. Silence filled Bolan's earpiece for a moment before it returned to life with a dial tone buzzing in Bolan's ear. Van Zant fired to life the phone lines and proceeded to spend another twenty minutes calling a variety of hardmen, rousting most from sleep. Bolan assumed the day shift hadn't been scheduled to come on duty for a couple more hours.

Call after call, the content was the same: convene at a predetermined spot, catch a pair of chartered planes that would be there waiting for them. The planes, chartered personally by Vega, would fly them to an unknown destination. Cars would be waiting for them on the other side, ready to transport them to the drug lab.

During Van Zant's second round of calls, he summoned a small army to his home to clean up Bolan's mess, fortify the house.

For a second time, the earpiece fell silent. It remained so for more than a minute.

Bolan removed the earpiece, turned off the listening device and started the car. It was time, he decided, to get while the getting was good.

The longer he stayed, the later it got, the greater Bolan's risk of attracting police attention either from a passing patrol car or a suspicious vehicle complaint filed by a neighbor. Failing that, as Van Zant's battalion of thugs arrived, Bolan risked identification by and a gunfight with edgy hardmen who overnight had lost nearly a dozen of their own. The Executioner worried little about his odds in such a confrontation. But he had no desire to turn this quiet suburban street into a battlefield where residents might get hurt as they stepped out of their homes to jog, to go to work or to snag the morning paper.

Slipping the rental into Drive, Bolan left behind the posh neighborhood and contemplated the exchange between Vega and Van Zant. It had left him with more questions than answers. He still had no idea where Vega had disappeared to or how many hospitals his people planned to hit. The latter worried Bolan most as his mind flashed back on the police photos of the cop, Jon Sanchez, who left behind a widow, herself a dying woman, and the photo of the unassuming pharmacist whose only crime had been working on a low-inventory night.

Vega was a greedy, bloodthirsty parasite—of that Bolan had no doubt. And with Bolan's failed attempt to eliminate him through a quick hit, the guy now was gunning for Bolan and the brave DEA agent whom the soldier had saved from a near-certain death.

Bolan planned to hit Vega. Hit him hard for the widows and orphans left behind in the hospital raids, for the families torn asunder by the ravages of drug addiction.

Vega and Victor Sampson were taking their bloody trade to a new level. In Bolan's mind, they constituted a clear and present danger. He planned to snuff out the danger, violently if necessary.

First he had to find Vega. He started toward the motel—his temporary base of operations—so he could pick up Glynn, check in with Stony Man Farm and pick up any necessary equipment. He was going to need all the help he could get.

SIPPING HIS WHISKEY and coffee, Harry Van Zant mulled Vega's words as the warm liquid trailed down his throat, smoldered pleasantly in his stomach. If this guy really was a federal agent as the boss assumed, then it was possible to track him down. Sure, Orlando was crawling with drug investigators, but someone with the right connections could find out anything he needed to know in a short amount of time.

After decades in the drug business, Van Zant had the connections on both sides of the business. He could place a few calls to Orlando PD, the local DEA and FBI offices, and find out who this bastard was. And he could do it in a matter of hours.

Harry Van Zant loved to party. Drugs. Women. Alcohol. He kept all in great supply. And he was generous with these things, especially when it came to greasing cops with them. Most cops would tell Van Zant to go fuck himself when he tried to bribe them, so he selected his targets carefully. He checked around, found out who was on the take, who had financial trouble, marital problems, drug or alcohol addictions and cultivated them as snitches. Troubled people sought life preservers; Harry Van Zant pretended to offer just that—a sympathetic ear, free drugs, a loan, a woman. Whatever it took to hook the poor bastards.

Then he owned them. And, like property, he used them whenever and however he wanted. He knew of busts hours, sometimes days before they came down. With that knowledge, he and Vega could make command decisions about whether to let a raid happen, in effect throw the cops an occasional bone so they didn't suspect treachery, or whether to pull up stakes and protect their holdings.

The contacts were what made Harry Van Zant his boss's most trusted lieutenant in a business where job security meant more than a steady paycheck. It meant the difference between life and death.

Right now, Vega was unhappy with him. The routine about Tahiti and chasing women was bullshit—unless he started to produce results. So it was time to make some calls, find out the name and location of this icy-eyed bastard. He'd hit the motels and airports, find his target and take him out.

6

Blades Airport, Jacksonville, Florida

Vega heaved the cell phone across the room, swore loud and long.

Tommy "Cooker" Johnson and the other man in the room turned to stare at him. The drug lord returned the stare, then felt an uncharacteristic flush of self-consciousness and composed himself. The man beside Johnson, David Estevez, Vega's personal bodyguard, went to retrieve the phone, avoiding eye contact with his boss as he bent to pick it up.

The airport was a small facility located on the outskirts of Jacksonville. Built in the 1950s, the place consisted of a small airstrip, a few hangars and a small terminal. Once a popular destination for corporate charters, it had eventually become a haven for drug dealers and other criminals who required air travel to run their organizations. Although the previous generation had balked at their changing client list, the latest operators encouraged patronage by drug smugglers and killers—as long as customers did nothing to bring the law crashing down upon them.

Vega preferred the relative anonymity it offered him compared with airports closer to his own home. It was the first place to which he and his crew had headed after the attack on his house.

Johnson appraised Vega coolly. "What's the problem, Emilio?" he asked, his voice a lazy drawl.

"That big son of a bitch who raided my home, he just shook down Van Zant. Now we have four more dead. God knows what the guy is going to do next."

Estevez turned toward Vega, listening intently. Johnson yawned loud and long, then let a goofy smile overtook his face.

"My friend, you need some real muscle," he said. "These guys of yours, they're okay for busting heads on junkies and pushers. But they're obviously outclassed with this guy. You need some help."

Estevez gave Johnson a mean stare, but remained silent. The man from Nashville ignored Estevez and instead settled his lanky frame onto a metal chair outfitted with cushions covered in cracked orange plastic. He wore faded jeans, sandals and a black concert T-shirt. When he sat, his pant leg hiked enough to reveal the muzzle of an autoloading pistol strapped to his hairless, mushroom-white ankle.

"I don't need you to tell me how to run my business," Vega said. "Estevez knows plenty of muscle. Van Zant does, too. I want you to show me how to keep making this painkiller once we start production. You do that and I'll be happy."

Johnson stared absently out the window.

"Whatever, man," he said. A loud exhale underscored his boredom. "I've seen this shit before. You need a specialist. I can make some calls, get you some backup before this whole thing blows in your face."

"My first priority is getting the hell out of Florida. You're going with me. After that, you can call anyone you want."

"Suit yourself."

Vega stared at the skinny man with his bald scalp, his alabaster-shaded skull ringed in oily strands of white-blond hair. He had chartered a plane to bring Cooker Johnson here, and the man had landed just in time to do an about-face and skip town with Vega. The drug lord hated Johnson, despised the skinny man's arrogance, his know-it-all attitude and lack of respect. But he was the linchpin in his plans, a status that bought him room to shoot off his mouth. He had damn near exhausted the privilege.

"I can make this stuff, you know," Johnson said. "I analyzed the samples you sent me while I was in Nashville. Should be fairly easy, if you get me the equipment."

"You'll have equipment," Vega said. "We're seeing to that right now. We'll get you money and people, too. You just keep up your end of the deal."

"Why do you and Sampson need me, anyway?"

"*We* don't need you."

"What the hell does that mean?"

Vega looked at the guard. "David, see if they got that plane fueled and ready to fly."

"Sure," Estevez said. He exited the terminal through a glass door and crossed the tarmac to check on the small ground crew's progress as they fueled and inspected the plane. The drug lord watched him for a moment, then turned to Johnson.

"You're working for me," Vega said. "Just me."

"No shit."

"I want you to oversee production of the Vitalife knockoff. You can run the laboratories instead of Sampson's corporate morons. Those guys know chemistry and pharmaceuticals. They're stupid when it comes to street drugs. They make things nice and slow. They stick to FDA rules. I need someone who can pop this stuff out quick and dirty. Do it on a national basis."

Johnson continued to look bored. He tossed a cigarette onto the black-streaked linoleum floor, watching as it burned itself out.

After a long pause, he spoke. "I can do that. But it's going to cost you. I make a lot of money processing coke and making crystal meth. Make it worth my while and we'll talk."

"I'm offering you a way to make some real money, build a

new empire," Vega said. "You want making junk in motel-room bathtubs, be my fucking guest."

Johnson jabbed another cigarette between his lips and lit it. He turned to Vega, twin streams of smoke billowing from his nostrils like a dragon. He sneered as he spoke.

"Who says I don't make money now? I got a dozen guys working for me in Tennessee. I account for twenty percent of the man-made street drugs in Nashville. You think I'm cooking meth in a goddamn bathtub somewhere like white trash? Fuck you. I'm a pro."

The drug lord consciously tightened his lips to keep from smiling. He had found a tender spot. Now it was time to salve the idiot's smarting ego to his own advantage. When it came to negotiating, Vega could charm and disarm with the best of them. Failing that, he could bargain very hard.

"I know you're the best at what you do, Johnson," Vega said. "That's why I'm asking you to join me. I need your skills to make this happen. But it's going to happen either way, so if you won't do it, I'll have to find someone with similar skills."

"Good luck. Assuming I agree to this, how much money would I make?"

"Five percent of everything we sell. After expenses," Vega said. He leaned forward, winking. "And you'll have power. You'll be my right-hand man."

Johnson barely blinked at the carrot dangled before him.

"Fifteen percent," he replied. "And you can keep your high rank. All I want from you is money. Fifteen percent off the top line. That means before expenses. *Comprende,* partner?"

"Fifteen percent?" Vega asked, his voice rising. "Why the hell should I even bother doing this if I'm giving away everything I make?"

Johnson stared out the window and nursed his cigarette. "It's your call, man. I got a job either way."

Johnson's words—his arrogance—stoked a caldron of rage in the drug lord's gut. He jabbed his hand inside his jacket, pulled his Glock from its holster and lunged at the man. The suddenness of the attack seemed to surprise Johnson, who turned wide-eyed as the threat registered with him.

The skinny chemist threw up a hand to protect his face. His other hand grabbed for the pistol holstered on his ankle. He shouldn't have bothered; Vega knocked him from the chair and fell on top of him before fingertips reached the frayed cuff of his jeans.

Johnson gasped as he struck the floor and Vega's weight crushed down upon him. The drug runner rapped the gun against Johnson's face with an audible crack. Blood sprayed as the barrel split the man's lips, cracked a tooth. Vega shoved the pistol barrel against the tip of Johnson's nose.

"Look, you prick," the drug lord raged, "I didn't even give my son that kind of cut. You take five percent off the bottom line. You know, after everything's paid for. And you just take it for the Vitalife sales, not the coke, crack, grass or heroin I sell. Agree to those terms or I'll spread your damn head all over this floor, find me someone else to do the job. You decide."

Johnson struggled for a moment, then stopped. A massive shadow fell over them and the slamming of a submachine gun's charging bolt to the rear of Vega told the drug lord why. Estevez had returned from the airfield.

"David, this bastard wants to make big money, wants to make more than my boy did. What do you think of that?"

The drug lord didn't give Estevez a chance to respond.

"I think it shows bad judgment," Vega said. "I don't know if I want to work with someone with such poor judgment. You know what I'm saying? And if I'm not going to work with him, we may as well kill him."

"I can do that," the guard said.

Johnson searched Vega's eyes, probably trying to gauge whether the intimidation tactics were a trick. Judging by Johnson's sudden change of heart, he realized Vega would kill him without a second thought.

"We can work something out, Emilio," Johnson said. Crimson bubbled in the corner of his mouth, and his words slurred slightly as he spoke. "You don't need to do this."

"So now five percent is fair?"

"Yeah. It's fine. It doesn't need to go this way. I swear."

Vega returned the Glock to its shoulder rig, then stood to his full height.

"You're right," the drug lord said. "It doesn't have to go this way."

He slammed his right foot into Johnson's ribs. The cooker screwed his face, groaned and tried to roll into a ball to protect himself. Another kick put him on his back. Then Vega stepped on the drug chemist's throat and applied enough pressure to gain his full attention.

"Take his gun."

The big guard switched the SMG to his left hand, bent down and pushed up the leg of Cooker's faded jeans. With a thumb and two fingers, he pulled the 9 mm Smith & Wesson from the ankle holster. He stood and slipped the pistol into the pocket of his jacket. Vega removed his foot and held out a hand.

"Now, you want to talk? Or should I have David lean on you a little more?"

"No, Emilio. We can talk."

Vega extended a hand. Johnson eyed the drug lord warily, but took the hand and pulled himself to his feet with the drug lord's help. He wiped blood from his mouth.

"Get the man a towel, David. And some ice if you can find it."

"Sure," Estevez said. "The plane's almost ready to go. Just another couple of minutes. We got ice in the cooler and some towels on board."

Vega clapped his hands. The storm cloud passed from his face, and his lips spread back into a smile. "Wonderful. We'll talk out the finer points of our deal in the air."

"Nothing to talk about, Emilio," Johnson said. "I'm your guy. But what's Sampson going to say about your bringing me along?"

Vega shrugged. "I don't care what Sampson thinks. I'll tell him I recruited you to oversee one of our future labs. Tell him his people are still in charge. That's all he needs to know. You just keep your damn mouth shut."

"You're going to have to tell him sometime."

"You let me worry about Sampson. We've got a plane to catch."

Johnson shot him a puzzled look, but said nothing. Instead, he nodded and exited the terminal. Another smile tugged at Vega's mouth. He apparently had broken Cooker Johnson, at least for the moment, and that was good. He demanded total obedience from his people. Street criminals like Johnson gave it easily enough. Flash them money, prestige, women or drugs, and they reciprocated with loyal service. Failing that, violence was a good driver and often bought deeper allegiances than material things.

An angry, fearful look in Johnson's eyes told Vega that he owned Johnson. He had seen the look in enough men and women that he could name it as easily as a sunrise.

Victor Sampson was another matter altogether. Months of working together told Vega he would never own the man. At best, Sampson would stick to his original promise of a fifty-fifty partnership. Vega knew the rich industrialist never would surrender control, full control, of the Vitalife operation. From the drug lord's way of thinking, that meant their partnership would be short-lived.

Short-lived, indeed.

Just like Victor Sampson.

7

Orlando International Airport

An armored sedan and a team of agents were waiting for Ray
Pitt when he arrived at Orlando International Airport. From the
minute he stepped from the private charter plane and crossed
the airfield, he was surrounded by worried-looking men and
women, eyes darting around for possible assailants. As DEA
director, Pitt was used to the treatment. He was both grateful
for and exhausted by it.

A wiry agent, with black hair trimmed close to the skin on
the top and sides, stepped from the armored car to greet Pitt.
Eyes obscured by mirrored sunglasses, the agent offered a
hand. Pitt took it and smiled.

"Good to see you agent Cronin," Pitt said.

Dan Cronin was special agent in charge of the Orlando office. Cronin didn't return the smile, but Pitt had expected that
and knew it was nothing personal. Having the director's security on your to-do list was a heavy burden, and Pitt knew Cronin

took the responsibility seriously. Chances were he wouldn't relax until Pitt left town again in two days.

"It's good to see you, too, sir," Cronin said. "We can transport you to the motel. Our security teams already swept your room and the building. Orlando PD pitched in with some help, too. Everything is secure."

"I knew you would take care of things, Dan," Pitt said. The praise caused the corners of Cronin's mouth to relax into his best version of a grin. Dressed in a navy-blue suit, Pitt felt the sun creating a pocket of heat between his jacket and his shirt. He wiped sweat from his brow. "Let's get into the air-conditioned car. Or else this heat may be the thing to take me down."

Seated in the back of the limousine, Cronin situated himself across from Pitt. He pulled a leather briefcase onto his lap, opened it and withdrew a handful of papers. Shutting the briefcase, he set the papers on top of the leather bag and began rifling through them.

"The summit begins at 1:00 p.m.," Cronin said. "We'll be meeting with the police chiefs, U.S. Postal Service and customs officials at Orlando PD's main headquarters. Police from Jacksonville, Miami, Tampa, Orlando, Daytona, Ormond Beach, as well as sheriffs from major counties, will be there."

Pitt nodded. "What's the mood?"

"Tense. The local authorities are wary of us. That's a polite description."

Pitt nodded. Having been an assistant police chief for the Washington, D.C., department, he knew the legendary enmity that existed between federal law enforcement and local police. Having been on both sides of it, he tried to handle multiagency operations with sensitivity. Sometimes it worked, and sometimes it didn't. Pitt stopped focusing on the latter a long time ago. It helped him keep his sanity in a pressure-cooker job.

"You think the local chiefs will cooperate?" he asked Cronin.

"I think so. The depth of cooperation is the real issue. No major city police chief would openly snub the DEA. But whether they really want to work together or just pay lip service so we mention them in the press release is the real question."

Pitt sank back into the leather seat. He knew Cronin was

right, but his work here was critical. The latest operation he planned to propose was so important that it was going to go regardless of whether the locals cooperated. Both the President and the attorney general had told him as much. Egos be damned and full speed ahead.

Pitt's bosses had asked him to identify Florida's three biggest drug importers and take them down, with or without local law enforcement's help. The President was prepared to offer him a blank check as far as federal resources—attorneys, money, boats, soldiers and weapons. In exchange he wanted heads on pikes, figuratively or literally.

From a tactical standpoint, the strike made sense. Knocking down Florida's biggest domestic drug exporters meant a lighter flow of drugs along the Interstate 75 corridor, a prime drug conduit between Florida and Michigan. The President wanted a prime bust to present for his next state-of-the-union address, a big arrest to underscore statistics proving the administration's get-tough stance in the war on drugs. Pitt's job was to produce the visual aid.

Lucky him.

Pitt reached into a black leather valise and pulled from it a folder detailing the program, dubbed Operation Thunderbolt II. The latest effort was to rival or surpass its predecessor. More drugs, more property seizures, more arrests. Pitt just hoped the sequel included a lower body count, at least on his side. The director had personally attended the funerals of each agent killed during Operation Thunderbolt. He had visited the families, mourned with them, listened to them as they vented anger and sadness at him, his agency and the drug dealers who had shot and killed his people.

His people.

He considered every DEA agent an extension of himself. When one did something wrong, got caught taking a bribe or succumbed to drug addiction while in the field working undercover, Pitt felt it. When an agent died in the line of duty, grief washed over him, dulling his senses for days, as if some force had extinguished a light in his soul. Pitt always let the families know how much he hurt for their loss. Sometimes they believed him; sometimes they didn't. Regardless of their reaction, he never let it go unsaid.

It was the least he could do for those who made the supreme sacrifice for their country.

Thumbing through the folder, Pitt weighed Thunderbolt II's hit list. Pitt knew of all three men, of course, but he was especially familiar with Emilio Vega, who had lost his son during the first Operation Thunderbolt. He couldn't help but marvel at the drug runner's arrogance. His bloody trade cost him his flesh and blood, yet he continued to practice it. Vega knew of no other way to live—of that much, Pitt was sure. And if seeing his own child zipped into a body bag hadn't taught the drug lord a lesson, Pitt hoped a second assault against his drug empire might finally show the man the error of his ways.

Pitt considered it a personal failure when they hadn't nailed Vega during the operation. As was typical in organized crime, the drug lord had insulated himself with enough people to make prosecution impossible.

Vega paid his people well, and those not swayed by money remained loyal out of fear. The drug lord had connections in federal prisons that could make a stay in jail either heaven or hell. Keep quiet and live easy in prison where bribed guards looked the other way while you continued to break the law. Or talk and end up with your throat slit during a manufactured riot. And in the unlikely event the organization couldn't get you directly, they'd come for your children, your spouse, your parents. Vega's power made it damn near impossible to turn his own against him, which made prosecuting the bastard a nightmare.

But Ray Pitt didn't plan to give up. He and the other officers involved in Operation Thunderbolt's second incarnation would succeed where previous efforts failed. Even, he decided, if it meant getting blood on his own hands in the process.

Downtown Orlando

RAGE AND HATRED swept through the young Hispanic as he stared through his windshield, watching Ray Pitt disembark from the government car and head into Orlando police head-quarters. A group of agents and aides followed as the drug cop entered the building.

Juan Vega was unsure what brought Pitt back to Orlando, but he planned to find out. It wasn't critical to his mission, but it would satiate his curiosity. What he wanted most was to put a bullet in Pitt's head. He planned to accomplish this goal before the clock struck noon.

He drove a few blocks away, parked along the curb. He hated to put so much distance between himself and his escape vehicle, but he had little choice. Parking in the police department's garage put him closer to the building, but it also would make for a difficult escape. If all went as planned, he would silently kill Pitt and escape before anyone discovered the murder. Then he would ditch the gun and forget the whole sordid mess.

Perhaps even forget the pain of losing his brother.

Juan Vega had always been considered the weaker son, the one who needed protection, the one who needed to go to business school and work in the relative safety of one of his father's money-laundering companies. His mother—God rest her soul—had demanded that he endure such a sheltered existence. Ernesto Vega had been asked to join the family business—the *real* family business—while Juan toiled running a small bank.

What the younger Vega boy had taken over barely qualified as a bank. It had one office, no tellers and a massive computer system that transferred money electronically between Orlando and banks in the Cayman Islands and Aruba. Employees issued credit and debit cards that allowed his father and other members of his father's selected clientele to tap into their riches easily. Juan had personally helped establish a data system that protected the transfers from the prying eyes of everyone from federal agents to securities regulators.

The elaborate system protected his father's empire from asset seizures, from the prying eyes of the government's army of forensic accountants.

Accomplishing that, the young man took the bank legitimate, created a branch network, hired real tellers and loan officers. Within a matter of years, he changed the organization from a sleepy wirehouse to a thriving bank with millions in assets.

At first his father had worried the success might draw too much attention. Juan Vega had put those fears to rest by using the legitimate institution to further insulate his father's business dealings from investigators. Weaving legitimate and illegitimate transactions, he created a practically impenetrable money-laundering machine. Tirelessly he worked, relying on a diet of cocaine and amphetamines to supply his drive and ambition. Always he succeeded.

Still, his father hardly noticed.

It was always the drug trade—and Juan's older brother, Ernesto—who commanded Emilio Vega's attention. No matter how great his achievements, Juan always languished in his brother's shadow. Ernesto's death had only cemented that, transforming the older sibling from family favorite to martyr and hero. The legend of Ernesto Vega had inflated to such an unrealistic magnitude that the younger son had given up hope of ever overcoming it.

Victor Sampson changed all that.

Juan Vega liked Sampson the moment he met him. Sampson was a businessman. They talked the same language, and Juan Vega could tell Sampson respected him. He also said several times that he understood the family's pain well because it was his pain, too.

Normally he would consider such a statement sentimental bullshit uttered by a man with an agenda. But Sampson had lost his own son. He seemed sincerely concerned for Emilio Vega's younger son, something his own father had never mustered up for him.

He had started to consider the older man a confidant, perhaps even a father figure. Sampson's only demand was that Emilio Vega not know of their friendship. The drug lord, Sampson reasoned, might think Sampson had ulterior motives, perhaps even hatred for Emilio Vega because their sons had died together.

Nothing could have been further from the truth, Sampson assured the younger man. His own son's death had forced Sampson to reassess his life, had forced him to come to peace with himself and others. He was looking for a friend, perhaps even a replacement for his lost child.

As Juan Vega grew to trust the man, he told him of his secret desire to kill Pitt, to strike a blow for his family, help regain its honor. He expected a law-abiding citizen like Sampson to laugh or distance himself. Instead, the man listened intently, admitted his own hatred for Pitt and offered his help.

Juan shared his plan with Sampson, who provided suggestions. The industrialist's security team also consulted with the young banker about ways to eliminate the DEA director. They trained him in ways to kill a man with bare hands or a silenced pistol. Sampson's personal assistant, Richard Ahern, went so far as to locate the perfect weapon for the hit, called in some markers to get it stolen from the police department.

No shirker, Juan invested plenty of his own time into making the mission happen. He contacted the same dirty cops who regularly helped his father, found the dirtiest, most vulnerable of them all and secured his help. Under Ahern's tutelage, he learned to use the stolen pistol—a Beretta 92. How to field-strip and clean it, pack a clip with alternating rounds of hollowpoint and hardball ammunition, where to dispose of it after the hit.

He did all this and continued to run the bank. The effort required that he snort more cocaine, pop more pills than ever before. Was damn close to costing him his marriage, but he cared little. Killing Ray Pitt would make the whole effort worthwhile.

8

"So you think they'll still raid the Georgia hospital?" Brognola asked Bolan as the two spoke via telephone.

Bolan sat on the edge of the motel room bed, feeling the broken springs pushing against his behind. Glynn, who already had called her DEA superiors, stood next to the window, peering through the curtain at the parking lot. Bolan pressed the receiver against his ear so he could hear Brognola over the rattle of the air conditioner. He watched a cockroach scurry under the scarred dresser that sat against the long wall opposite the bed.

"Sounds like it, Hal. Van Zant was too scared to tell his boss I knew of the raid. Whether he'll continue to lie is debatable. They stand to lose a lot of people if they do. Either way, Van Zant may have thrust himself into the Hank Nickel category."

"Small loss," Brognola said. "Do you think he was talking straight on the phone? Or did he know you were listening?"

"It's possible he suspected," Bolan said. "Van Zant knew I had overheard his previous phone conversation while I was in the house. Both men were cautious. But that could be out of habit. It's hard to tell."

"We can send a team to Buckhead today," Brognola said, "to make sure the hospital's safe. But that doesn't bring us any closer to finding Vega."

"What did you find out about Victor Sampson?"

"Richer than you and I will ever be. He and his family have been in Florida for generations. They've made a mint in pharmaceuticals and medical supplies. Legally his record is clean. Nothing but a couple of inquiries by the Securities and Exchange Commission regarding stock trades. None of those were of any substance, and he never got in any trouble. He and his company have the typical baggage—mounds of civil lawsuits, occasional embezzlement cases in which they act as the plaintiff, industrial-espionage complaints. But here's the interesting part."

"What's that?"

"His son was another matter. He was up to his neck in the drug business. The illegal drug business. And his boss was Emilio Vega."

"Van Zant told me he lost a son in Operation Thunderbolt."

"Not before he killed a DEA agent. Junior was so coked up at the time, no one's sure whether he knew what he was doing."

"So Sampson's on the war path."

"Absolutely," Brognola said. "The man wields considerable clout on Capitol Hill. He practically owns several congressmen because of the money he sinks into their campaigns. Hedges his bets and gives equal amounts to both parties to steel himself against changes in the political wind. Plays golf with a lot of media moguls and has tons of influence there, too. All perfectly legal. No bribes. Nothing to draw attention to himself."

All legal, sure, but not necessarily right. Bolan had learned a long time ago there often were miles between the two.

Brognola continued. "Our sources tell us Sampson has launched a war on the DEA. His congressional cronies push for an investigation of the agency and its practices. They get the

DEA's funding cut. Always some back-door bullshit. It's a dirty war, corporate style."

"So Sampson gives Vega the expertise and equipment he needs to reproduce the drug."

"Right," Brognola said. "And the resources. He has a ton of talented chemists and all the necessary equipment. Besides, he profits from a competitor's drug—Vitalife—without sinking a dime into its development."

"And Vega gives him what he wants—revenge," Bolan said. "He creates more headaches for the DEA and he feels better, at least temporarily. I assume his offices are here in Orlando?"

"Yeah. You going to see him, Striker?"

"It's the best lead I have at this point. Hell, it's about the only lead."

"Be careful. Sampson keeps pretty rough company. His family's personal security team is comprised of cutthroats and mercenaries rather than private cops. When you're worth billions, it makes good sense to do so. Most of these guys have a criminal record somewhere, whether it's with the military or in some other country."

"I'll watch my back, Hal."

"You always do."

"I may have to take this guy down," Bolan said. "Is the Man prepared for that kind of heat?"

Brognola exhaled audibly. Bolan knew his old friend was weighing the political ramifications of what Bolan was telling him. Nearly no one knew of the Stony Man program. Most believed Mack Bolan dead and certainly didn't know of his on-again-off-again partnership with the federal government. Chances were Sampson's death would never be connected to any of the above. Still, Bolan wanted Brognola to understand the potential risk to the President and the program going in.

"I'll deal with the Man," Brognola said. "You deal with Sampson."

"Right. Also, have Bear check something for me. I want to know whether Vega has an airplane and where he keeps it. If it flew this morning, I want to know that, too. Same goes for Sampson"

"Each probably has a fleet, but give us an hour. We'll find out what we can."

Brognola gave Bolan Sampson's home and work addresses, both of which he jotted in his war book. Bolan clicked off the phone and set it on the bed next to him. Glynn turned away from the window and looked at him.

"We're going to see Sampson?"

Out of habit, the Executioner started to protest but stopped himself. Glynn was a trained federal agent, and a tough one at that. She had decided to involve herself in this long before they met. She didn't need coddling. But she did need a reality check.

"Yeah, we're going to see Sampson. After that, I'm going to find Vega."

A HALF HOUR EARLIER, Sampson was pulling the fat end of his silk tie into a Windsor knot when a knock came at his door. He tightened the knot, brushed imaginary wrinkles from his starched white shirt and turned from the mirror to face the door.

"It's Richard, sir. May I come in?"

"Of course, Richard."

The young man entered, a portable phone clutched in his left hand, a scowl on his face. Dressed in a navy-blue suit, he wore his earpiece and mirrored sunglasses. Sampson knew the younger man probably had been up two hours already, checking overnight security reports, giving Sampson's car of choice a final sweep for explosives or tampering, covering any other last-minute details.

The former Green Beret was efficiency personified. Sampson imagined the young man had been a good soldier before his court-martial. He was loyal and took direction without argument. When Sampson had found him, the young man was preparing to go to military prison for sexual assaults against several of his female comrades. Sampson hired him through his family's usual method of recruitment. He offered him a job, knowing the young man's only marketable skill was soldiering. In exchange, Sampson pulled strings in Washington to get the young man's sentence suspended as quietly as possible. Gratitude mixed with money forged strong loyalty, and most of Sampson's people stayed as long as he would have them.

Were he given to such sentimentality, he probably would consider Ahern like a second son. Such feelings eluded him, though. He barely was able to muster paternal warmth for his own flesh and blood, especially after his son had sullied the family name with his overt criminal connections.

Sampson considered Ahern and the host of other men ready to take a bullet for him employees, like a chemist or a janitor. Nothing less. Nothing more.

Ahern walked to Sampson and handed him the phone.

"It's Mr. Vega, sir."

Sampson took the phone and Ahern stepped back, feet shoulder's width apart and hands clasped behind his back while Sampson placed the phone to his ear.

"Emilio," he said, "how are you?"

"We have trouble, Victor," Vega said. "I was attacked last night just after I left your home. This morning the same man went after Harry Van Zant. Someone has tied me with the hospital raids and knows about the labs."

Sampson felt as though he might vomit. The nausea and fear turned to anger.

"Dammit, Emilio, how would they know that?"

"We were infiltrated. A woman DEA agent got into our organization. Harry Nickel told her about the whole thing. I don't know whether she had specific places and dates, but she knows the general plan."

A tickle of fear passed through Sampson's stomach. His shoulder and neck muscles tensed at the news.

"Does she know about me?"

The drug lord's voice turned cold. "It's always about you, eh, Victor?"

"Does she know?" Sampson repeated, his own voice steady.

"Possibly. Probably not. I never mentioned you to Nickel."

Sampson took little comfort in the words.

"You need to deal with Nickel," Sampson said. "And the woman."

"He's been dealt with already," Vega replied. "A federal agent killed him last night, along with several of my men. I was nearly killed myself. I'm in hiding. The police swarmed the house. My lawyers have been on the phone, stalling them. Telling them I dropped out of sight for my own safety. The police want to offer me protective custody."

Sampson almost laughed at that. "Surely they've talked to the DEA agent," he said.

"Of course they have. They want to charge me, but protect me. They have a good case against me as far as threatening the woman and Nickel. I'm sure she knows enough about the operation to cause trouble, too."

Sampson began to feel lightheaded. "What does this mean for us?"

"Not a damn thing," Vega said. "My lawyers can stall them forever. By the time they convene a grand jury to indict me, I can leave the country. Run this operation from Colombia or somewhere else. Those bastards took down my son. They won't take me down, too."

"Of course, Emilio," Sampson said. "I never expected you to fold under pressure."

Sampson admired the drug lord's tenacity and toughness. In the months he had known Vega, the drug lord never had exhibited anything akin to weakness. That infuriated Sampson when it came to dealings between the two, since he operated best when able to intimidate others. But Sampson couldn't help but envy the man's nerve when it came to adversity.

He just hoped Vega's steely disposition didn't make him do something stupid. Courage was only useful when backed by brains and logic. Vega had plenty of brains, Sampson knew, or he already would be in a federal penitentiary. Logic, on the other hand, seemed in shorter supply with him.

He looked forward to the time when Vega was less of a factor in this operation. Soon, a second son's death would weigh on the drug kingpin's mind and heart. The distraction would allow Sampson to take control of the Vitalife operation and get revenge on Vega for allowing the businessman's son to get killed last year. Sampson would enjoy both; the only question was which he would enjoy more.

"Just be careful, Emilio," he cautioned. "You're very important to this operation. What about the woman. What's being done to find her?"

"I've handled it. We have sources in the police department, just like they have sources in our organization. I have people trying to find out where she and the male federal agent went to. I should know within the hour."

"Then what?"

"We take care of her and that big bastard who shot up my house. We'll handle them both."

"Just be careful. If something happens to them, you're the first person the authorities will come after."

"I've already thought of that," Vega said, irritation evident in his voice. "They'll be lucky to find the bodies they need to prove someone died, let alone trace it back to me."

Or more importantly me, Sampson thought. But he said, "It sounds as though you've thought of everything, Emilio. I never should have doubted you."

"You're learning. You need to get out of there, you know."

"Now? I have a board meeting in a matter of hours. Directors have flown in from all over the country for this."

"Cancel it, Victor. That crazy bastard might be coming after you next. He doesn't operate like a regular cop. He's killed nearly a dozen of my men, without shouting a warning or flashing a search warrant. He plays by his own rules. At best, he might force the lab location from you. At worst, you could end up dead. Come to the lab."

"Why to the lab?"

"No one knows the location. I've got a crew coming out here to harden things up. Can you think of somewhere better to hide?"

Sampson paused and realized he couldn't.

"I'll be there by this afternoon, Emilio."

"Of course. I'll see you then."

Vega disconnected the line. Sampson did likewise and handed the phone back to Ahern, who had remained in a parade rest staring at a wall during his boss's conversation.

"We might have company," Sampson said. "Get my jet ready. And secure the estate."

Richard uttered a crisp "Sir." The former soldier turned on his heel and left the room.

After the younger man left, Sampson returned to his dresser, opened the top drawer and withdrew from it a lacquered cherry box. He extracted a nickel-plated .380 autoloader with rubber grips and a loaded clip from the box. He slid the clip into the pistol, chambered a round and locked the safety before putting the pistol back on the dresser. In his years of carrying the .380, he had never used it in firefight. But Richard and his predecessors had drilled Sampson in its use. He knew that, if backed into a corner, he wouldn't hesitate to fire on someone.

Morally, killing was not an issue for him if it furthered his agenda. He preferred to have others do his dirty work, but he also knew he gladly would kill someone if it came to that. Especially if the insane Fed or the woman got too damn close.

9

The way Harry Van Zant figured it, the icy-eyed bastard needed to die if Van Zant had any hope of living.

A member of Van Zant's network—a dirty narc named Robert Baker—had turned up an address where the two federal agents were staying, a third-rate motel Van Zant knew well. He had consummated several drug deals at the motel when he started as a street-level pusher for Vega. Now he rarely even saw a kilo of cocaine or a rock of crack himself. Moving drugs was a secondary concern for him. He leaned on trouble employees, kicked ass on aggressive rivals and handled other business details for his boss.

The latest detail: killing two federal agents, a task in which Van Zant personally planned to participate.

On the outside, the enforcer acted like the quintessential professional. As reinforcements arrived, he briefed them quickly, inserting emotion only when it furthered the cause, but otherwise remaining aloof. He armed the men with information and weapons from his private arsenal. He sent gunners to Orlando's smaller airports, fortifying them in case the son of a bitch already had decided to skip town.

As the two carloads of gunners headed toward the motel, Van Zant sat in the back seat, staring ahead with cool disinterest.

Inside, though, the thought of confronting that cobalt-eyed bastard again elicited more fear than the enforcer cared to admit. He knew he had stared death in the face once today, felt its cold, fetid breath close to him before it mercifully had decided to spare him.

Secretly, the memory made Van Zant want to run. But running wasn't an option; it never was in his business. Bungling and betrayal invited death as surely as facing the guy who had so easily entered his house and killed his guards. Better to find the guy—this time armed and accompanied by reinforcements—than to screw up and invite Vega's wrath.

"This the place?" the driver asked, pointing through the windshield at a ramshackle motel with three cars in the parking lot.

"Yeah," Van Zant said. "Pull in here. Up next to the office. One of you find out which rooms are occupied. Tell the guys in the other car to hang back."

The crew wagon halted in front of the office. Through the window, Van Zant saw an old man at the counter, arms propped on its top. He regarded the motel's visitors with a suspicious gaze. The glass-and-steel door was propped open, and an oscillating fan blew steadily on the counter.

"Chuck, go talk to the guy," Van Zant said.

"Sure, Harry." The big gunner stepped from the car, his right hand tucked in his jacket, and swept his eyes over every window and door in the motel. Satisfied, he stepped into the office. The second crew wagon stopped behind Van Zant's car. Gunners disembarked from the car and eyed the building.

Van Zant was about ready to tell them to sit their asses back in the armored Mercedes when three doors down from the office, a glass window pane exploded and an assault rifle's muzzle poked through the curtains, spitting fire and raining slugs across the hood and windshield of Van Zant's car.

Death was back. Harry Van Zant knew it in an instant.

He just hoped this time it had come for the black-suited Fed and not him.

BOLAN HAD CHANGED into a pair of jeans, a black short-sleeved shirt and a pair of black leather sneakers. He wore the Beretta in a shoulder rig outside the T-shirt and planned to cover the weapon with a light jacket when they went to visit Sampson. He was packing the Uzi and the Colt Commando, which had been outfitted with an M-203 grenade launcher, into the canvas duffel bag when tires crunched gravel outside his window.

One look through the dirty glass told him his life and that of Madeline Glynn were in danger if he didn't go in to battle mode. Bolan sized up the situation. Van Zant was sitting in the crew wagon's front seat, chewing his lower lip. Two gorillas stepped from the rear of the second vehicle. The one closer to the building fished in his jacket for something, either a cigarette or a gun. Bolan guessed the latter.

The Executioner grabbed the Colt Commando from the bed and called for Glynn. She stepped through the door, her DEA badge and a holstered 9 mm pistol clipped to her belt, her forehead creased with concern. Bolan snatched up the Uzi with his left hand.

"You know how to use this?"

"Sure. Why?"

He handed her the submachine gun. She hefted the weapon and checked its load even as she continued to focus on Bolan. He had taped a second clip to the one jammed inside the Uzi's handle. Between that and her pistol, Bolan hoped, she would have enough hardware and ammunition to survive this latest assault.

"Harry Van Zant's outside looking for retribution," the soldier said, grabbing his combat rig and slipping into it. "He's not alone. We're going to have to fight our way out of this."

The color drained from Glynn's face for a moment. She inhaled heavily, and let her training take over.

"What about bystanders?"

"Negative," Bolan said, fastening the combat harness. "The

rooms between us and the office are empty. The place usually does most of its business on lunch hours. I saw no one else in the parking lot. My guess is that besides us, the motel clerk is the only one here. I plan on drawing fire away from him."

"I can call for backup."

Bolan shook his head and stepped toward the window. By the time the police arrived, the fight would be finished. In the best-case scenario involving the police, he and Glynn would live, but be waylaid as he spent hours making statements, possibly being forced into custody, protective or otherwise. He could almost guarantee the local police would force him to leave Orlando. Brognola could work miracles from Washington, but two firefights in twenty-four hours involving Justice Department Agent Mike Belasko would raise enough hackles to ensure Bolan a seat on the next plane out of Florida.

Local cooperation had its limits. He had hyperextended them.

Bolan raised the assault rifle and smashed its telescoping butt against the brittle window, letting tattered curtains shield him from falling shards. Pulling the assault rifle to his shoulder, he pushed the muzzle past the curtain and through the window frame, drew down on the first crew wagon's hood and squeezed the trigger. The bullets caromed off the car, ricocheting in several directions away from the vehicle.

The soldier pulled the curtain from its rod and climbed through the window, laying down cover fire with the Colt Commando as he stepped onto the sidewalk. Gunmetal glinted as car windows rolled down and Van Zant's men brought their weapons into the open. The hardman who only seconds before had walked into the office poked his head around the door frame in time to catch a swarm of 5.56 mm shredders as they tore through his head and neck.

Bolan saw two men scrambling outside the rear vehicle. One reached for a gun, while the second pulled at the rear passenger door's latch, trying to push himself back inside the car for cover. The Colt Commando stitched a line of crimson across the man grabbing for his gun, forcing him to perform a jerky pirouette before he hit the ground. The other thug had opened his car door and thrust his shoulders and head into the vehicle. Before the man gained too much cover, Bolan unleashed a fusillade of slugs that caught the gunner in the hip, twisted him and threw him onto the broken asphalt. He clutched his side, screaming for help.

The Executioner drew down, ready to drill a mercy round into the guy's head.

Acceleration of the lead crew wagon's engine and the sound of screeching tires killed that idea.

The soldier spun on his right heel and ran, sticking close to the building as he did. He guessed he had another ten rounds left in the Colt Commando's clip, but it was the high-explosive round in the grenade launcher he was betting his and Madeline Glynn's lives on.

He whirled as the car turned the corner, tires squealing as the vehicle rocked to a halt. Bringing up the Colt Commando, he shot the HE round through an open window. As it sailed into the car, Bolan thrust himself away from the vehicle and to the ground, feeling bits of gravel and glass biting into his forearms. He lost his grip on the Colt, watched it skitter across the asphalt and covered his head as hellfire rolled through the crew wagon's cockpit. Bolan heard screams from inside the vehicle as shrapnel and flames gutted the car's interior, the vehicle shuddering under the force of the contained explosion.

Bolan got to his feet, his right hand clutching the Beretta. He bent to grab the Colt Commando in his left hand, gripping it as he passed and kept walking. A nauseating mixture of cordite, burned plastic and singed flesh filled his nostrils as he approached the car. Van Zant sat in the back seat, covered in blood. The enforcer screamed and grabbed at his wounds, trying to staunch the torrents of blood with his hands. The Beretta sighed once, propelling a 9 mm Parabellum round into the man's head, granting him a merciful death. Bolan also dispatched whispering death into a second man who had lost part of his face, but not consciousness, as the man writhed and screamed wildly in the back seat. The driver was slumped over the wheel, dead, his body destroyed by the explosive round.

The stuttering of a subgun at the front of the motel caught Bolan's attention and alerted him that Glynn was in danger. Clutching the assault rifle in both hands, he double-timed it from the burning car and headed for the front of the motel.

A HOLLOW PIT OF FEAR opened in Madeline Glynn's stomach as she watched Belasko tumble through the window, his assault rifle blazing. Before this hellish couple of days started, she had been involved in one other firefight. In that instance, the suspects smartly had surrendered before anyone was killed. Intuition told her she wouldn't get that lucky this time.

Violence erupted suddenly in her line of work. She knew that, accepted it, but never got used to it. She handled it as well as, if not better than, many of her peers. But not, it seemed, like Mike Belasko. He was more soldier than cop. He sprang into battle like a machine, a warrior born.

Her? She had been a law-school student, a Gary, Indiana, native who turned to the DEA after her little brother was shot and killed execution style during a drug deal gone bad.

His death had come as a wake-up call for Glynn. The young woman knew drugs were out there, had been offered marijuana and coke at countless high-school and college parties. But she never realized the toll the drugs exacted on families until she saw her little brother in a casket. Her haggard parents, too shell-shocked to grieve, had blamed themselves as they buried their son.

That day in the funeral home she realized that her family's drama was one that played out repeatedly across the country. Her heart told her it had to stop. Not that Glynn ever joined the DEA with illusions of single-handedly ending the war on drugs, but she knew she could win a few battles, make a dent in the drug trade.

If that meant taking on Vega's goons in a gunfight, so be it.

She cradled the Uzi in both hands and walked toward the front of the motel room. Glynn heard feet scuffling outside. The DEA agent pushed herself against a wall, trying to remain out of the line of sight of anyone brave—or stupid—enough to poke his head into Mike Belasko's room. Someone rattled the door handle, tried to open it and found it locked. Glynn figured the men either would shoot off the handle or climb through the window. She also figured these gunners were traveling in a pack. A lone man probably would have hopped back in the car and headed home to lick his wounds. Belasko had taken down the two shooters in the rear of the car; that meant the driver and probably another man were at the door.

Considering the odds, the heightened tension, Glynn figured it best to get the drop on these guys rather than risk a head-on gun battle.

Pressed against the wall, she moved toward the door that connected Belasko's room to her own. Easing herself through the door, she let the Uzi's snout lead the way as she entered the room. She allowed herself a quick sigh of relief as she saw the space was empty, the security chain still hooked in place. Crossing the worn carpet, she peeled back the curtain and saw two men positioned outside Belasko's window. A shorter one, armed with a semiautomatic pistol, pointed at the empty frame. The second, a man shaved bald with a spiderweb tattooed on the crown of his head, nodded, stepped back and pulled his submachine gun to the ready. The little one was going into Belasko's room through the window, while the big one provided cover.

Allowing the gunners to separate opened Glynn to attack from behind. She mulled for a moment with the notion of hiding under the bed, but immediately dismissed it. Her heart, pride and training wouldn't let her behave like a coward. And from a purely practical standpoint, sandwiching herself between the grimy floor and a mattress more likely would pin her down and speed the likelihood of discovery rather than offer her protection.

If she were to get out of this, she'd have to do it by facing her attackers head-on.

She made sure the Uzi was set at full-auto. Then, reaching toward the door, she palmed the gold security chain and slid it back. To her, it sounded as loud as a rock slide. Neither man seemed to notice. Her hand dropped to the doorknob, and she began to twist it.

An explosion from behind the motel startled Glynn. The impact shook the rickety building, knocked pictures from the wall, spilled plaster dust to the floor.

In the aftermath, she heard the screams.

They stopped almost as quickly as they had started. She thought of Belasko for a moment, hoped he was on the giving rather than the receiving end of the mayhem erupting behind the building.

Focus, dammit.

Realizing the two intruders would also be distracted, she decided to use the explosion to her advantage, zero in mentally on her own situation rather than worrying about the fight behind the building. Having even a second's more concentration than the enemy, she realized, would make all the difference in whether she survived.

Peering again through the window, she saw the small guy had frozen, one leg in the window, the other still on the sidewalk, pistol pointed upward. He looked at the big gunner, who raised the SMG defensively, pointing it at the edge of the building in case the firestorm swirling behind the building raged around to the front.

"We've got to go," the small man said, his voice muffled but audible through the glass. The big man nodded and stepped back, giving the smaller man room to extricate himself from the window.

Allowing the pair to leave would provide them a chance to confront—and possibly kill—Belasko. It was time for her to move. Popping open the door, she snaked an arm outside and pointed the Uzi at the two men. She exposed as little of her head and body as possible, using the cocoon of the motel room for cover.

"Federal agent," she said, "drop your weapons. Raise your hands."

The big man turned, searching out Glynn with the SMG. She squeezed the Uzi's trigger, pummeling his midsection with a storm of 9 mm slugs. The impact shoved the bigger man backward into his smaller comrade, knocking them both over. The smaller man wiped blood from his eyes and raised his weapon toward Glynn. She stroked the Uzi's trigger and fired a burst into the small man's center mass.

A blur at the corner of the building caught Glynn's attention. She shifted her weapon and her eyes toward the blur, and drew down as a figure rounded a corner. Belasko had both hands turned slightly up. One still held the assault rifle. He looked grim.

"We need to go," he said.

Glynn felt herself bristle at the notion of abandoning the scene of a shooting. It flew in the face of her training, the law and her morals. She started to protest but stopped when she heard sirens in the distance. Her adherence to the rules already had cost Belasko a chance to nail Vega, perhaps forever. Who knew how many young men like her own brother Vega had profited from as he peddled death on America's streets?

She and Belasko couldn't end the war on drugs, sure. But they could win this skirmish.

If they moved now.

"Let's do it," she agreed.

10

A half hour later, Waters stood in the motel parking lot and surveyed the carnage. Anger and worry vied for his attention as he wondered what the hell had happened to Mike Belasko and Madeline Glynn. He also couldn't help but wonder how the local authorities would sort out the mess this guy from Justice had just handed them.

We're from the federal government. We're here to help.

Yeah, right.

Since Belasko had arrived in Orlando the previous day, he had ripped a deadly swath through town. And ever the cynic, Waters couldn't help but wonder what the guy's visit would do for the FBI's annual crime statistics for Orlando. His money was on the local homicide rate spiking like a football.

Still, there was little Waters could do to stop Belasko, even if he wanted. A mandate had been handed down by no less than the chief of police to help the Justice Department with its investigation. Not that Waters's boss had anticipated this kind of carnage in his town, of course. But the chief was emphatic in his demands, as though pressure had come down from a level higher than Waters could imagine.

Waters stared at Harry Van Zant's bullet-riddled corpse and knew philosophically he had no quarrel with Belasko. The big federal agent probably had prevented five times as many deaths as he had caused by taking down Vega's army of killers. Waters realized that. He also liked the guy. He had tried like hell not to, but Belasko's sincerity had won him over. Something about the Fed made it damn near impossible not to trust him.

That made Belasko part of a very small fraternity, as far as Waters was concerned.

It also made Belasko's disappearance that much more worrisome. Waters assumed the guy had gone under his own power. No one was going to take prisoner a guy capable of inflicting this kind of damage. If they had any brains, they'd kill him rather than let him walk away. Besides, both rooms had been picked clean of any belongings. A hit squad never would have stayed long enough to clean out a target's personal effects—especially not when those targets were federal agents.

Belasko had left of his own accord; that much Waters could deduce. In the final analysis, though, that deduction told him shit, since he still had no idea where Belasko was.

Part of Waters hoped Belasko was leaving town. Another, perhaps more rational part, knew the man would only leave if he determined his work in Orlando was finished. The big guy sure as hell wasn't fleeing in terror.

Waters spotted Tom Jackson, a black patrol sergeant, talking to a withered man with a hell of a mouse under his left eye. Jackson nodded and took notes in a small spiral notebook as the little man spoke and waved his arms. Waters walked to him. Jackson turned, saw Waters and grinned.

"Hey, Cap," Jackson said. "I can see why you wanted us protecting this guy."

Waters returned a weary smile of his own. "Yeah, he's freakin' helpless," Waters said. "This gentleman a witness?"

"Name's Gerald Bettencourt," Jackson said. "He's the manager here."

The little man, dressed in faded jeans and a white T-shirt stained orange-red by spaghetti sauce, extended a bony hand to Waters.

"Call me Jerry," he said, smiling. A three-year-old could count the teeth in this guy's head, Waters thought.

"What the hell happened here, Jerry?" Waters asked.

"Not sure," the little guy said, shrugging. "Some big guy, really well dressed, came into my office. Asked me about the gentleman down the way. I asked him if he was a cop. Guy laughed at that. Then, we heard gunshots, me and the big guy. He hit me. Hit me for no reason."

"What happened then?" Waters asked.

"I fell against the wall. Knocked me cold. When I woke up, I found all this."

He swept a slender arm across the parking lot, which was a black sea inhabited with shell casings, broken glass, blood and bodies. "There's more around back, too," he said. "It's just awful. Looks like a goddamn war zone. Reminds me of Nam."

Waters ignored the color commentary. "So Mr. Belasko wasn't here when you woke up?"

Bettencourt pursed his lips, scratched the stubble on his cheeks and wrinkled his forehead for a moment, as though confused.

"Belasko?" he asked. His face brightened. "You mean Blanski. That quiet man with the dark hair? Naw, he was gone. So was that pretty little thing he brought with him this morning. She got a separate room. But that don't fool me. Know what I mean?"

He shot Waters a wink. The detective looked at the motel manager grimly. He pressed with another question.

"So Mr. Belasko identified himself as Blanski? Does that strike you as odd he gave each of us a different name?"

"Not at this place."

"The man who hit you, did he say what he wanted with Mr. Belasko? I mean Blanski?"

Bettencourt squeezed his eyes shut and shook his bald head emphatically.

"Nope. Just asked me which room the guy was in. Didn't even give me Belasko's name. Just a description. Don't take a genius to figure out I'm not overbooked. But I told him to kiss my ass. My motel ain't a palace, but I watch out for my customers. I run a respectable motel."

Waters doubted it.

"I figured the guy who hit me was a private eye. We get some of those around here, you know? Asking about my customers. Lots of people check in as husband and wife, even though they ain't."

Again Bettencourt winked at Waters. Again Waters ignored him.

"Did you see Mr. Belasko leave?"

"Naw, he was gone when I woke up. Him and the lady both. Place was as quiet as a graveyard. Know what I mean?"

Waters stared at a dead gunner lying on the sidewalk in front of the motel. The man rested on his back, in a pool of his own blood, his abdomen ravaged by bullets.

Waters nodded. A graveyard.

He knew exactly what Jerry Bettencourt meant.

"YOU DOING all right?" Bolan asked as he drove.

Glynn nodded, but continued to inhale and exhale greedily.

"Do you need me to pull over?" he persisted.

"Goddamn it, just keep your eyes on the road," Glynn said. "I'll be fine. Just give me a minute."

"Sure."

He stared ahead and continued to navigate the car toward Victor Sampson's suburban Orlando home. If the businessman had fled, Bolan would try the man at his office or check with Stony Man Farm to see if Kurtzman had found more information. He also planned to ditch the rental car in case Waters or other local authorities decided that they had had enough of Mike Belasko and wanted to take him off the streets.

Bolan stole another glance at Glynn. She was pale, but her breathing seemed to be slowing. He felt for her. He had taken many lives during his career, but he also never took death lightly. Neither, apparently, did Madeline Glynn. She obviously was no killer; she was a woman who wanted to make a difference and had become embroiled in something horrible.

Bolan wished he could assure her the worst was over. He knew better.

This war had just begun.

Bolan would do his best to ensure she emerged from this battle safely. But he also knew his best didn't always guarantee results. Things didn't always work that way. Bolan wished they did. But hard-won experience told him otherwise.

He glanced again at Madeline Glynn and squelched a desire to ask her if she wanted to bow out. The determined look on her face told him all he needed to know. She was in for the duration. As much as that concerned Bolan, it also pleased him. Glynn had proved herself a tough ally. She had been through hell and kept coming back for more.

He couldn't help but admire her tenacity and courage.

Over the next few hours, she would need it. In spades.

Orlando police headquarters

AS THE SON of a wealthy drug dealer, no one knew better than Juan Vega that rank had its privileges, but the truly privileged were those with money.

That morning's privileges had included Ray Pitt's itinerary and an Orlando PD visitor's badge stuffed into an envelope. Both had been waiting for Vega in his mailbox when he stepped out to fetch the morning paper. The young man couldn't help but smile as he recalled finding them there. His father's name—and its accompanying promise of either violence or rewards—carried a lot of pull. A couple of phone calls to a coke-addicted Orlando PD detective had secured for Juan everything he would need to hunt down and kill Ray Pitt.

Pitt would be no pushover; that much Juan knew. The middle-aged law officer still looked lean and tough, despite the hours Juan imagined Pitt had spent behind a desk. He was sure the man was armed, too. And a contingent of DEA agents trailed Pitt as though he were a messiah. Getting him alone and getting the drop on him wouldn't be easy.

Still, Juan would do his best.

Perhaps this time, his best would be good enough for his father.

In the end, taking down Pitt might become a suicide mission. That was okay, too. The drug dealer's son had decided long ago he preferred to burn out in a blaze of glory rather than subject himself to a lingering death shuffling papers behind a desk in his father's bank.

Emilio Vega may never understand his son's seemingly reckless actions. Victor Sampson, on the other hand, comprehended them easily. He had seemed awed at the young man's eagerness to do the unthinkable—assassinate the director of the DEA. Juan, who rarely inspired awe in anyone, basked in the admiration. Enjoyed it so much that he wanted to feel it again. He thirsted for someone—anyone—to respect him. Someone other than those mindless kiss-asses he employed or the automatons searching for scraps at chamber of commerce and civic club luncheons.

Respect from a captain of industry such as Victor Sampson would do fine. Respect from Emilio Vega would be even better. If getting his father's respect entailed spilling blood, so be it.

Parked near the police station, he reached inside his jacket and extracted the Colt Python he normally carried from his shoulder holster. Though he liked the weapon, he knew it was impractical for what he planned. Ahern had convinced him of that much. He reached over the front seat and with his fingertips found the handle of a metal suitcase. He grasped the handle, pulled the case up over the backrest and set it on the seat next to him. Popping the top, he extracted the stolen Beretta, which was already loaded, and slid it into the shoulder holster secreted under the light jacket of his custom Italian suit. He pocketed the sound suppressor and an extra clip of ammunition.

The sound suppressor could mean the difference between a covert kill and escape or immediate discovery and capture. He worried for a moment over whether a surveillance camera might snap a shot of him while he was inside the police department. In the end, though, it didn't matter whether one did.

Over the past few months, he had let his hair grow long and allowed his beard to thicken. A pair of tinted, nonprescription glasses also helped to disguise his face while strategically placed padding in the jacket of his suit created the illusion that his frame carried several pounds more muscle than it actually did.

Once he finished the job, he would return to his clean-shaved look, ditch the bulky clothes and lose the fake glasses. No one, Ahern had assured him, would ever link the young banker to the crime. Ahern's assurances and strong doses of cocaine had steeled his nerves as he prepared for the hit.

Juan sniffled, pulled his car phone from its moorings on the console and hit buttons to activate a programmed number. After three rings, panic seeped in. What if that bastard cop stood him up? He needed an escort to access the bowels of police headquarters. Once inside, the unrestricted-access visitors pass would allow him to get as close to Pitt as was necessary to kill the man.

On the fourth ring, a scratchy voice answered, "Baker, fraud."

"It's me."

"Okay. Got the stuff?"

"What the hell do you think?" The "stuff" was cocaine. His father was one of the nation's biggest drug dealers. It had been like stealing a few shots of whiskey from Daddy's liquor cabinet to get the drug.

"No need to get shitty," Baker said. "Just wanted to make sure you were going to make this worth my while."

"I'll make it worthwhile. Don't worry."

"I'll be right down."

Juan killed the connection, exited the car and started for the police department. The sun warmed his face and a light breeze tousled his dark hair. After this day, everyone—police and criminals alike—would know his name. Not a bunch of work-a-day wimps, but real men with a real impact on the world would like and, perhaps, fear him.

Hell, Emilio Vega would beg his only remaining son to work by his side.

And he graciously would accept. Carry on the family tradition. Perhaps even pass it down to another generation.

If he lived through today.

Juan self-consciously checked his reflection in the passenger-side window of a nearby parked car, saw the Beretta was hidden and continued on toward the police department. He realized how close he was to making history and decided to allow himself to whistle as he walked.

"WAS SHE HURT?" Dan Cronin asked.

Pitt stared across the big table at the younger agent as he talked on a mobile phone barely the size of his palm. The two men were seated in a conference room in Orlando PD's headquarters, waiting for the police chiefs to arrive. Cronin looked and sounded concerned about whatever he was hearing. Occasional glances toward Pitt cued him that he also should worry.

Pitt didn't need another problem. Soon enough, he was scheduled to meet with the state's top cops, try to bring them all under the umbrella of a single, focused drug bust. The last thing he needed was one more concern. Experience, and what his wife called his "unabashedly cynical world view," told him the last thing he needed was the first thing he was going to get.

"Keep me posted if you find her," Cronin said. "Okay. Thanks."

He clicked off the phone, set it on the table and stared at a pile of papers, lost for a moment in thought.

Pitt decided to break the silence. "What's wrong, Dan?"

"Madeline Glynn, one of our undercover operatives, apparently was involved in a shoot-out at a local motel. Now she's gone."

"Gone? Gone where?"

"Not sure. Our agents, along with Orlando PD, have scoured the scene. Apparently another federal agent was involved, too. Afterward they disappeared, along with his car and all their belongings. Left behind more than they took, though. Eight bodies. A burned-out car. Handed Orlando's homicide team a nightmare."

Pitt sank into his chair, exhaled loudly and rubbed his temples with the thumb and index finger of right hand. "Great. Just great. She was working on Vega." During the last week, Pitt had familiarized himself with all the DEA's various efforts against Vega and other targets of Thunderbolt II.

Cronin nodded. "She had been undercover in his organization for a couple of months. Word is she got made yesterday. Vega was going to kill her. Then this other agent appears from nowhere and saves her."

"Why weren't we told any of this sooner?"

Cronin shrugged. "It's a case of the right hand not knowing what the left hand is doing," he said. "Your purpose here is top secret, so no one felt it necessary to report the attack against her to anyone at the director level. The files you've been studying are at least a week old."

"Beautiful. Who's the other agent?"

"Not sure. He may be Justice Department. One of the cops at the scene identified him as Mike Belasko. But we can't find anything about the guy. It's like he appeared out of nowhere."

"Could be," Pitt offered. "Maybe he's a spook."

"If he's with the Agency, lord knows no one will ever own up to it."

Pitt knew that was true. "So who did they kill this morning?"

"More of Vega's thugs. It looks like these gunners came to the motel looking for them. It's not clear whether Emilio himself ordered the hit, or these guys acted independently. His lieutenant, Harry Van Zant, was among those killed. Van Zant had the clout to order the hit himself without his boss's blessing."

"So while I'm here trying to raise a posse against Vega, two agents—including one of my own—are shooting apart his organization."

"It gets worse if you think about it," Cronin said.

"Thanks, Dan."

"No, really. To be pulling the nasty shit Belasko's been pulling here, he must come with high-level Washington credentials. If you know what I mean."

Pitt did. "Son of a bitch," he said.

The DEA director had just been handed the political equivalent of a live hand grenade with the pin pulled. He was busting his ass to arrest Emilio Vega, now, another Washington bureaucrat, probably also acting under presidential orders, had parachuted in a cowboy to do the exact same thing, in a more overt manner.

Pitt's chances of working out a deal with the local police departments had just slipped to less than zero. Regardless, though, he wasn't ready to roll over that fast.

"One of the officers at the scene knows this Belasko?" he asked.

Cronin nodded. "Met with Belasko and Glynn late last night, early this morning, actually. His name's Waters. He's a detective here."

"I want to talk to him."

Cronin started to reply, but stopped as the door opened behind them. A tall, slim black man with precisely cut white hair entered the room. Pitt recognized him immediately as Orlando Police Chief Sebastian Davis. Pitt rose and extended his hand toward Davis who took it. Hard eyes told Pitt the reciprocated handshake was more reflex than a symbol of genuine welcome.

"Good to see you, Seb," Pitt said.

"Looks like you folks got an early start on Thunderbolt II."

Pitt felt his body tighten into battle mode, a defensive reply ready to burst forth. He checked himself and relied on his diplomatic skills.

"Look, Seb, we're still trying to piece together what happened. I'm sorry you're having to deal with it, but from what I've heard so far, the woman was defending herself. She didn't do anything your officers wouldn't do."

Davis nodded and waved a hand at the seats. The other chiefs weren't due for hours. Plans had called for Thunderbolt II's main base of operations to be in Orlando and Pitt had set aside the morning for the men to forge better cooperation and clear the air about any misgivings Davis might harbor toward the DEA's latest effort. Under the circumstances, though, Pitt figured that time could be sheer hell, or a chance to mend some fences, depending on Davis's attitude.

At Davis's direction, Pitt and Cronin sat, followed by the chief.

"I talked with Detective Waters personally," Davis said. "He met agents Glynn and Belasko yesterday, and based on that and preliminary evidence, believes they acted in self-defense. I'm inclined to trust him."

"Agent Glynn is not a loose cannon," Cronin said. "If she fired on someone, I'd bet it was justified."

Davis glanced at Cronin as he spoke, then returned his stare to Pitt.

"I'll be blunt," the chief said. "I'd love to bust Vega and the others targeted by Thunderbolt II, but I'm not going to put my men and women in the line of fire for the DEA's greater glory. We've had good relations before, but if this string of shootings indicates a new definition of local cooperation, you can pack up and get out."

Pitt picked through a series of possible replies, searching for the least offensive. Davis was angry, justifiably so, and trying to goad the DEA director into a fight. Reason and patience were the most effective weapons Pitt had at his disposal.

"Look, Seb, I want this thing to work," Pitt said. "If there's a reason for me to apologize for these shootings, I'll do it. But if they're good kills, I'll stand behind my people. You'd do the same thing and don't tell me otherwise."

"But I'd also take them off the streets and investigate the hell out of them and their actions. Far as I know, both of these people still are running loose. That's unacceptable."

"I'll do what I can to get Glynn under wraps," Pitt said. "I also can call Washington, see if I can get someone to put a leash on this Belasko before he hurts someone else. You still willing to participate in Thunderbolt II?"

Davis's face remained stern. "As long as there's someone left to arrest once the federal government finishes with my town, I'm in."

11

Seated in his private plane, Victor Sampson tried to concentrate on the balance sheets perched on his lap, but his mind repeatedly drifted back to his conversation with Emilio Vega. It had been more than an hour since the two spoke. Still, the nausea and fear continued to roll over him in massive waves. If the federal government knew of their plans, it could bring the operation, Sampson's reputation and, perhaps, his life to a sudden end.

Sampson wasn't one given to panic and self-doubt. He considered those refuges for the weak and unsuccessful, neither a fraternity he cared to belong to. Nevertheless, pangs of fear too powerful to ignore passed through him.

The money. Think about the money, he told himself. And the sweetness of revenge. All that would make this hell worthwhile.

Success would mean a windfall for him. The drug went for fifty cents per milligram when bought legitimately. On the street, it fetched at least four times that much, and people bought it by the pound. The chance for easy, tax-free cash once they rolled out the drug nationally was mind-boggling.

The death toll would probably be equally mind-boggling as Vega and he flooded the streets with the drug.

Despite his earlier protests to Vega, Sampson cared little about whether people died. His pleas to the drug lord for more time had been a ruse. If they got caught, he wanted to blame Vega for forcing through the counterfeit drug, even though it carried with it such a high death rate. Sampson eased his conscience with fantasies of bedeviling the DEA while making lots of money in the process. Some would say the billionaire already had obscene amounts of cash. Too much cash, in fact.

Sampson would counter that there was no such thing.

Then there was Vega.

Sampson considered turning the man's son into an assassin his masterstroke. It had taken time and guile, but Sampson had managed to do it. The young man hungered for attention, validation. Sampson sensed that the minute he met Juan Vega and knew it was an Achilles' heel to exploit. Bolster a fragile, shattered ego, and people would walk over fire to please you. Sampson had learned that rule applied everywhere—boardroom, bedroom, wherever. Find the weak, build them up and create an ally. During his career, he had conscripted an army of such people—loyal to a fault, ready to do his bidding, willing to endure occasional upbraiding to get another morsel of approval dropped in their path. Like a mouse running a maze for a food pellet.

Sampson had dispatched his latest mouse on a death mission. For his own part, though, Sampson considered it the proverbial win-win situation: Pitt died a bloody death, or Vega's son was killed in the process.

Perhaps both, though Sampson considered that scenario too perfect to hope for.

Of course, the executive considered the DEA culpable for his son's death. But he really blamed Emilio Vega. The drug lord had taken in Sampson's son, turned him into a criminal and failed to protect him when the DEA raided an Orlando warehouse looking for drugs. Hadn't the elder Vega told Sampson's son not to draw down on federal agents armed with submachine guns? Hadn't his son known better? What had driven him to be so loyal? Those questions tormented Sampson when he weighed them in his mind.

That's why usually he found it best to vanquish such thoughts and forge ahead.

Sampson planned to get even with Emilio Vega and make money in the process. The fear shifted into a sense of power, and Sampson felt better. More deaths—be they DEA or Vega—would heighten the sense of well-being now flowing through his body.

Orlando, Florida

MACK BOLAN WAS in the car and within five minutes of reaching Victor Sampson's suburban estate when the secure cell phone on his hip vibrated. A bout with interstate construction had slowed his and Glynn's progress from the motel to the billionaire's sprawling mansion. Bolan plucked the phone from his belt, flipped it open and put it to his ear. "Yeah?"

"Striker, I've got some information you might want." The voice was Aaron Kurtzman's.

"Go," Bolan said.

"Sampson is leaving town. Actually, left town. His people filed a flight plan with the FAA this morning calling for him to travel to Atlanta. Plane left Orlando Executive Airport about a half an hour ago."

"You're sure Sampson was aboard?"

"Not one hundred percent, but it stands to reason. We've intercepted e-mails coming in and out of his company's executive offices through some creative hacking. Rumor has it Sampson abruptly canceled a board meeting this morning and left the directors cooling their heels in Orlando, while he flew the coop, ostensibly because he got called out of town on an emergency."

"Any clues as to where he's going in Atlanta once he gets there?"

"Negative," Kurtzman said.

Bolan did a quick calculation in his head. "Can you ask Jack to ready the plane for takeoff within a half hour?"

"Will do," Kurtzman said. "Hey, Striker, Hal wants to talk to you."

"Put him on."

Silence filled the line while Brognola joined the secure connection. In the meantime, Bolan turned the rental and started toward the airport. Brognola's deep voice boomed onto the phone as the car nosed in a new direction.

"The Man said do what you deem necessary," Brognola said. "It took some convincing, but he finally conceded that losing Sampson was politically better than a new street-drug epidemic."

"Good choice on his part," Bolan said. "Correct me if I'm wrong, but I hear an unspoken 'but' in there."

"You're not wrong, Striker. He'd prefer the guy went to trial, of course. But he knows ultimately he can't control what you do in the field. Those are his words, almost verbatim."

"Sounds like plausible deniability to me, Hal. Like if any trouble comes out of this, we hang while he helplessly shrugs his shoulders and smiles when asked about it at press conferences and cocktail parties."

"I won't leave you hanging," Brognola said. "You have full license to do what you want, as far as I'm concerned. Without any repercussions, legal or otherwise."

From anyone else, Bolan would consider such talk meaningless chest thumping. From Brognola, though, he took it as assurance that his old friend would back him up, regardless of the mission's outcome. It was the kind of support Bolan needed to perform his job. Without it, he would have severed ties with the government long ago to focus solely on his own war.

"There's another wrinkle, Striker. While we've been busting Emilio's chops, the DEA's been trying to convene a multiagency task force to take him and his associates down. That agency's director is in Orlando even as we speak trying to pull the whole thing together."

Bolan felt anger burn hot through his skin. "What does that mean for us?"

"Probably nothing," Brognola said, his irritation audible.

"Far as I'm concerned, they can convene all the task forces they want. In the meantime, you keep doing things your way. But you can count on what little local cooperation you've enjoyed to dry up soon. From what we're hearing, they want you and Glynn off the streets."

"And if they succeed, what then?"

"I'll have you back in action within an hour if I have to come down there and kick someone's ass myself," Brognola said. "We aren't there to play politics. You're only concern is finding Vega and Sampson and stopping them. You've got the Man's backing on that. The locals won't want to pick that fight. And I can handle Ray Pitt."

"Thanks, Hal."

"You might want to tell Glynn what's going down. Give her a chance to bow out if she wants. She might not want to run afoul of her agency director."

"I wouldn't blame her if that was the case," Bolan said.

"Me, neither. You need some help? I have Able Team in Maryland on a mission. I can tell them to pack up and meet you in Atlanta."

Bolan smiled grimly. The mother-hen routine was practically a reflex for his old friend.

"Got it in hand, Hal. You folks just keep providing me with intelligence. I'll handle the fieldwork. Anything changes, I'll let you know."

"We'll keep running names and numbers on our end," Brognola said. "Watch your ass."

The two men hung up on one another. Peripheral vision told him Glynn was eyeing him, waiting for a recap of the conversation.

"What wouldn't you blame me for?" she asked.

He gave it to her briefly. "Ray Pitt's in town, convening a drug task force," Bolan said. "He doesn't like my methods. He wants us to stop what we're doing and come home. You can pull out if you want. It's your call."

She stared through the window, squinted against the sun's glare. "My last orders were to stick with you," Glynn said. "My people haven't told me any different. So you're stuck with me until I hear otherwise. I can't abort a mission on your say-so."

Bolan nodded.

"You turned around. Where are we going?"

He told her about Sampson's last-minute decision to cancel his board meeting and head toward Atlanta.

"Buckhead's close to Atlanta," the Executioner said. "So it seems like our best lead at the moment for finding Sampson and Vega."

"You think the prototype laboratory is there?"

"It would stand to reason. Sampson's pilot filed a flight plan out of habit, which helped us find him. Unfortunately Emilio's pilot didn't do the same thing. Otherwise, we could confirm his destination, too. Put the two guys in the same place."

"It would be a good piece of evidence."

Bolan let the last statement slide. Mounting a case against the two men was the least of his worries, especially where Vega was concerned. His objectives were much simpler: identify, isolate and destroy.

He planned to accomplish all three in short order.

Roswell, Georgia

VEGA COULDN'T HELP but grin his approval as he scanned the exterior of what would soon become the first in several drug-producing laboratories. Sampson had located the building in a suburban Atlanta industrial park. The two had discussed setting up shop in a seedier section of the sprawling city, but Sampson, in a rare moment of inspiration, had rejected the idea. Police looked for drug labs in bad sections of town. He reasoned, and probably rightfully so, that the same facility in a pristine industrial park would go virtually unnoticed. Especially since they had established a front company—a food-wholesale business complete with a staff, equipment and trucks—to cover the facility's true intent.

The drug lord recalled the ribbon-cutting photo that appeared in the local paper touting the new construction project and its promise of new jobs, and snorted out a cynical laugh. Little did the mayor, chamber of commerce president and city council realize they were welcoming a criminal facility in their midst as they stood at the construction site, donned their plastic hard hats, gripped gold shovels and took credit for their ingenious economic-development strategy.

The irony, Vega decided, was beautiful. So was the facility.

Sampson's logic was counterintuitive, but made sense. Create a facade of openness and legitimacy to repel real scrutiny. Grudgingly the drug kingpin admitted to himself that Sampson's instincts were good. A byproduct, he was sure, of the man covering his own ass at others' expense.

The food-wholesale front would allow them to ship as much product as necessary to anywhere in the country. A state-of-the-art computer system would allow Vega and his people to track shipments large and small and remain in contact with their sprawling network of mules.

"What the hell is this thing?" Johnson asked as he regarded the two-story glass-and-brick building, the well-manicured lawn, the flower gardens. "Looks like a health club, not a drug lab."

"You're entitled to your opinion," Vega said. He turned to face the drug maker. "Just shut up and keep it to yourself."

Johnson flinched, probably recalling his earlier beating. Estevez still held the drug maker's pistol in his jacket pocket, leaving him defanged.

"Sure, Emilio. Just a little nicer than what I'm used to, is all," Johnson said.

Estevez navigated the car around the rear of the building, pulled up to a delivery bay and honked. The big door yawned open, exposing a cavernous room filled with forklifts, wooden pallets and stacks of flat, unassembled cardboard boxes. Two men dressed in forest-green uniforms with their first names stitched over the right breast pocket stood in the concrete-and-steel cavern. Vega assumed both were armed, but he knew the real firepower lay out of sight, as a security team monitored the bay every time a door opened, ready to rain down gunfire on potential threats.

Estevez pulled the car into the loading bay, parked it and killed the ignition. The three men exited the vehicle while a second crew wagon of gunners entered through an adjoining bay door. A small man dressed impeccably in a navy-blue suit offered his hand to the drug lord.

"Mr. Vega, welcome. It's wonderful to have you here."

The drug lord almost ignored the man's hand, but caught himself. He considered Bill Thomas, a vice president for Sampson's pharmaceutical concerns, a worm. But he was a valuable worm. He had made the laboratory a reality, understood its operation intimately. Vega might need his loyalty down the road, at least temporarily, after he ousted Sampson.

The drug lord took Thomas's flaccid hand in his own, released it immediately as though he had touched something vile. To cover his disgust, Vega tossed Thomas a contrived smile that exuded warmth. His eyes remained cold.

"Bill, good to see you," he said. "I assume all is going well here?"

Thomas stood a little straighter and his face beamed. With the index finger of his right hand, he pushed wire-rimmed spectacles up the ridge of his pinkish nose.

"Yes sir," Thomas said. "Ahead of schedule and under budget, as promised. We certainly appreciate the cash infusion you provided."

Vega wondered whether the young executive realized the money came from a drug dealer rather than a venture capitalist. Or whether he cared, for that matter. Thoughts of stock options and board seats probably blinded the executive to the reality of what he was doing. Most likely he saw his success with the lab as another feather in his cap.

The more likely scenario, though, was his help was bringing him that much closer to getting a bullet in the head. Ultimately, Vega wanted his own people running the show; Thomas wasn't one of them. He would outlive his usefulness soon enough. End of story.

"I assume production will begin on schedule?"

"Absolutely. Within a month we should be pumping out two thousand tablets every two days. Another month after that, production should double. That's enough to really make a difference."

"Come again?"

"As far as sending this painkiller to underprivileged countries. It's really a wonderful project we're embarking on, making a cheaper version of the drug to send to Third World countries. Very noble cause."

So that was Sampson's cover story. He wondered whether Thomas actually believed it or clung to the lie as an alibi. There were just too many things overtly suspicious about the operation for someone of Thomas's intelligence to believe. Regardless, Vega played along.

"Yes," he said, "very noble."

"Victor Sampson has a soft spot for the poor," Thomas said.

"Sampson doesn't know poor," Vega said, his voice taking on a cold edge.

Thomas looked stunned. "Did I say something wrong?"

The kingpin clapped Thomas on the shoulder and laughed. "Forget it. I have someone here I want you to meet. Tommy Johnson, this is Bill Thomas."

Thomas held out a hand. Johnson nodded but didn't return the gesture. Instead he continued eyeing every inch of the delivery bay as though memorizing it. Vega felt his rage rise again at Johnson's indifference, but checked himself. "Mr. Johnson is a chemist. I want you to show him the entire operation. So he can help out."

Thomas continued looking like a deer in the headlights, but said, "Of course. I'm sure Mr. Sampson will appreciate the help."

"I'm sure," Vega said.

A mobile phone trilled behind Vega. He turned to look at Estevez, who already was digging the phone out of his pocket. Vega turned away his gaze, but continued to listen.

"Yeah? Aw, man." A loud exhale. "When did that happen?

Shit. Emilio's here. You want to tell him?" A short laugh. "Dumb question. Well, here you go, anyway."

"What the hell's happening now?" the drug lord asked.

Estevez held out the phone but remained silent. Vega snatched it from his grip, looked at Thomas then Estevez. "Get him the hell out of here." The gunner escorted Thomas and the others from the room.

Vega stuck the phone to his ear. "Emilio."

"Emilio? This is Donny."

The drug lord tried to place a face to the name or voice, came up blank and snapped, "Yeah? What do you want?"

"It's Harry, Emilio. He's dead."

A cold trickle of fear started just under the hairline on Vega's neck and rolled slowly down his spine. "When did that happen? How?"

"He took a crew looking for that Fed who busted up your house. He found the guy at a motel. Tried to take him down, but the guy killed Van Zant and the other gunners."

"Shit, how does that happen?"

"He's like a one-man army, I guess. From what our contact at the PD is saying, this Belasko guy was firing automatic weapons and tossing grenades around like it was a war zone."

"Sounds like that's exactly what it was," Vega said. "And you pussies are losing the war. What are the cops saying?"

"Guess the guy split. Couple of detectives stopped by Van Zant's house. Wanted to ask some questions about why Van Zant would attack a federal agent. We didn't tell them shit, Emilio. It was close, though, man. We had just cleaned the bloodstains from the carpet when they came."

In a panic, Vega forgot his usual phone protocol. "Yeah, you got it tough. Listen—get whatever gunners you have left. Take a plane and get your asses out here. Bring cash. Bring guns. Bring some balls, too, huh? I want this place like a goddamn fortress before the evening."

"Sure, Emilio."

"You got anybody staking out the airports, trying to catch this guy in case he leaves town? Maybe you ought to find him before he finds me and blows my brains out, what do you think?"

"Got it covered, Emilio. Guys are positioned at a couple of the suburban airports right now. Got people at Orlando International, too, but that's a long shot. I don't expect him to catch a passenger jet loaded down with all his weaponry."

"I think you're finally using your head," Vega said. "Let me know how it goes."

The drug lord killed the connection, realizing that goddamn Fed continued to ratchet things up several notches, pushing him harder with every step. Tired, angry and scared, he decided it was time to push back. Hard enough to draw blood.

12

Orlando, Florida

Bolan parked the rental car in the lot of the airport, popped open the door and stepped into the heat. Within moments, his shirt began pressing against his skin and the sun burned against his black hair, heating it like a leaf under a magnifying glass. Bolan wiped away the sweat and donned a pair of mirrored sunglasses, scanning the collection of small hangars, a terminal and acres of airfield.

"How long until the plane is ready?" Glynn asked.

She, too, had stepped from the car.

"Five minutes tops," Bolan said, without looking at her. "There's a plane waiting for us here."

"A plane waiting? You have more connections than I thought, Mike."

"It's not as glamorous as it sounds. And it's not mine."

"I was kidding." Glynn gathered her hair into a ponytail with her left hand and fanned her neck with the long strands to cool it. She eyed the airfield briefly and said, "Am I supposed to be looking for something?"

Bolan shrugged. "Trouble, I guess. I wouldn't be surprised if someone was waiting for us."

"How would they know?"

"How did they know about the motel? I'm not saying there is a problem. I'm just saying there could be."

"You're paranoid."

"It serves me well."

Bolan's combat sense begged for an audience. Whether it sensed a new danger or remained triggered from the encounter at the motel mattered little. The Executioner knew better than to ignore it. He always gave the prickly feeling his full attention even on the rare occasions when it turned out to be wrong.

He opened the car's back door, leaned his big frame inside and grabbed the duffel bag filled with weapons. He couldn't shake the edgy feeling grating against already raw nerves. He inventoried the parked cars—a silver BMW Z3 two seater, a red Mercedes convertible, a Dodge Viper and a Jeep Cherokee sport utility vehicle, all of which probably belonged to executives taking early-morning flights to business appointments elsewhere. The asphalt was beaten to a dull gray by tires and sunlight and pocked with holes. Lines of weeds marbled the parking lot with wavy green lines. Bolan turned his gaze to the airport terminal, a large building walled with windows that stretched practically from floor to ceiling. The cars were parked along the road, leaving the front of the terminal building exposed.

The building looked empty, as did the tarmac. Then he saw it, the signal that had triggered his radar. A white Lincoln and a black Mercedes sedan, both parked along a service drive stretching along the back of the airfield. He recognized both as crew wagons.

The plane wasn't visible from his vantage point, and he felt a sudden, cold pang of fear as he thought of Grimaldi.

The chatter of machine-gun fire, the dull smack of bullets against metal and shouting from the airfield gave his fears substance.

Bolan pulled the bag from his shoulder and dug into it. He slid into the combat harness containing extra ammunition, strapped on the Desert Eagle and fisted the Colt Commando in quick, economical movements. Glynn came up from behind. He handed her the Uzi charged with a fresh clip. Again a second clip was taped to the first in an over-under configuration. She took it from him and chambered a 9 mm round.

"I've got to get to Jack," Bolan said, almost to himself.

"Who's Jack? The pilot?"

Bolan nodded.

"You think they got to him?"

"I hope not. Stay here until I call you."

"What the hell?"

"Just do it."

Bolan eyed the distance between the car and the terminal. He estimated about fifteen yards of open asphalt and concrete separated the two. He rose into a combat crouch, passed Glynn and moved around the front of the car, ready to exploit the cover provided by the line of automobiles.

As he moved among the cars, a man in a beige suit appeared in the window. The man's eyes widened in alarm at the sight of Bolan. An SMG cradled in his arms began spitting fire. Bullets smashed through the bank of windows and sent a waterfall of glass shards cascading to the ground. The more shots he unleashed, the better his aim became, the bullets gradually going from chewing a line toward Bolan, slamming into the cars that surrounded him.

The warrior crouched, drew down on the shooter and squeezed the Colt Commando's trigger, peppering his opponent with 5.56 mm rounds. The shooter jerked for a moment as the shots slammed into his torso before the impact knocked him to the ground.

By this time, two more gunners ran through the terminal, SMGs blazing. Bolan squeezed off another burst, picking off the lead gunner in the process. The Executioner swiveled the rifle toward his second attacker, who was firing into the parking lot through the terminal's shattered front, and started to draw a bead on him. A burst of autofire roared from the right and behind, pounded into the man and killed him.

Bolan turned and saw Glynn crouched and approaching him. Her face was angry. A trail of smoke seeped from the Uzi's muzzle.

She shot Bolan a dark look that said "Stay here, my ass," then returned her gaze to the terminal. Bolan did likewise, seeking a new target. Seeing none, he rolled to his feet, returned to a crouch and started for the terminal, traversing the parking lot in a zigzag fashion. The warrior felt exposed, but was willing to risk it. He imagined the shooting and shouting somehow were tied to Grimaldi. He wanted to make sure his friend was okay.

God help these bastards if he wasn't.

FIVE MINUTES EARLIER, Grimaldi was seated in the small passenger plane's cockpit. His hands moved quickly over the instrument panel as he ran the plane through a final preflight check. He wanted the craft ready to move when Bolan arrived.

Whenever Bolan was ready to hit the trail, Grimaldi put himself into high gear and did whatever it took to make Bolan's job easier. Few commanded Grimaldi's respect as did Bolan. Long ago, the warrior had saved Grimaldi from a career of ferrying wiseguys and thugs, helped him regain his self-respect as he replaced a Mob career with something more meaningful. Under Bolan's direction, Grimaldi had moved from being part of the problem to becoming part of the solution. He repaid Bolan with unflinching loyalty.

Minutes earlier, just before Grimaldi began warming the engines, a ground crew had finished refueling the plane. As always, the Stony Man pilot found himself entranced by the craft's high-tech navigational gear, the explosion of multicolored digital readouts, the small but powerful computers that made up the instrument panel. From the exterior, the plane appeared to be a typical light commuter craft. A check of its flight number would have linked it to a nonexistent corporation in Maryland. A look inside told the real story. The mechanical instruments and systems had been stripped away, replaced with the latest in military flight and navigational technology.

Shouting from outside pulled Grimaldi from his thoughts. He raised himself from the seat, stepped into the cabin and peered through a window to see what was causing the ruckus.

A couple of heavies were pushing around the two young men who comprised the ground crew. One of the gunners was a bodybuilder, a pretty boy with highlights in his hair and an earring in his left earlobe. He wore jeans, a T-shirt and expensive athletic shoes. The other man was dressed similarly, but small, wiry and formidable looking. He had the deep reddish brown skin and creased features of a Native American. The big one yelled at the two kids and pointed at the terminal. Obediently both started toward a rear door heading into God knew what.

The thugs started toward the plane. Whether they were looking specifically for this plane or checking every craft parked on the small airfield mattered little to him. He assumed both men were skilled fighters. Grimaldi, a quick-handed expert in savate, was no slouch, either. But with the odds two against one, he saw no reason to risk it.

In long, smooth strides, the pilot returned to the cockpit, reached under the seat and withdrew a micro-Uzi holding a 20-round magazine. Grabbing two more clips, he placed the extra ammo into the pockets of his blue flight suit. Turning toward the primary security computer, Grimaldi punched in a code that locked the system until he or Bolan entered a second set of numbers to free the system. If neither man entered the disarming code within fifteen minutes, hidden munitions would destroy the aircraft.

Grimaldi set the Uzi to autofire, returned to the cabin and knelt next to the door.

He tucked the Uzi against his leg and peered out the door. The shorter man saw him, pointed and yelled. "You, get your ass out of that plane. Now."

The smaller man started for the craft and reached his left hand behind his back, presumably for a gun. The bigger one left no doubt of his own intentions as he clawed at the butt of an autoloader holstered in his left armpit.

That was all the stimulus Grimaldi needed.

He poked the Uzi's snout above his left leg and triggered it. The machine pistol spit a stream of 9 mm Parabellum slugs that tore into the smaller thug. The rounds chewed the man open from right hip to left pectoral as Grimaldi swept the weapon up. Before the first hardman hit the ground, the pilot aimed at the second target, caressing the trigger. He held the weapon firm and let the concentrated burst batter the man's chest. Grimaldi released the trigger, and the man crumpled to the ground in a dead heap.

The Uzi clutched in his left hand, the pilot started to stand, but saw two more gunners moving from the building toward the plane. Spotting the corpses on the asphalt, one man pointed at the plane and cried out. He brought up an SMG and fired on the craft as he moved sideways to find cover. The second gunner triggered an M-14 as he raced behind a big steel trash receptacle.

Grimaldi scowled as the rounds hammered against the plane's skin. The special armoring most likely would prevent the shooters from inflicting too much damage in the short term. The pilot couldn't help but question how long the craft would withstand the constant pounding. Maybe forever. Maybe not, if these guys had heavier ordnance with them.

For a moment, Grimaldi wondered when Bolan would arrive. The thump of a grenade, the thunder of gunshots and commotion from somewhere else at the airport gave him his answer.

Grimaldi couldn't help but smile.

The big guy never missed a flight.

AS HE NEARED the building, Bolan reached into a pouch slung over his shoulder and fisted a stun grenade. The device was similar to those used by police officers who wanted to disorient suspects before storming into a building. He plucked the pin from a canister and tossed the bomb through the now empty window frame. Between gunshots, he heard a metallic clank after the device sailed through the window and disappeared into the building. Someone shouted as they spotted the grenade. Because of the terminal's square footage, Bolan followed up with a second device.

The warrior averted his gaze, covered his ears with his hands and waited out the blast. His palms muted the blast only slightly and even in broad daylight the flash was visible outside the building As the blast died down, Bolan was on his feet and moving into the building.

He stepped through the frame of a destroyed window and pressed himself against the wall, the Colt Commando held ready. Amid the acrid smoke, he heard groans and swearing as those inside recovered from the shock of the blast. Fleetingly he wished he could have used something more potent, but knew better. There had to be hostages in the building, innocents who needed protection. Even as Bolan took down the gunners outside, he tried to contain the shooting to prevent workers and passengers—if, indeed, any still were alive—from getting caught in a cross fire.

Bolan heard footsteps from behind and wheeled toward the sound. His assault rifle was tracking a target before he stopped moving. Glynn stood behind him, her hands raised, one still clutching the Uzi, her eyes wide. Bolan scowled, turned back around and continued into the building.

A shape to his left bolted from the smoke, headed in the direction of Bolan and Glynn. The soldier spun at the waist toward the runner and peered through the white haze that filled the room. He held his fire, waiting for a critical sign of danger to trigger the weapon. A twenty-something woman of Asian descent ran toward him, her hands raised, her breathing labored, probably more from fear than exertion. Still stunned from the explosion, she seemed to look right through Bolan and was running aimlessly in search of an escape route.

He grabbed her arm roughly and shoved her past him and toward the terminal's shattered entrance, thankful he had hesitated to fire. Propelled by the shove, she passed Glynn and exited the building through the shattered windows. She tripped as she went through the glassless window, fell to the ground, then raised herself to her feet and continued running, scuffed but apparently no worse for wear.

The mixture of gunners and innocents was going to make navigating the besieged building difficult.

Bolan shifted positions again, careful not to remain in one spot too long. He crouched and listened for signs of danger— the scuffle of a foot, the clicking of a pistol, the telltale rasp of breath as someone tried to sneak upon him.

He didn't have to listen too hard.

A big shape spitting gunfire bore down on Bolan. The warrior stroked the trigger, punching several rounds into his attacker. Even as the Executioner eased off the trigger, he was moving, searching for his next target. Pistol shots slammed toward his former position, tearing large holes in nearby walls.

A shotgun blast weighed in with a deafening boom.

The mechanical click of a pump-action shotgun warned Bolan and Glynn of another impending shot before they spotted their attacker. Glynn brought up the Uzi and tapped out a short burst toward a man armed with a Winchester shotgun. A cry accompanied by the boom of a shotgun's accidental discharge told Bolan her slugs had hit their mark even before he saw the man go down.

The haze had begun to dissipate, and shadows were transforming back into easily identifiable figures. Two of the shapes were joined together, walking toward the front entrance. One of Vega's hardmen, with a young woman in a business suit clutched tightly against him, approached Bolan and Glynn. The man had looped his arm around the woman's neck, pressed a gun muzzle against her head. He seemed to have his senses about him, as though he had been far enough from the grenades' disorienting blast to suffer only minor effects. The woman was slender, the man ample. Two other people, both apparently hostages, lay on the floor. One clamped his hands against his ears and groaned, while the other vigorously rubbed his eyes, blinked and tried to reorient himself. Bolan sighted down the Colt's barrel, sought a clear shot, but found none. Still, he held the rifle steadfast.

The hardman probably weighed 240 pounds, much of it gut, and stood at just less than six feet. Pieces of him oozed out around the woman, but a decent kill shot didn't present itself. Just injuring the man would put the hostage at risk.

"I'm going through that front door," the guy said, his beefy forearm pressuring the woman's head up at an excruciating angle. "I'm taking a car. I'm taking her. You can't stop me."

Bolan wondered for a fleeting moment whether the man was right.

ARMING THE UZI with a fresh clip, Grimaldi fired on his opponents until the machine pistol clicked dry. He popped out the clip, inserted a new one and repeated his onslaught as he decided how best to proceed.

I could exchange gunfire with these bozos all day, he thought. This situation requires a quick fix.

In a crouch, Grimaldi ran to the armory cabinet situated at the rear of the airplane. Keying in a pass code on the computerized lock, he popped open the steel door, grabbed three more magazines for the micro-Uzi and shoved them in his pockets. He fisted a frag grenade, resealed the armory cabinet, which contained an assortment of pistols, SMGs and rifles, and headed for the door.

Sporadic gunfire suggested Bolan was in trouble. Grimaldi planned to help out where he could. But first he had to get out of the airplane and get to the terminal.

Both men had gathered behind the steel trash receptacle, which offered the best cover on the airfield other than the interior of Grimaldi's armored plane, and continued to fire upon the craft, apparently hoping to score a lucky shot against its sole occupant. Grimaldi armed the grenade, tossed it and watched as it struck the asphalt and rolled behind the trash receptacle.

Hurling himself on the floor and away from the airlock, Grimaldi heard the explosion, followed by a clipped chorus of screams as flames and shrapnel tore through the gunners. In the contained space between the steel bin and the brick wall, Grimaldi had no doubt both men had died nearly instantaneous deaths.

Pulling himself to his feet, Grimaldi crept down the steps onto the airfield and approached the airport's main building. As he neared it, he saw smoke and the occasional muzzle-flash.

Pressing his back flat against the terminal, Grimaldi edged along the wall until he reached the building's back door. He reached across the door, grabbed the handle and pulled it toward him.

He stopped cold. A big man clutched a scared woman and pushed a pistol against her temple. Bolan was crouched on the floor, aiming his assault rifle at the man. A pretty redhead lay on the ground a few yards away from Bolan, propped on her arms as she drew down with an Uzi.

Grimaldi had a clear shot at the thug's backside, but didn't dare take it. He considered himself a decent shot, probably plenty good enough to hit the fat man with the hostage. Whether he would inadvertently hit the woman by sending a bullet through her captor was another matter. Trick shots weren't his business.

For Mack Bolan, though, they were a specialty.

Grimaldi pushed the glass door as close to the outside wall as he could and reached around with the micro-Uzi. He drew down on the fat guy.

"No need to get tense there, brother," Grimaldi said, his voice even.

The pilot's words startled the hyped-up hardman and caused him to make a fatal mistake. The big man wheeled toward Grimaldi, pulling the woman with him as he came around. The motion momentarily shifted the man's arm, jerking the pistol muzzle away from his hostage's temple and aiming it instead at the ceiling. The new stance also exposed a healthier portion of the gunner to Bolan, who seized the moment by pumping a single shot into the thug's head.

Covered in her captor's blood, the woman screamed and stepped away from him as his corpse hit the floor.

Glynn and Bolan rose from their respective positions. The DEA agent stepped to the woman, took her shoulders in her hands and began speaking softly to her, trying to console her and usher her away from the body. Bolan walked to Grimaldi as other hostages began to raise themselves from the floor. Both men surveyed the carnage around them. After a few seconds, the soldier turned to face his friend.

"It's time to leave," Bolan said.

"I think we'd best get out of town before we get tossed out," Grimaldi agreed. "There's only so much magic Hal Brognola can work with his connections. It'll take a pretty big wand to straighten out this mess."

Grimaldi turned toward Glynn, letting his gaze linger.

"Who's the lady, Sarge?"

"Madeline Glynn. DEA. She's going with us."

"To Atlanta?"

"Yeah."

"Atlanta it is," Grimaldi said. "Gather up your friend and let's go."

13

Detective Robert Baker looked disheveled, but no more than usual, Juan Vega thought, as the strung-out cop ambled toward him. Baker was a member of Orlando's fraud team who had picked up a coke habit sometime during his days as an undercover officer. When his superiors discovered the addiction, they yanked Baker from undercover work, put him in rehab and reassigned him to the fraud unit.

From what Vega knew, Baker had learned just enough in rehab to hide his using so he could function while continuing to snort cocaine. His superiors either bought his line of crap or had resigned themselves to having a cokehead among their ranks. Either way, Baker had been more than happy to turn informant to score with the lady cocaine. Juan knew Baker had been one of Harry Van Zant's best sources within the department. He had switched allegiances easily.

"Morning Mr. V.," Baker said, extending a hand.

The young businessman took Baker's hand, shook it and released it. "Robert, good to see you."

They walked toward a windowless door, Baker leading the way. The cop passed a plastic card through a reader, waited a moment, then grasped the handle and pulled the door open. He swept his left arm across his midsection, beckoning Juan through the door.

"After you," Baker said.

Juan proceeded through the doorway. His most recent snort of coke had left his senses alive, his heart soaring. As he moved deeper into police headquarters, he pulled the visitor's pass from his jacket pocket and clipped it with his right hand to his left jacket lapel. The laminated, all-access pass should allow him to travel through the halls unmolested.

Or at least he hoped so.

He had come too far to get caught now.

The pair entered an elevator, descended into the basement and headed to Baker's office. Once inside the office, Juan set his briefcase onto the desk, popped the top and pulled from it a plastic-wrapped brick of cocaine, which he set on the desk. Baker's bloodshot eyes widened when he glimpsed the prize.

"This is for you," the young banker said. "With my father's and my compliments. Now, where is Pitt?"

Baker looked up at the drug lord's son. His expression turned from happiness to suspicion. "Just what you got in mind for this guy anyway?"

"I want to talk with him. What? Did you think I came here to kill him or something? I'm a banker, for Christ's sake."

Baker laughed. "Naw, I didn't think you'd kill him. But it kind of raises eyebrows when a drug dealer's son takes an interest in the DEA director."

"Whose eyebrows has it raised?"

"Just mine."

"You're sure?" Juan covered the cocaine with his hand, pulling it back toward him.

"Yeah. Yeah, I'm sure. Don't go freaking on me. Just wondered what you wanted to talk to him about, is all."

The younger Vega's mind raced for a suitable lie, one that

might cover his tracks down the line. An idea formed in his mind. He looked from side to side, unable to shake his fear that someone might be listening, then stared at Baker trying to appear as earnest as possible.

"Can you keep a secret?"

"Of course, I can."

"I mean a big secret."

"Jesus."

"All right. My father's tired of the game," Juan lied. "He wants to turn himself in. Things are falling apart. He wants to give up, but he wants to do so under his own terms."

"Bullshit."

"No, really. He wants me to negotiate the deal with Pitt. But it needs to be secret. No one must know."

"Wow," Baker said. Stunned, the cop leaned back in his chair, fished in the breast pocket of his shirt for a cigarette with the first two fingers of his right hand. "That's big. Almost unbelievable."

"Believe it," Juan said.

And he hoped the idiot did. Otherwise he might have to take down two cops instead of one. Normally he knew an experienced police officer would never bite on the line of crap he was casting. But Baker, his senses dulled by drugs, seemed willing to believe anything. With Baker looking at a brick of cocaine, Juan imagined the guy's street cop instincts were an irritating buzz gnawing at his brain from the distant end of a very long tunnel.

"He's in the third-floor conference room, with the chief," Baker said. "They don't have a scheduled break until noon. You could catch him then. Or maybe before that when he goes to the can or something."

"That would be perfect," Juan said.

"I can go with you," Baker offered.

"I'd prefer to handle this alone."

WATERS STEPPED into his office, dumped his coat in a heap on his paper-strewed desk and sank into his chair. He massaged his temples with stubby fingers and shut his eyes for a moment, trying to purge the headache that gathered behind his forehead like a storm cloud. Images of the charred bodies and the bloodshed at the motel sprang forth from his imagination, and his eyes flicked open automatically.

The detective had seen a lot of bodies during his career. The causes of death varied: car crashes, overdoses, serial killers, domestic violence. Name it, he had seen it. But for sheer, unadulterated destruction, he never seen anything like the mess at the motel. Belasko—with some help from Glynn—had methodically killed eight gunners with stunning precision. And had done so in self-defense. From what the coroner said, the bastard even put a bullet into several of the victims' foreheads, like a mercy shot.

As much as Waters hated to admit it, he found himself simultaneously repelled and intrigued by Belasko's methods. The big federal agent had just rid Orlando of a small contingent of leg breakers, urban terrorists who had preyed upon innocents and criminals, hurting and killing whomever they liked.

In some ways, Belasko's actions would make Waters's job easier, at least temporarily. Apparently the killings were sanctioned by someone with enough clout to make Orlando's mayor and Florida's governor bow. As far as Belasko's movements there were concerned, Waters's job had been to sit on the sidelines and collect data, not to investigate or prosecute the federal agent.

That was until that morning.

None other than Police Chief Sebastian Davis had summoned him to discuss, as Davis said, "the Belasko-Glynn situation." From the police chief's somber tone and the fact that Waters was getting a rare personal audience with Davis, Waters surmised he wasn't going to enjoy their talk.

Probably the opposite, in fact.

Releasing the pressure on his temples, he leaned forward in the chair. No sense in delaying the inevitable, he decided. Standing, Waters grabbed his jacket with two fingers and flung it over his left shoulder. The best he probably could hope for was to emerge from the meeting with a good tongue-lashing. That and maybe a good cup of coffee.

Roswell, Georgia

"SO VAN ZANT TALKED with this agent Belasko sometime before his death?" Sampson asked Emilio Vega.

The two men were seated in a conference room inside the sprawling building housing the drug laboratory. Ahern and another of Sampson's security guards stood behind the billionaire, watching the exchange. On the other side of the table, Estevez and another gunner flanked Vega.

"I assume they talked. Harry got close enough to get himself killed. So they probably talked."

Sampson narrowed his eyes at his partner. He leaned his elbows on the table and stared at Vega.

"Don't get cute with me, Emilio," he said. "This is important."

The drug lord jutted his face across the table, returning Sampson's stare.

"I'll decide what's important here, Victor. Remember that."

"Not," Sampson said, "if you keep screwing up. We're equal partners, Emilio. That's something you need to remember."

Vega glared, but Sampson robbed him of a chance to reply.

"I want to know—is this federal agent aware of the Buckhead raid?"

The drug lord shook his head no. "Harry told me he didn't breathe a word about it."

"You believe him?"

"Harry was a good man, Sampson. The best. Better than you or this battalion of candy-asses you tote around with you."

Sampson watched as Vega's gunners stifled laughs. Estevez, who stood at least six feet four inches tall and weighed 225 pounds, studied the nails of his left hand and shook his head. The other gunner stared at a wall and smirked.

"At least my men are still among the living," Samson said.

Vega slammed an open palm on the table. His cheeks burned crimson, his eyes bulged. The thunderclap created by his hand startled Sampson. The executive took a deep breath and let his hand slip beneath the table, moving fingertips precious inches closer to the .380 pistol holstered in his jacket pocket.

He returned Vega's dead-eyed glare. He'd be damned if he would let the drug-dealing son of a bitch intimidate him. He'd backed down more than one narcissistic, sociopathic CEO in his life. Given time, he knew he could do the same with this overblown drug pusher.

In the meantime, however, Vega's tantrum continued unabated.

"That's because your men don't do shit, Victor," he said. "They follow you like puppies, carry your bags for you. Pussy shit. My guys lay their lives on the line. If it wasn't for them, we wouldn't be where we are right now."

"Which is exactly where, Emilio?" Sampson replied. "Sitting in a half-finished drug laboratory in an open field, hiding from crazed federal agents? Thank you very much for accomplishing all this. It's sheer genius."

"You don't like the deal? You don't like it? I can cut you out, and don't think I won't."

"What exactly does that mean?" Sampson asked.

Smiles drained from the faces of Vega's gunners. Each intensified his focus on the exchange. Ahern, too, had stepped closer to Sampson, almost imperceptibly so. Sampson noticed Ahern had put his hands on his waist, letting his jacket bunch up over his wrists. A seemingly innocent gesture, Sampson knew it positioned Ahern's shooting hand closer to a pistol holstered in the small of the guard's back.

"It means I don't need you. I can make this damn drug on my own. I included you out of respect for your son. To avenge his death. To get even with the DEA. Your son was a good man, not pampered like you."

"Don't talk to me about my son, Emilio," Sampson said, his own voice rising. "You didn't know him. He was just another mule to you. Just somebody else to sell drugs and line your pockets with money. You didn't know your own son. You want me to believe you had a soft spot for my child?"

Vega jumped up from his chair, which clattered to the floor. His two hardmen hovered near him, ready to back him up.

"You don't talk to me about my son, you bastard," the drug lord said, bellowing. He hacked at the air with his index finger, pointing wildly as he yelled, "I'll kill you."

It was only after his outburst that Vega realized his predicament. Before his discarded chair hit the ground, Ahern had drawn the Beretta 92 and set it dead center on the drug lord's heart. Sampson was pleased with Ahern's battle reflexes.

"I don't think," the executive said, "you want to pick that fight with me, Emilio. Can we at least agree on that much?"

Vega glowered at Sampson. His breath chugged in and out in loud pulls. Estevez and the other bodyguard stared at Ahern, but also kept their hands visible.

Sampson's voice dropped to just above a whisper. "Now, shall we decide which cancer hospital to hit instead of Buckhead? Or should we just dissolve our partnership? The outcome of such a dissolution, I think, would displease you."

Never letting his eyes stray from Sampson, the drug lord snapped the fingers of his right hand. Estevez bent, grabbed the fallen chair and righted it. The muzzle of Ahern's pistol remained trained on Vega, but Sampson could see Ahern's eyes roving, tracking the bodyguards' movements. Sampson had no doubt his guard would murder Vega and Estevez before either could complete a single threatening move. Sampson knew his other mercenary would kill Vega's other bodyguard before he could draw a gun.

Apparently Estevez also sensed this and didn't try his luck. He took a hand off the chair and stepped away as Vega lowered himself onto the seat. The drug kingpin shot Sampson a look that told him their fight was on hold, but far from over.

A warm satisfaction passed through Sampson's body. He wouldn't have it any other way.

"I think, Emilio, we should jettison the Buckhead raid. Find another target and move ahead with that."

"Just like that, I'm supposed to find another target?"

"There are plenty of others," Sampson said. "It would cost us a day or so, but it's better than sending out a team to get ambushed by the police. Another bungled raid would lead the authorities right to us. It takes only one person giving information to blow the operation before we make a dime from it."

The drug lord nodded. He seemed to agree, albeit grudgingly so.

"Okay, you made your point. We'll postpone it. Keep everyone here. Probably best to have reinforcements until we figure out what the hell's going on. We might need the backup."

Sampson clapped his hands. "Good, it's settled." He rose, smoothed his jacket with his hands. "I assume you can select another target."

Vega stayed seated. Smoldering rage emanated from his body and filled the room like a tangible force.

"Fuck you, Sampson. Nothing's settled here. We both know that."

"Of course we do, Emilio. We can continue this discussion now or resume it later. It's your choice."

The drug lord looked away, his face twisted in disgust, and dismissed the billionaire with a wave.

"Get out of here, Sampson. You make me sick."

The executive exited, tailed by Ahern and the other mercenary. Despite his neutral expression and comparatively polite demeanor, Sampson felt anger swirl through his chest and stomach. Sure, he knew damn well things weren't over between them. In fact, he planned to make things much worse for Vega. And soon.

VEGA BARELY HEARD the door click shut behind Sampson as he left the room. The drug kingpin was too lost in seething thoughts to give the man any more attention.

As Sampson and his entourage had departed, Estevez followed close behind them, putting his considerable bulk between them and Vega, making sure he would take the first bullet. He didn't turn back to his boss until Sampson's last man shut the conference room door and Estevez locked the door.

"Guy's playing a dangerous game," Estevez said, huffing and rolling his shoulders like a fighter psyching himself for a title bout.

As far as Vega was concerned, the show of machismo was too little, too late.

"So far he's winning the game," Vega said. "That's unacceptable. You better do something to make things more acceptable. Quick."

The big guard stopped rolling his shoulders and looked at the ground.

"Sure, Emilio," he said. "I'll gather the guys. We'll make sure he doesn't get the drop on you again. I'll see to it myself."

"You do that," Emilio said. "And check with the guys in Orlando. Make sure they downed that stupid Fed. Last thing we need is him popping up here and making more trouble for us. We got enough of that right here."

Too much trouble, in fact, the drug lord thought. Too goddamn much.

14

Orlando, Florida

The insistent burn in his crotch told Ray Pitt that the morning's first two cups of coffee had worked their way through his system. He needed to hit the head, and soon, but was waiting for a break in his dialogue with the police chief to make it happen.

The DEA director and Davis had continued to spar over territorial issues as they waited for Davis's detective to arrive. The tension in Pitt's shoulders, the grinding of his teeth, told him his last ounces of diplomacy were ebbing from his body, fast. Needing to make a trip to the bathroom wasn't helping his disposition any.

"Look, Seb," Pitt said finally, "I hear what you're saying. But I'm not going to give you a heads-up every time I send an agent into Orlando. It just ain't happening."

Davis started to reply, but Pitt held up a hand.

"Let me take a break and we can pick this up in a minute," Pitt said. "Where's the can?"

Davis gave him directions. As he left the conference room, Pitt turned right and made his way down the hall. He barely noticed the well-dressed, bearded Hispanic man standing to his left as he traversed the corridor. To his surprise he felt a chill, and the hairs on his neck prickled as he neared the bathroom. He attributed the sensations to an overactive air conditioner and kept going.

JUAN VEGA FELT as though his heart would rocket through his rib cage as Pitt approached, then passed him. The young man's palms moistened, his hands trembled as Pitt stalked past him, nodded absently and journeyed to the bathroom. The banker returned the nod and then buried his face in a nearby water fountain. The younger Vega wasn't a carbon copy of his father, especially with his appearance altered, but they shared enough physical similarities that even a dumb pig such as Pitt might make the connection if the man put enough effort into doing so.

Juan held his breath, listened as the DEA director's steady gait carried him down the hall. The man was pushing ahead, apparently unaware of the danger just yards behind him. He either hadn't made the connection, or he purposely was playing dumb. As cool water trickled down Juan's chin, dribbled between the hairs of his beard, he chanced a look back at his quarry.

Pitt passed through the bathroom door without a second look. The young man smiled. The bathroom would be perfect.

God willing, it would be empty of others. Pitt would be preoccupied, and Juan could end this with a single silenced gunshot. He started down the hallway. With his right hand, he reached inside his jacket for the Beretta. With his left hand he felt around in his jacket pocket for the sound suppressor.

Within seconds, it all would be over. The drug lord's son would assassinate the man who had helped murder his brother. Juan also would finally gain his father's respect. It all seemed so easy.

So much gained from a single gunshot. Excitement tickled his stomach as he joined the pistol and the sound suppressor and continued walking. As he neared the men's-room door, his pace and his heartbeat each hastened a notch.

He paused for a moment, wishing he had time to enjoy a line of blow before killing Pitt. He vowed to reward himself with one hell of a party—right after he murdered his first cop.

He pushed open the door and entered the bathroom.

AT FIRST, Pitt hardly noticed being joined in the bathroom. Spending the morning in a restricted area of the department had allowed him something he rarely enjoyed on the streets: a sense of safety. As door hinges squealed, he assumed the fellow bathroom patron was a police officer. He finished drying his hands, wadded up the paper towel, turned and prepared to throw it away.

His blood ran cold.

The Hispanic he had seen moments before stood in front of him, a silenced pistol leveled at Pitt's head. Instinctively Pitt raised his hands, but thought of the Glock holstered in the small of his back.

"What's this?" Pitt said.

The Hispanic smiled. "You don't know who I am, do you?"

What was this game?

Pitt shook his head. "Should I know you?"

"Not yet," he said, "but your successor sure as hell will."

His successor? An invisible fist sucker punched Pitt in the stomach.

"What are you talking about?"

"Let me tell you."

WATERS STEPPED from the elevator, hitched up his pants and tucked in his shirt. As he fussed with his shirt, he noticed a small tan splotch on the breast pocket. He scowled. The stain had appeared a couple of weeks ago, and at the time had seemed a minor inconvenience. Now, as he was about to get face time with the chief, this small blemish amplified his every insecurity. Waters knew it would be the first thing that picky bastard saw when Waters entered the room. The son of a bitch would slip into judgment mode, assume Waters's work was as sloppy as his appearance and ignore everything the guy said. Waters had heard enough stories about the chief to know this was true.

God, he hated this.

The detective started down the hallway, walked past the bathroom door and toward the conference room. The closer he got, the drier his mouth became. Waters had faced down criminals of all types. He hit them hard, peppering them with questions, threats and sarcasm. When they tried to intimidate him, he laughed in their face. Cajoled them. Shamed them. Whatever it took to establish the pecking order. Same went for their high-priced lawyers who were big on volume and vocabulary, but shy on balls.

The department brass was another matter. Waters realized he had been following the chief's express orders when he let Belasko hit the streets after the first round of killings, opening the door for Belasko to kill again. He knew in his heart that the federal agent had done Orlando PD and the city a colossal favor by killing Vega's army of thugs.

He also knew that when Chief Davis's ass fell on the firing line, it would become Waters's fault. Somehow. Orders be damned. Davis was a good cop, but he also had to do a balancing act between law enforcement and politics. Had to put on his spit and polish and kiss the city commission's ass when the job called for it. Sometimes that meant letting the shit roll downhill where it smacked squarely onto the street cops. If Davis ran true to form, it was Waters's turn at the bottom of the hill.

Waters stopped at the water fountain and took a drink. Hoping to stall a few more seconds, he decided to go to the bathroom.

"YOU DON'T KNOW ME, but you know my father," the young Hispanic said.

Pitt scanned through his mind, trying to place his assailant's face, while also weighing his options, all of which looked bad. The gunman blocked the only door out. Loose items, such as trash cans, that could be turned into weapons rested just out of Pitt's reach. A grab for his own gun would mean instant death. So would a yell for help.

His best defensive weapon, Pitt decided, was his mouth. Talk to the young man, either stall him or convince him not to shoot.

The guy wasn't a professional hitter, or Pitt would already be lying on the bathroom floor in a pool of his own blood rather than discussing the kid's heritage. Pitt might be able to turn the inexperience to his own advantage.

"Who's your father?" Pitt asked.

The DEA director spoke quietly, pressuring his diaphragm as he did to keep his voice strong, confident. He noticed the young man's eyes were bloodshot and glazed. He sniffed like an allergy-plagued man in a field of tall grass. Pitt immediately pegged him as a cokehead.

Great. He had to reason with someone whose mind was beyond reason.

Pitt felt his irritation rise as the young man ignored his question, choosing instead to fit a smug grin across his face. "C'mon, son, who's your father?"

The young man said, "My father? Emilio Vega. Know him?"

Damn, Pitt thought, this keeps getting worse. "Sure, I know him. He send you to do this?"

The young man shook his head. His posture straightened, and his face beamed with an unabashed pride usually reserved for children. "I did this myself."

"Okay," Pitt said, "you must be Juan. Why do you want to kill me, Juan?"

Pitt asked the question, but already knew the answer.

"You killed my brother."

"That wasn't me, son. Someone else did that."

"Fine. The end result is the same. Someone's got to pay a debt to my father and my family."

Pitt wanted to explain to this punk that the last Vega to die did so because he chose to sweep a warehouse with submachine gun fire, endangering a team of federal agents in the process. Pitt had personally written a letter of commendation to the sniper who had plugged Vega's son.

Pitt wanted to explain that he cared a hell of a lot more about the three agents who died during Operation Thunderbolt than he did about that homicidal maniac Juan Vega called a brother.

Sure, he wanted to explain all that and more to the young man. He also knew better than to try.

Instead, the DEA director said, "Hey, sorry about your brother. How 'bout we talk this over."

"I'm not here to talk."

The knuckles of the young man's shooting hand whitened against the pistol's grip. Hands still in the air, Pitt tensed, ready to simultaneously scream and lunge.

WATERS HEARD murmurs through the heavy steel door of the bathroom, but paid little attention to them. Instead, he concentrated on the upcoming meeting, imagining the chief's questions, formulating answers to them, then doing the same with the inevitable follow-up questions. The scenarios and conversations ran through his head at top speed, like a VCR stuck on fast-forward mode.

Practically entranced, he pressed the middle two fingers of his right hand against a metal hand plate and pushed open the door. He bulled his way in, lost in his own thoughts.

He stopped dead.

Before him stood two men. The older guy was grabbing air and facing Waters. The younger man, his back toward Waters, pointed a pistol at his hapless victim.

Hearing Waters, the younger man turned to face the detective, his pistol leading the way. Waters had no idea what he had walked into, but the silenced Beretta spoke volumes to him. It didn't take a criminal-justice major to peg this guy as something other than a brother officer.

His big frame already filling the door, Waters knew he was committed and had neither time nor space to backtrack and grab cover. So, like a tank, he continued forward. One hand jabbed inside his jacket for his side arm. His other arm jutted forward as he plunged ahead.

It was do or die. That much Waters knew.

A growl escaped his lips and he kept moving.

A pistol muzzle locked on him. The silenced weapon coughed once as the detective pressed forward.

THE SLUG from Juan Vega's pistol slammed into Waters's abdomen. The detective doubled over, wheezing for air and fell to the floor. Crimson spread quickly through his shirt, soaking the fabric around the bullet hole perforating his stomach.

Pitt, meanwhile, had fisted his 9 mm pistol. He didn't know who the poor bastard was, but wittingly or unwittingly, the guy had saved his life. He planned to return the favor.

Juan Vega lowered the pistol and aimed it at Waters's chest, ready to slam a second shot through him.

"No," Pitt screamed.

Vega turned, the pistol's snout seeking a target. On autopilot, Pitt raised his own weapon, fired.

The pistol bucked four times in Pitt's hand as slugs drilled through Juan Vega's sternum and throat before ripping out the other side of his body. The bullets' impact slammed the bearded man against the wall. He slid down, smearing the wall with crimson. Blood frothed from his mouth, and his eyes registered surprise as his rear end settled to the floor.

Pitt stepped over the fallen detective. Keeping his own weapon trained on Vega, Pitt kicked away the silenced pistol. He did likewise with Waters's abandoned Glock, which also had fallen within the suspect's reach. Chances of the drug kingpin's son breathing, letting alone lunging for a weapon and firing on Pitt, were nearly nonexistent. But Pitt had his training.

Footsteps thundered down the hall toward the bathroom.

The DEA chief knelt beside the young Hispanic man. The first, hastily placed bullet had pierced his abdomen. The second apparently had smacked into his chest, probably tearing through his heart and killing him instantly. Pitt holstered his weapon, turned and rolled over the man who had thrown himself at Vega. Though blood was matting his hair against his skull, he was breathing. As Pitt settled the man on his back, the man's jacket fell open, revealing a detective shield pinned to his belt.

The footsteps neared, but slowed. He was sure the officers in the hallway were trying to gauge what they might be walking into before entering.

"This is Ray Pitt. DEA. Can we get paramedics in here?" Pitt heard himself shout. For the first time, he realized his ears were ringing from the gunshots. "We have an officer down."

Officers swarmed the room, pushed Pitt from the downed detective and began trying to make him comfortable. Someone shouted for a first-aid kit. Pitt leaned against a bathroom stall, looked at the dead Hispanic and felt vomit push at the top of his throat. He looked away, took some deep breaths and watched as the uniforms, now armed with medical equipment, treated the fallen officer. Pitt's pride wouldn't let him get sick in front of all these cops.

"Ray, what the hell happened here? Who shot Captain Waters and who's that on the floor?"

Pitt turned and saw Sebastian Davis standing in the bathroom door. Agent Cronin stood next to him, his pistol drawn, but rested flat against his thigh. The flood of officers had parted like the Red Sea for Moses, allowing the police chief and the DEA agent access to the already crowded room.

Tersely Pitt explained the situation.

A short female officer, a lieutenant, approached Pitt and Davis. Though still feeling lightheaded, Pitt glimpsed the rectangular name tag, which read D. Stevens, so he knew whom he was talking to. Still in shock, he had to read it twice before it registered.

"Sir, we're going to need to take a statement from you," she said.

She turned to Davis. "And we need to clear these people out of here as soon as Waters is transported. This still is a crime scene. We need forensics to scrub this place down. Right now it's a circus in here."

"I'll take his statement," Davis said.

The woman shot her boss a no-nonsense look and shook her head firmly. "We can't do that. You may be a witness," she said, "when a grand jury considers the shooting."

She turned to Pitt. "We'll also need to take your weapon and admit it into evidence."

Pitt almost blew his stack. A grand jury? This had been a

good shooting. Any idiot could see that. He started to protest, but stopped himself, realizing he was letting emotion override experience.

Every police shooting underwent a grand jury.

He should be no different.

In his heart, though, he knew this incident would be completely different.

Considering his own high-profile job, the identity of Juan Vega's father and the nature of Pitt's mission to Orlando, Pitt knew he probably could expect the scrutiny to become excruciating and the conspiracy theories to take on a life of their own.

Davis nodded. "You're right, Stevens. You should do it."

The chief turned to Pitt. "Sorry, Ray."

"It's no problem, Seb," Pitt said. "I understand."

Unconsciously he had holstered the weapon when he bent to check on Waters. He pulled the gun and holster from his belt, handed them to Stevens. He'd have Cronin get him a replacement before he left Orlando. Hell, before he left the building, for that matter.

Pitt watched as paramedics loaded the detective onto a stretcher and carried him from the room. The sea of police officers, both investigators and gawkers, again parted to allow the paramedics' passage.

"He'll be okay, right?" Pitt asked no one in particular.

He felt a hand on his shoulder. "He'll be fine, Ray," Davis said. "It could have been a lot worse."

Pitt wondered how, but squelched a sarcastic reply. He turned to Davis. "You'd better have them seal the building, Seb. This guy didn't just walk in here with a gun and a vendetta without help. Probably need to clamp down on the information flow, too. When Emilio hears about this, he's likely to go ape shit."

"Already on it, Ray," Davis said. "You go back to the conference room, grab a cup of coffee. I'll give you a few minutes to collect your thoughts before I sic Lieutenant Stevens on you."

Davis gave Pitt a smile, probably the first one the men had

shared since Pitt arrived in Orlando earlier that day. Despite their differences, the guy was trying to put Pitt at ease, and the DEA director appreciated it. He imagined Davis felt partially responsible for the younger Vega getting into the building in the first place.

For his part, Pitt felt no need to assign blame to Davis. He wanted the guy to find the bad seed within the department, sure. But he wouldn't come down on Davis because a bad cop sold out the whole department.

Besides, judging by the growing blood debt between the federal government and Emilio Vega, Pitt had more pressing things to worry about.

He expected Emilio Vega to respond to his son's death in kind. And once again Pitt expected to be smack in the center of the bull's-eye.

15

"Got a call coming in from Bear," Grimaldi said over his shoulder to Bolan. "Can you take it?"

Bolan nodded. Seated in the airplane's passenger section, he had fieldstripped the Colt Commando and was cleaning its components as Grimaldi, Glynn and he journeyed to Atlanta. Tilting his torso forward for balance and to protect his head from the ceiling, Bolan walked to the cockpit. He settled into the copilot's seat and donned a spare headset.

"Striker."

"Things are heating up in Orlando," Kurtzman said.

"We got out before the good guys tried to shut us down. Couldn't have blamed them if they had."

"I'm not talking about the scrapes at the motel and the airport."

"What, then?"

"Emilio's other son, Juan, is dead."

"Shit. When?"

"Just a little bit ago. Found out by tapping into Orlando PD's computers. Cops are gossiping among themselves via e-mail. They've sealed the building, ordered a media blackout, the works. My guess is they have an hour, two at best before the whole thing explodes in their faces."

"What happened to his son?"

"You know Ray Pitt?"

"Know of him."

"Pitt shot the guy dead. Guess Emilio's son sneaked into Orlando's police headquarters, tried to kill Pitt and ended up dead himself."

"Does Emilio know?"

"Too soon to tell. You can bet he'll find out soon enough. It won't be good when he does, either."

"That's the classic understatement," Bolan said.

"My stock in trade," Kurtzman said. "Hey, Hal wants to speak at you. Got a sec?"

"Go."

As the warrior waited for Brognola to take the line, he felt irritation grind at him. He wasn't sure how the assassination attempt fit into the larger picture, if it fit at all. It could mean a meltdown within Vega's organization, perhaps a dissension for Bolan to exploit. Or it could indicate his quarry had switched objectives, leaving the Executioner proceeding down a blind path. He hoped the latter wasn't the case; he had no patience for indulging in a prolonged cat-and-mouse game with Sampson or Vega.

Brognola joined the secure connection and the two men greeted each other.

"You're en route to Atlanta?" Brognola asked.

"Should be on the ground in about fifteen minutes," Bolan said. "What can you tell me about Juan Vega?"

"Clean until today," Brognola said. "He has no criminal record. He's a banker. He actually ran his own bank for ten years. It's a small community job in suburban Florida. We assume he launders money for his father, but he's been smart enough or lucky enough not to get caught. Otherwise, there are no apparent links between him and Daddy's business. He files all the proper papers with the FDIC, IRS and Comptroller of the Currency. He was active in the community. Seemed like an upstanding guy."

"Unlike his brother," Bolan said.

"Unlike his brother," Brognola repeated. "Revenge is the most obvious motive. The DEA killed his brother. He kills Pitt. The family is avenged. In a twisted way, it makes sense."

"But it doesn't seem like a plot he would hatch on his own."

"Not at first blush. Could be the kid had a dark side, though. Or his father put him up to it. If Daddy's still pissed about his number-one son dying last year, maybe he wanted to kill Pitt himself, but didn't have the balls."

Bolan mulled that for a moment. "Doesn't play, Hal. Emilio has enough hired muscle to kill Pitt ten times over. I'm not convinced he would endanger his remaining son in a suicide mission."

"You think somebody else gave Juan a nudge?"

"Maybe. Might be one of Vega's people trying to undermine the boss. Could be Sampson."

"Getting revenge?"

"Makes some sense," Bolan said. "Maybe he blames Vega for his own son's death. Seems an odd partnership in the first place, considering the thread connecting them. Anyway, their motives should be academic soon. I plan to wrap this up today."

"How can we help?"

"I need some face time with one of Emilio's lieutenants. I want to get a precise location for the drug lab. He have any people in Atlanta?"

Brognola paused. "Eduardo Mendoza is Emilio's Atlanta connection. If Vega is in town, Mendoza knows where the guy is staying."

"Then I need an audience with Mendoza. I want to do this as a soft probe, gather intel and get the hell out quietly as possible. The last thing I need is Vega and Sampson knowing I'm in town before I find them."

"I can call Leo Turrin," Brognola said, referring to the undercover federal agent who doubled as a semiretired mafioso. "Leo might be able to grease some wheels, get you some face time."

"Okay," Bolan said. "But tell Leo to distance himself as much as possible. I don't want this to come back on him if it goes bad."

"Leo's a pro," Brognola said. "He won't do anything to compromise his cover. Who should he tell Mendoza to expect?"

"Tell him John Delgado, a midlevel drug buyer from West Virginia. I should be able to pass as an American with Latino roots."

"I'll have him set up the meet."

The weariness in his old friend's voice didn't escape Bolan's notice. "What's eating you, Hal?"

Brognola sighed. "Look, Striker, we both know the assassination attempt changes things. Once Emilio finds out, he's liable to do anything, including hunt Pitt down himself. The Man's breathing down my neck to do something. He's worried. Frankly, so am I."

"What's Pitt's status?"

"Right now, he's at Orlando PD's headquarters. Plans are to get him out of there and back to his home in Bethesda, Maryland. In the meantime, he's surrounded by an army of police officers and DEA agents in case of further aggression. The running theory is junior had inside help penetrating the PD. Whether it was hostile or just a bribe, we don't know. The faster we get him out of Orlando, the better. Carl is en route to Bethesda to oversee security."

"Good choice," Bolan said.

Carl Lyons was the leader of Able Team, and the Executioner had known him since the earliest days of his War Everlasting, back when Lyons was a young police detective. He implicitly trusted the brash warrior to handle the job. If gunners attacked Pitt and encountered Lyons in the process, they would know they had hit something hard.

If, that was, they lived long enough to think about it.

"Yeah," Brognola said. "It's a good choice—if Carl gets through this without turning it into an incident."

"Don't count on it," Bolan replied. "I need Rosario down here to help me. How soon can you get him to the naval air base in Georgia?"

Another pause as Brognola did a quick mental calculation. "A few hours," he said.

"Get him there," Bolan said. "He's going undercover with me."

"Right. What else do you need?"

Bolan ticked off a list of equipment. Brognola promised to have everything in place by the time Rosario Blancanales arrived at the air base. The big Fed also pledged to have Kurtzman electronically ship dossiers of Mendoza and his key people to Bolan.

The two men signed off. Bolan sank deeper into the copilot's seat. He stared through the windshield at the blue sky and wisps of clouds, listened to the steady hum of the plane's twin engines as he considered the changing face of the mission. The assassination attempt and the likelihood of reprisal against Pitt added another battle front. The inclusion of Lyons and Blancanales did little to ease his mind. Bolan was preparing to enter the mouth of a lion and asking friends to do likewise. Lyons and Blancanales were soldiers—damn fine soldiers—and would follow their orders. As often entered his mind, he hoped he wasn't asking either to perform a final mission. He rose from the seat and returned to his rifle, preparing himself for the next battle in his War Everlasting.

Naval Air Station, Marietta, Georgia

WITHIN MINUTES of landing, Bolan had settled into a private room at the air base. Spartan in its furnishings, the quarters offered a single bunk, a steel desk, a midnight-blue cushioned chair on rollers and a stout night table. Pulling a laptop from his bag, he hooked the device into the base's fiber-optic network, booted up the computer and began downloading files sent to him by Stony Man Farm through an ultrasecure network virtually impervious to outside tampering.

During the remainder of the flight, Bolan had briefed Glynn on the attempt on Pitt's life. Upon their arrival at the base, she had disappeared to find a phone so she could discuss the situation with her superiors in private. Grimaldi was getting the plane serviced and also scouting the base's inventory of helicopters in case the hit on the drug lab required air power. Bolan imagined it would.

He estimated he had at least another two hours before Blancanales's arrival.

The Stony Man files on Mendoza and his security chief, Robert Guirrez, offered detailed snapshots of each man's life. Bolan soon found himself engrossed as he scanned the electronic documents memorizing data—physical, personal and legal—for both men. According to his dossier, Mendoza had worked for Vega's predecessor in Atlanta before Vega gained a foothold in the market. He'd tried to partner with Mendoza's boss, who told him to go to hell. His counteroffer included having the man's throat slit, his tongue pulled through the gash and exposed in the classic Colombian necktie. His wife and the families of two brothers suffered a similar fate.

Not surprisingly, Mendoza and Guirrez decided to get on board with Vega, and within days of the hostile takeover, Vega controlled large portions of Atlanta's drug trade. By all accounts, Mendoza was most adept at staying alive. He survived by pleasing Vega and anticipating the drug lord's needs.

If anyone in Atlanta knew Vega's whereabouts, it was Mendoza. That put him on Bolan's must-see list.

A knock at his door jarred him from his reading. He quit the classified documents, turned off the computer and approached the door. As he grasped the handle, he called, "Who is it?"

"Madeline. Let me in."

Bolan let her in and shut the door behind her. She had changed into a pair of jeans, blue canvas tennis shoes and a dark blue T-shirt with a U.S. Navy insignia emblazoned on her right breast She carried a Glock wrapped in a shoulder holster in her right hand. Freed from its ponytail, her hair fell around her shoulders and framed the ivory skin of her face in red curls. Anger burned from her eyes and tightened her lips into a thin line.

"They're making me go home," she said.

Bolan knew who "they" were. "Why?"

"With Vega's organization possibly coming for Ray Pitt, the brass won't condone me going after Emilio alone. My team's little undercover operation has exploded into the agency's number-one priority. They're summoning lawyers, creating strike forces. The U.S. attorney is talking with Vega's lawyers. Supposedly they're willing to deal."

"It's a stall," Bolan said. "They've been talking since yesterday when I hit his house and he went underground. Vega won't give up."

"I know," she said. "My guess is Vega's biding time, perhaps to get himself out of the country."

"Where he can kill Pitt later without facing U.S. reprisal," Bolan said.

She shook her head in agreement. "Vega's worth billions. He can buy asylum anywhere. My bosses figure he'll put a price on Ray Pitt's head, let the hitters line up to kill him. In the meantime, Vega and Sampson can synthesize the cancer drug overseas, probably easier than they can make it here. Their plan continues undeterred, and they make lots of cash."

"You're going to follow orders."

Glynn shrugged. "I don't have a choice. Doing otherwise could cost me my career, make me a pariah within the DEA. It's best that I bow out while I still can."

"You're okay with that?" Bolan asked.

"Truthfully, Mike, I'm not sure what I'm okay with," she said. "Part of me feels relieved to back off. I'm not a commando, I'm a federal agent. After all the death I've witnessed—hell, that I caused—part of me wants to hole up in an office and shuffle papers for the rest of my life. Another part wants to see this through to the end. Does that make sense?"

"Perfect sense."

"The fighting is wearing me down. It scares the hell out of me. Do you think that makes me a coward?"

The thought had never occurred to Bolan.

"You've proved yourself to me," he said. "This fight's not worth your career. Or your life."

"Thank you," she said. "What about your life?"

Bolan didn't avert his gaze. "I give it willingly if it comes to that. I don't dwell on life and death. Otherwise, I'd be paralyzed and would be of no use to anyone."

"I can't imagine you paralyzed," Glynn said. "You seem like a man of action."

Bolan didn't need his ego stroked. He deflected the compliment.

"Whatever the hell that means."

She looked hurt for a moment. Then she seemed to shrug it off, and her eyes regained a playful sparkle Bolan hadn't seen since she first arrived with him at the motel in Orlando.

"I could show you," she said, "what it means for me."

She moved in closer, and Bolan felt warmth pass through his stomach and settle pleasantly into his groin. He didn't stop the approach. The animal attraction he had felt at the motel returned, gripping him like an unstoppable force. The battle weariness that had conquered his muscles yielded to excitement.

Softly he cupped her chin in one hand, searching out her eyes with his own. "You understand this is just for now," he said.

"I understand."

Bolan felt good about Glynn, had almost since they had met, and knew he had a lull in the battle. The DEA agent looked up at him, her lips parted slightly, the corners of her mouth curved in a slight, expectant smile. He looped an arm around her waist, pulled her to him, sought her mouth with his own. As they connected, she melted against him. He felt the pressure of firm breasts, slender waist pushing into him. He let his free hand graze along her backside. Moist lips surrendered against his own. He kissed her harder and began tugging at her shirt, which was tucked into the waist of tight jeans. She broke contact with his mouth and nuzzled against his chest as he did so.

"When do you leave?" he whispered, wanting to know, but not wanting to break the moment.

"I guess when we get tired of this."

"That could be a while."

"Tell me about it."

NEARLY TWO HOURS LATER, Bolan got a call from Rosario Blancanales, who said he would arrive at the base's airfield within fifteen minutes and get to Bolan's room shortly thereafter. Bolan and Glynn quickly showered, dressed, said their goodbyes and she departed to make final travel arrangements for herself. Twenty minutes later, Blancanales, escorted by a young Navy ensign, appeared at Bolan's door and entered the room. The Navy man set down a large canvas duffel with a heavy thud and left the room.

Blancanales unhooked a second canvas bag from his shoulder and set it next to the first. He knelt beside the bag, unzipped it and exposed a small cache of weapons. He withdrew a Heckler & Koch G-3 rifle, set it on the floor, then an M16A1 outfitted with a sound suppressor and an M-203 grenade launcher. Finally he pulled out two pistols—a SIG-Sauer P-226 and a .40-caliber Glock—and their holsters.

He looked at Bolan. "I noticed you ordered some expensive suits, lots of cash and a briefcase. What's the plan?"

"How much did Hal tell you?"

Blancanales shook his head. "Not much other than to get on a plane and get to Atlanta. I didn't stop to ask questions."

The Executioner nodded. Brognola and Bolan inspired that kind of loyalty. He gestured toward the single chair. "Sit down. I'll explain what comes next. It's going to be more taxing than the airplane ride."

Bethesda, Maryland

CARL LYONS WHEELED his car into the driveway of Ray Pitt's brick two-story home. The structure, adorned with brass light fixtures and meticulously landscaped, sat in a sprawling development fronting a golf course. Lyons's first instinct was to wonder how a glorified cop—even a high-level federal bureaucrat—could afford such luxury. He set aside his distrust, reminding himself that not only was Pitt drawing a pension from the Washington, D.C., police department while also working a full-time job, but the guy also came from old money. Anticipating Lyons's suspicious nature, Brognola had provided a full financial disclosure up front.

Lyons braked the rented Pontiac sports car, slammed the console shifter into Park and popped open the door. Before he set a foot on the driveway, though, two men decked out in suits, shades and earpieces appeared. Lyons guessed both were DEA foot soldiers, but he let the fingers of his right hand encircle the butt of a small revolver stuck between the seat and the console, just in case. One approached Lyons directly while the other arced around the vehicle, his hand underneath his jacket. It was a good strategy: it split the newcomer's attention and ensured at least one agent would have a clear drop on the new arrival if he decided to get hostile.

At least these guys aren't total idiots, Lyons thought. There might be hope yet for this mission.

"I'm Agent Moses, DEA. Can I help you?" the man closer to Lyons asked. His thick black hair was cut in a high and tight military fashion, his mustache trimmed in a precise line about a millimeter off the length of his top lip. He outweighed Lyons by a good thirty pounds and had the bulk and stiff-jointed gait of a serious bodybuilder.

Lyons stepped from the car and extended a hand. The air was fresh and moist from an earlier rainfall.

"Jon Irons. I'm with Justice."

Lyons extended a hand, which the agent took in a quick, firm grip. The guy squeezed hard, probably more as a show of superiority than warmth. The agent's lips tightened in a thin line as he openly appraised this stranger tapped to lead the protection detail. Lyons returned the stare.

"This is Agent Donaldson. We were told to expect you. You come highly recommended."

Lyons escaped the guy's grip, nodded absently and scanned the house, memorizing the number and location of doors and windows, estimating their height from the ground, determin-

ing if decorative brick fences surrounding a small garden offered an intruder easy access. Or a viable shield should a gunfight erupt on the front lawn.

Finally he said, "I come highly recommended because I'm
extremely good."

The agent's lips whitened, but his eyes remained inscrutable
behind the sunglasses. His anger barely registered with Lyons,
who didn't bother to see how he was impacting the second
agent. His orders hadn't included making friends.

"I'm sure you're good," Moses said in a voice that clearly
stated the opposite.

"You realize I'm running the show, don't you?" Lyons asked.

He continued to get a lay of the land and mostly ignored the
two agents.

"Yes," Moses said.

Finished with his real-estate appraisal, Lyons settled his
eyes first on Moses, then Donaldson.

"Good. Now, why the fuck haven't you asked me for identification?" Before either could reply, Lyons fished a leather
case containing his Justice Department credentials from his
pocket and tossed it to Moses. The agent plucked the wallet-
sized case from the air even as Lyons started toward the house.

"When's our guy coming home?" he asked over his shoulder as he approached the trunk of his car.

Chastised, Moses scanned the identification intensely before
answering. "Couple, maybe three hours."

"How many of you are there?"

"Five counting Donaldson and myself, Agent Irons."

"You can cut the 'agent' bullshit and call me Irons."

"Yes, sir," Moses said.

Donaldson had joined him and was scanning Lyons's fake
ID. Lyons grabbed his weapons and equipment from the trunk
and dumped the bags at the agents' feet. He leveled his gaze at
the two men.

"Take this shit into the house and look alive while you're doing
it," Lyons said. Before either could move, he brushed past them
and headed for the maroon door adorned with a brass knocker.

"Guy's a prick," Lyons heard Moses whisper to Donaldson.

The former Los Angeles police detective allowed himself a grin. By all accounts the guy was right. Indeed, Lyons was a prick. And if Vega or his thugs dared to show their faces here, he would happily demonstrate to both the drug runners and the DEA agents how big a bastard he really could be.

Downtown Atlanta

BOLAN AND BLANCANALES walked through the revolving doors of Easton Tower, a twenty-story office and residential building. A blast of artificially cold air hit Bolan in the face, arriving just ahead of a cacophony of voices, clicking heels and tumbling water from big fountains located in the lobby's center.

Bolan wore a black suit, charcoal-gray shirt and black shoes. The Beretta 93-R was snugged in the armpit of the specially tailored jacket. Dressed in a tan, summer-weight suit, Blancanales carried the Glock in shoulder leather and the SIG in a waist holster. Both men carried briefcases stuffed with cash and wore mirrored sunglasses.

The cache of assault rifles and submachine guns was sealed in the trunk of a Mercedes Bolan had purchased from a car lot on Atlanta's seedier side. Obviously used to dealing with the dark side, the car dealer hadn't flinched when Bolan plunked down thirty thousand dollars cash nor when he slid the dealer another five grand to sidestep title changes, IRS paperwork and other red tape related to the buy.

As far as he was concerned, the car dealer said, the transaction never occurred. That suited Bolan fine; he hoped to keep a lower profile in Atlanta than he had managed in Orlando. It also helped him establish credibility as a criminal should Mendoza run traps on him.

With Turrin's network of criminal contacts, Bolan and Blancanales had secured an audience with Mendoza. The warrior's plan called for him to initiate a cocaine buy from Mendoza, steer the conversation toward Vitalife and pique Mendoza's interest in selling him that drug, too. If Bolan dropped enough cash, he reasoned, he might gain a private audience with Vega.

Bolan and Blancanales traversed the lobby, a riot of marble, glass, chrome and fluorescent lights. Wading through a flood of well-dressed executives talking into cell phones, security guards regarding the crowd and janitors pushing mop buckets and brooms, they reached the bank of elevators and found the express car to the penthouse. Blancanales punched a security code into a number pad and they waited. Kurtzman had the liberated the building's floor plans, security codes and guard schedules with a few keystrokes of a computer. Bolan and Blancanales had studied the material, gaining a working knowledge of the structure.

The pair climbed into the elevator car and Bolan selected the eighteenth floor. As the elevator began its smooth ascent, Blancanales turned to Bolan.

"You sure Mendoza won't recognize you after all the damage in Orlando?"

Bolan stared ahead, shook his head. "I took care of it."

During his raids on Vega's and Van Zant's homes, Bolan had relieved the security systems of digital disks carrying footage of his raids. Kurtzman had followed up with a long-distance assist by infecting the computer-operated security with system-destroying viruses. As long as Vega himself wasn't in the room, Bolan should go unrecognized. Other than piercing blue eyes, his olive complexion and other features were pedestrian enough that he shouldn't raise an eyebrow from Mendoza. Or so he hoped.

From everything Turrin had reported to Brognola, Mendoza was operating business as usual. He had a full schedule, and it had been no small feat for Turrin to secure Bolan and Blancanales an audience with the guy. If all went as planned, the Executioner would dazzle Mendoza with cash and talk. If it went bad, Bolan planned to cancel Mendoza and his future appointments permanently.

The elevator stopped on the eighteenth floor, the door glided open and a muted electronic bell announced their arrival. Bolan found himself faced by his own reflection in mirrored elevator doors situated across the hall. Four penthouses, one per corner, and a series of corridors occupied the building's top floor. The warrior checked his watch. They were right on time for their appointment with Mendoza.

At the door, Blancanales knocked while Bolan hung back. The door opened slightly and one of Mendoza's hardmen peered into the hallway, sizing up Bolan and Blancanales. A security chain held the door fast as the guy checked out the two visitors.

"We're here to see Eduardo," Blancanales said. "I'm Rodriguez. This is Delgado."

Letting the chain fall free, the man opened the door wide, ushering the men in. As Bolan and Blancanales scanned the opulence that surrounded them, a dead bolt slammed home from behind, sealing them inside Mendoza's lair.

Getting inside, apparently, was the easy part. Getting what they needed, then getting out would be the hard part.

Roswell, Georgia

WORD OF HIS SON'S DEATH hit Emilio Vega like a sledgehammer.

The drug kingpin's knees buckled, and he stumbled backward two steps before colliding with a table. Nausea and pain wrung his stomach like a wet towel. As he swallowed his own vomit, he turned away from his men and waved an arm at them.

"Get out of here," he said. "I gotta figure this out."

Most of the gunners filed through the door. Estevez stood over his boss and set a hand on his shoulder. The drug lord shrugged off the hand and walked away, stopping inches from a wall and staring straight ahead.

"You need anything, boss?"

"Explain it to me again. How the hell did this happen?"

In a quiet monotone, the bodyguard explained again about the attack on Pitt. About Juan shooting a cop. About the DEA director taking down the young banker with four 9 mm slugs.

"That's not something my boy would do," Vega said. "I kept

Juan out of this shit. He's not like his old man. How could this happen to him?"

"Who knows, Emilio? Maybe he was pissed about his brother dying and decided to go after Pitt."

Vega spun. "You bet he was pissed. You bet he wanted revenge. Hey, I'm pissed, too. But what he did was stupid. Very stupid. I can't believe my son would do something so idiotic. Where'd he learn to be such a goddamn hothead?"

The bodyguard decided not to take the bait, but instead nodded in agreement and kept his words neutral. "Kid lost his head."

"Fucking Ray Pitt ought to lose his, too," Vega said. "Bad enough the damn DEA steals my drugs, my money and my cars. Now they've taken my family. I got nothing."

"You still got stuff, Emilio," Estevez said. "Don't go getting nuts. The Feds are chasing you. You don't need more trouble."

"The hell I don't. I'm not going to get trouble. I'm going to give it. I want Pitt dead by sunrise tomorrow."

Estevez knew he teetered on a thin line between advising his boss and telling the guy he was an idiot. He persisted anyway. "Emilio, man, you gotta stay focused. Sampson wants to edge you out. You stop watching him, and he's liable to take you down."

"He can't touch me," the drug lord said. "He tries, he dies. That's what I'm paying you for, dumbass—to watch my back. So watch it."

The muscles of Estevez's jaws rippled, and his fists clenched tight enough to crush stone into powder. He said nothing.

"So what are you staring at?" Vega said. "Find out where Pitt lives and kill him. Buy us the best people you can. I'm willing to drop big money on this. And you tell them to kill anyone else who's there."

"Clean sweep?"

"Million for Pitt. A hundred grand each for his wife and kid. Another fifty thousand for each federal agent killed in the cross fire."

"You got it."

"You have someone you can call?"

"I know some people in D.C. They'll handle it from start to finish. It'll be bloody. Attract some attention. But they'll kill him."

"That's all I care about. To hell with finesse. I want results."

"Okay. What do we do in the meantime?"

"We make sure this white elephant is running okay. Then I leave the country for a while. I've got money set aside. I can go to Peru or Colombia. Do a little business traveling. Hell, we can go overseas, grow some poppies, make some heroin. Get my hands dirty again. It'll be great."

Estevez waved a hand around the expanse of the room, letting it represent the drug laboratory. "What about all this?" Estevez asked.

"What about it? We got plenty of people can take care of the Vitalife operation, the cocaine trade. I can oversee things from overseas. That fat bastard Mendoza can play domestic babysitter. I planned to let him run the Atlanta plant anyway. I'll sit on my ass, get drunk and reap the profits. I need to party, let off some steam, grieve my boys. First we got other business to attend to."

"What's that?"

"I got to transfer the crown. Get Mendoza on the phone."

16

Downtown Atlanta

With Blancanales at his side, Bolan checked out the penthouse's living room and found it steeped in luxury typical of high-level drug dealers. The furnishings were expensive—heavy oak dining tables, cabinets and wet bar, couch and chairs covered by supple brown leather, thick carpets, paintings by French Impressionists. Several stacks of money and two mechanical bill counters sat on the dining-room table. Several cardboard boxes stuffed with cash littered the floor. Bolan noted the placement of the furniture, decided the wet bar and the dining table, if upturned, offered the best potential for cover should things turn bad. Hints of marijuana and tobacco smoke fouled the air.

Next, the Executioner appraised the most important furnishings—the army of gunners positioned throughout the room.

To his left, hardmen stood next to a sliding glass door leading onto a balcony. Weapons bulged under the fabric of cheap suits. Thick arms and shoulders strained the seams of their suit coats. By most standards, the men would be considered intimidating.

To Bolan, though, they were two more faceless thugs in a seemingly endless parade of leg breakers.

He pegged them as easy kills and continued to sweep the room with his icy stare.

Directly in front of Bolan and Blancanales stood a man the Executioner recognized from photos as Guirrez. Well dressed and efficient in his movements, the guy gave the visitors a look that screamed distrust. He assumed Guirrez was armed, though he apparently had a better tailor than his boys did and a weapon wasn't visible. Mendoza stood next to Guirrez, legs spread wide, supporting his weight like columns under a bridge. He cocked ham-hock hands on his hips and let his obese middle spill forward like long pent-up water crashing from a broken dam, swallowing the real estate below his belt.

Two more gunners stood at three o'clock and four o'clock. The same dead-eyed stares took in Bolan and Blancanales. These guys would be equally easy kills, if it came to that.

Guirrez, Bolan decided, presented the biggest threat. He exuded cool confidence and had enough brains to stay wary of strangers. If possible, he would catch the first bullet should things go bad. Chances were, though, the guy wouldn't make it that easy for Bolan.

The guard who'd opened the door approached the Stony Man warriors from behind. Seeing him from the corner of his eye, Bolan turned slightly and held up a hand to stop the man. The guard opened his mouth to protest but before he could utter a word, Bolan turned his attention to Mendoza.

"Eduardo, you can check us for wires if you want," Bolan said. "But no one's restraining me. And no one—I mean no one—takes my gun. There are seven of you, two of us. We're all strangers. The gun stays."

"I don't do business that way," Mendoza said.

Bolan dropped his hand. "Then I guess we don't do business. No skin off my ass, I can get drugs anywhere."

"Then just fucking do that," Mendoza said.

Bolan knelt and reached for his briefcase. Blancanales withdrew his sunglasses from his jacket pocket, started to unfold them as though preparing to leave.

Without looking at Mendoza, Bolan fired the parting shot in their standoff. "Hope Emilio doesn't mind you shooing away millions of dollars in business, my friend. Thank God I'm not the poor fuck telling him I cost him all that money."

Bolan turned his eyes up at Mendoza, gauging his reaction. The drug lieutenant stiffened briefly, then regained his composure. In a heartbeat, he transformed from hardass to diplomat, let a smile play across his lips, spread his hands wide.

"We can talk," Mendoza said. "What the hell? We'd get the drop on you before you got off a single shot at us."

As if to punctuate the point, a couple of the hardmen drew their pistols, let them hang at their sides.

"My thoughts exactly, Eduardo," Bolan said. "This doesn't have to be difficult."

Two of the gunners approached Bolan and Blancanales and checked them for wires. The hands of the guy searching Bolan hesitated for a moment when he found the Beretta, but he left the gun alone. He relieved Bolan of a pager and a digital phone and handed them to another guy to inspect for cameras and microphones. Blancanales endured the same routine from another guard.

"Guy's carrying, Ed, but he's not wired," the hardman said after the search. The man searching Blancanales reported likewise.

"Show us the briefcases," Mendoza said.

Bolan and Blancanales laid the cases flat on the floor, worked the tumblers of the small combination locks and popped the tops. Each stood and stepped away from the cases.

The guard who had just searched Bolan knelt beside the warrior's briefcase and spun it toward himself without lifting it from the floor. He emptied it of several stacks of bills, ringing himself in uneven piles of currency. He scanned the case's innards, scrutinized the hinges, combination locks and handles, any fixture capable of surveillance equipment. The gunner who patted down Blancanales searched his briefcase in a similar fashion. Satisfied, they returned the cash to the cases and sealed the lids.

Bolan wasn't sweating the search. The briefcases were clean, purchased off the shelf at an office supply store in Virginia by Stony Man armorer John "Cowboy" Kissinger. The only modification was two small wedges of C-4 plastic explosives hidden under the lining of Blancanales's briefcase. The C-4 charges would create a noisy, smoky concussion strong enough to knock a bystander to the ground, but cause little other damage. Either Bolan or Blancanales could ignite the charge by punching a code into their mobile phone. The code armed the send button, transforming it into a detonator.

The phones and pagers carried by both men were clean of microphones and cameras. Surveillance didn't figure into Bolan's plans for Mendoza. If it got to the point of blowing up the briefcases, the penthouse was seconds from becoming a killzone.

"You can take the cases if it will make you feel better," Bolan said.

"It would," Guirrez replied.

"Be my guest."

The guards set the briefcases at Mendoza's feet and stepped away from them. Mendoza nodded, waddled to a couch and fell into it with a grunt. He waved a thick arm at a pair of chairs positioned across from him.

"Rodriguez, Delgado, sit."

They sat. Blancanales crossed his left ankle over his right knee, settled into his chair and smiled. Bolan's old friend was known as the Politician because of his ability to negotiate and interrogate damn near anyone. Coming in cold and trying to secure help from a paranoid drug dealer, the Stony Man warriors had agreed from the outset that Pol's tact might prove a powerful weapon. If necessary, Bolan could play bad cop to Pol's good cop.

The Executioner had already established himself as the bad guy with his hard line on keeping his weapon.

Mendoza leaned back against the couch. Bolan noticed the drug dealer perspired and struggled for breath under his own weight.

"You two came a long way," Mendoza said between gasps.

Blancanales shrugged and kept his expression warm, approachable.

"From Virginia," he said. "It was no big deal. You come highly recommended. We want very much to do business with you."

"Make it worth our trouble," Bolan said.

Mendoza ignored him, sought the path of least resistance—Blancanales. "They don't have suppliers in Virginia?"

"They do," Blancanales said, "but they're idiots. In the last couple of weeks, the state police and the DEA have shut down two of our biggest pipelines."

"I heard about that," Mendoza said.

Bolan wasn't surprised. They had culled the information from real news reports, building their ruse upon a foundation of truth.

Blancanales continued. "That means product is getting scarce. It also means the men who got arrested could compromise us. Cause us problems with the authorities. Our boss doesn't like that."

Mendoza arched an eyebrow. "You mean Alberto Vasquez?"

"Yes," Blancanales said. "Alberto."

Vasquez was a small-time Virginia drug dealer, and a federal agent. He was deep cover, ready to go into semiretirement like Leo Turrin, but willing to vouch for Bolan and Blancanales if someone called and verified their story. Apparently Mendoza had done just that.

Blancanales kept the conversation going. "You know Alberto?"

"Know of him. Maybe I should check with him, see what he says about you two."

"Sounds like you already did check with him, Ed," Bolan said.

Blancanales gave Bolan a stern look. The soldier faked irritation, turning his attention to a nearby painting while Blancanales continued salving Mendoza's suspicions.

"Eduardo, please ignore my friend. Call if you must. I'm sure it would strengthen his confidence in you as a supplier. He appreciates smart, careful businessmen such as yourself."

Flattery, it seemed, got Blancanales everywhere. Mendoza sat a little straighter, visibly puffed out with pride.

"I've got to be careful," Mendoza said. "I work for Emilio Vega. He's a smart, thorough man. He demands the same of his people."

"As well he should," Pol said.

Bolan dropped a loud exhale and shook his head in disgust.

"Can you two stop kissing each other's asses long enough to make a deal?" he said.

"Give it a rest, John," Blancanales said. He turned to Mendoza. "Ignore him. He has no tact, no manners. We want very much to work with you. It would be our pleasure."

"How much of a pleasure?" Mendoza asked.

Bolan broke in. "About twenty million dollars' worth. That pleasant enough for you?"

Mendoza's bloodshot eyes flickered for a moment, but otherwise his round face remained emotionless. "That's a lot of money," he said. "I'd love to take it. But why us?"

"Because Mr. Vega is smart enough to keep from getting caught. Alberto sells a quarter-billion dollars in drugs every year. He has no interest in running low on product or getting arrested. I'm sure you can appreciate that."

"Sure," Mendoza said. A spark of mistrust still glimmered in his eyes, but Bolan could tell the potential for a big score was clouding his judgment.

Guirrez, the smarter of the two, continued to glare at Bolan and Blancanales with the intensity of a halogen searchlight.

"We want to spend lots of money with you," Bolan said. "But you have to prove to us the product is worth it."

"It is," Mendoza said.

"We also want some diversity," Bolan stated. "Not just coke, but some other stuff, too. Can you handle that or not?"

Mendoza leaned as far forward as his belly would allow. His eyes had narrowed in anger. Bolan knew he had hooked the son of a bitch's pride.

"We do more than coke," Mendoza said. "We got grass, hash, meth. We got all kinds of shit."

"Who doesn't?" Bolan said. "I can grow grass in my basement. I don't need to come to Georgia or Florida for that." He waved toward the briefcases. "You've seen our money. All I get from you is the stench of stale pot. You want the real money, show me that you've got the product. Or stop wasting my time."

"We can hook you up with all kinds of shit, man," Mendoza said. "You treat me with respect, and I'll get you great stuff. But you got to treat me right. Otherwise walk."

Bolan leaned against the chair's back support and pretended to contemplate Mendoza's words. Finally he dropped his shoulders and shook his head in agreement.

"All right, I can do that. How fast can you get us the cocaine?"

"Fast as you want. We can get anything."

"Like what?"

"You like pills?"

"Sure. Ecstasy, Vitalife, speed."

"We can get you all that."

"Bullshit," Bolan said. "Ecstasy and speed, sure. Any asshole teenager can get us that. Vitalife is hard as hell to get. We snatch every pill we come across because it's so controlled."

Mendoza dropped against the backrest of the couch, tried to cross his leg and cup the knee with his hands, but gave up after a few unsuccessful attempts. His voice dropped in a self-conscious whisper, and he looked from side to side before speaking, as though they were the only three men in the room.

"We can get you as much Vitalife as you want," he said.

Bolan feigned a suspicious look. "How?"

"That's not the question," Mendoza said. "The question is, how much will you pay for it?"

"Plenty. How soon can you get it?"

"Give me a few of days. I'll talk to Emilio. See what kind of price I can swing for you."

"I want to meet him," Bolan said, "before I agree to anything."

Mendoza shook his head. "He's got too much going on. Might be a couple of weeks before he's back in circulation."

Bolan gave another suspicious look. "Why? What's wrong?"

"Show the man some respect," Blancanales said. "We're trying to establish a partnership here, not pry into Emilio Vega's personal affairs."

Mendoza turned his gaze on Blancanales.

"Trust me, Rodriguez, there's nothing wrong with Emilio," Mendoza said. "He's just got a couple of big deals in the works. They're eating up all his time."

"I understand," Blancanales said.

"Where the fuck is he?" Bolan said, his voice exploding.

"You get the money for the coke," Mendoza said. "I'll talk to Emilio about the Vitalife. But you deal with me. You don't want the painkillers? Get the hell out of here."

Bolan began to reply, but stopped when Blancanales put a hand on his arm. "We want the Vitalife, Ed. We can't keep the stuff in Virginia. It sells as fast as it hits the streets."

"I still don't see why we can't deal directly with Vega," Bolan said.

"You don't need to see," Mendoza stated. "You just need to pony up the cash. It might speed things along if you shut your damn mouth in the process."

Bolan shot Mendoza a cold stare, then looked away.

Blancanales stared at Bolan. "I agree with our new friend. Maybe you ought to shut up and let us do business like civilized men. Stop trying to piss him off. He's trying to help us."

"Whatever," Bolan muttered.

A portable phone on the coffee table rang. With some effort, Mendoza leaned forward, grabbed it and stuck it to his ear. "Yeah," he said. He snapped to attention when the voice on the other side boomed through the earpiece.

"Hey, Emilio. Yeah, I'm working. Just talking about you with a couple of guys, as a matter of fact."

Roswell, Georgia

THE NOTION OF KILLING Mike Belasko made Ahern feel damn near giddy.

He hefted the metal gun case, set it on the desk and popped the top. He felt lighter since pulling the gun on Vega and his men. More confident. More in charge.

More like himself.

It had rankled the young security man to have the drug runner and his army of criminals look down their noses at him. Ahern was a soldier, a black-ops veteran who had pulled the trigger on more than a few of Vega's kind during his military career. He'd be happy to do the same thing again, this time to Vega.

It felt good to finally shed the milksop facade in favor of his true self. Ahern was a soldier, not a billionaire's errand boy, but a fighter, a warrior.

He had never stopped being those things. Even after the court-martial.

The U.S. Army had stripped Ahern of his rank, of his uniform, of his command. The arrest and conviction for multiple rape counts had caused the army to disown the once highly regarded soldier.

Unbeknownst to his superiors, they had only scratched the surface of his criminal activity.

He left the service with his skills, his warrior's heart and his record intact. And he owed it all to Victor Sampson. Sampson had heard of Ahern's conviction through one of his Capitol Hill sources. Always on the lookout for fresh mercenary talent, Sampson sought out and hired Ahern. The billionaire dropped bundles of cash, pulled strings, got the soldier freed from prison and his military record expunged. Sampson even secured for Ahern federal permits to carry concealed automatic weapons, all with a few phone calls.

Little did Sampson realize the military investigators had barely scratched the surface of Ahern's misdeeds. The sexual assaults were a side note in a much darker story.

Both as a soldier and more recently while exiled in the civilian world, Ahern kept his skills sharp by hunting people. He'd pick someone out of the crowd—man or woman, it didn't matter—trail the person through urban and rural jungles like a lion stalking an antelope and eventually kill him or her. A drive-by shooting. Sniping from a nearby building. A flash of sharp steel in an alley. The method mattered less than the outcome. And the outcome always was the same: a person died and Ahern experienced dizzying, but brief, peaks in his otherwise flat, gray emotional landscape.

The frequent travel required by his job allowed him to kill without legal reprisal. His association with one of the nation's most respected pharmaceutical tycoons coupled with his unassuming exterior all but insulated him from scrutiny. And—except for the moments when the blood lust nagged at him, driving him away for hours on end—Ahern clung to his boss like a loyal lap dog.

Like a good little soldier.

Ahern hefted the M16A1 from the case. With practiced ease he pulled the butt to his left shoulder, fisted the pistol grip with his left hand and sighted through the scope and directed the muzzle with his right hand. The weapon's weight and shape felt as natural to him as his right arm. He slid the gun from his shoulder, grabbed a 30-round clip from the suitcase and rammed it home. He charged the weapon, set the safety and placed it on the table.

Sliding out of his jacket, he removed his necktie and rolled up his sleeves. He slid a Kevlar vest over his head and secured the side straps. He pulled out a web belt fitted with a holster, a Beretta M-9, pouches of extra ammunition, and strapped it around his waist.

As he checked his weapons, he recalled his earlier conversation with Sampson, which occurred shortly after Ahern's exhilarating confrontation with Vega.

"Belasko is a soldier, Richard," the billionaire had said. "My Washington sources haven't found any information on him. Even my people within the Agency can't find anything on the man. But he's made it patently obvious he won't stop until he's dead."

"Yes, sir," Ahern said, hoping Vega would speak exactly the words he did.

"Emilio's men aren't up to the challenge. I'm counting on you and your people to make Belasko go away. After that, we can concentrate on Vega."

Ahern looked down at the M16A1, running a hand fondly across the dull black finish.

He smiled.

He planned to show Belasko—and Sampson and Vega, for that matter—a real soldier. Whether it took slamming a slug through Belasko's head or a knife through his heart, Ahern would give the Fed a real show.

It would be the last thing the bastard ever saw coming.

Downtown Atlanta

BOLAN COULD TELL Mendoza's conversation with his boss wasn't going well.

Mendoza's face flushed as he talked with Vega. The drug lord's voice came through the other end, audible but not discernible. Bolan assumed Vega had found out about his son's death and was dropping the bomb on his associate. Mendoza's words confirmed it.

"Man, boss, I am sorry to hear that," Mendoza said. "Those DEA bastards are getting crazy. What the hell were they thinking?"

More booming on the other end. The red splotches coloring Mendoza's cheeks deepened in color and spread across his face. He strategically muttered "Right, right," as Vega ranted from the other end.

"He never said anything to me about it, Emilio," Mendoza said. "God as my witness, Juan never talked to me about this."

More screaming.

"You're going to do what?" Mendoza said. He looked at Bolan and Blancanales self-consciously. "Hey, Emilio, man, let's switch to another line. I got guests. We need to talk privately."

Without excusing himself, but with some effort, Mendoza hefted himself from the couch. He disappeared into the rear of the penthouse.

Bolan wished Mendoza would stay in the room so he could

track the conversation. Vega was planning something. If it was hunting down his son's killer, Stony Man Farm and the DEA had covered the bases. If it was fleeing the country, Bolan needed to find the guy before he disappeared again.

The pace of the mission was hastening. It was time for Bolan and Blancanales to catch up and pull out ahead.

Apparently sensing the same thing, Blancanales stood.

"Let me have my phone," he said. "I'm going to make a couple of calls while we're waiting on Mendoza."

Guirrez unclipped a flip phone from his belt and tossed it on the couch in front of him.

"Here," the security chief said, "use mine."

MENDOZA STOOD in the master bedroom, stared through the window at the teeming Atlanta skyline and listened to his boss rant like a madman. He felt his heart race as Vega outlined his plans over the phone. Over the phone, for God's sake. He was talking about killing the DEA director on an open line. Normally Vega wouldn't discuss a trip to the bathroom over the phone, let alone hatch an assassination plot.

The guy had apparently gone off the deep end, and he was dragging down Mendoza right along with him.

"I'm blowing out of here," Vega said. "I can run things from abroad. I'm making you my North American chief, Ed. You're my pointman in the States once I leave. What do you think of that?"

The words hit Mendoza like a landslide. He sat on the edge of the bed, grateful for a chance to rest after walking from the living room to his bedroom. "'Preciate it, Emilio," Mendoza said. "But won't the DEA shut us down if you do what you're talking about?"

"What do you mean 'if'?" the drug lord asked. "I've already got the wheels in motion. Consider it done."

"They'll hit us hard after that."

"So let them hit us," he said, stretching the words for emphasis. "If you can't handle it, I'll find someone who can. I'm not turning my empire over to a pussy. So, can you handle it or not? Tell me now. I don't need surprises down the line."

The displeasure in Vega's voice caused Mendoza's life to flash before his eyes. Gooseflesh swelled from his normally smooth, bloated skin.

"I can handle it," Mendoza said. "Just trying to cover the bases."

"Always thinking, huh, Ed? That's why you're perfect for the job."

"Thanks, Emilio. I won't let you down."

"No, you won't. You making me any money?"

Mendoza brightened. If Emilio was throwing phone etiquette out the window, so could he. "Yeah, got a couple of live ones here now. Came looking for the usual stuff. They got excited when I mentioned your new product."

"What do you mean 'got excited'?"

"They're interested is all. No big deal."

"Who they with?"

"Vasquez out of Virginia. Lost a couple of suppliers up there and came down here to work with professionals."

"They told you that?"

"Yeah."

"And you believed them?"

"Sure, why not? They really want to do business with us."

"So you told them about our new product before we start selling it."

"Yeah."

"You are the dumbest of fucks, Ed. You know that?"

Mendoza felt flaccid chest muscles tighten, grinding his labored breathing to a sudden halt. Inhaling deeply, he asked, "What's the problem, Emilio? I thought you'd be happy to get the business."

"I've got crazy Feds chasing me all over God's creation. Meantime, you're bragging to strangers about my new venture. Guys who say the police have shut down everyone around them. How do you know the police didn't turn them, too? You should have checked them out better, made sure they were okay."

"I made calls, Emilio," Mendoza said, his voice cracking. "They have lots of cash."

"The FBI and the DEA have a lot of cash, too," Vega countered.

"They have credentials," Mendoza said. "They seemed legitimate."

"You make damn sure they are. You mess this up and I'll have your head."

Mendoza knew from experience it was best to be succinct. "I'll fix it, Emilio."

"Damn straight you will. I'll call later."

Vega ended the call. With a nervous flutter replacing his prideful boasting, Mendoza clipped his phone to his belt and headed back into the living room. He planned to give the boys from Virginia a closer look before closing the deal. For his sake, he hoped they stood up to the scrutiny.

BLANCANALES'S HEART SANK as he picked up the security chief's phone from the overstuffed couch. Outwardly he winked, smiled and thanked Guirrez, who returned the warmth with a stoic gaze and silence. Pulling a restaurant number from memory, he punched it into the handset. He pretended to get a busy signal, ended the call. As he did this, he moved closer to the wet bar and his own cell phone/detonator. The position also gave him the drop on two gunners, freeing Bolan to handle the two next to the sliding glass door.

Sure, Mendoza's decision to talk in private might have meant nothing. But Blancanales wasn't willing to take that chance. It was a safe bet Bolan wouldn't take that chance, either.

He repeated the dial-and-hang-up ritual and again swore, this time out loud. He turned and smiled self-consciously at Guirrez.

"Sorry. Phone's busy. Probably my eighteen-year-old. I left her alone. Wanted to make sure she's okay. Look, it's long-distance. Why don't I use my phone?"

"Whatever," Guirrez said. He apparently had lost interest in Blancanales and his use of the phone. Instead, the security chief was indulging himself in a staring contest with Bolan, who played along.

The Able Team warrior set Guirrez's phone on the bar top, picked up his own and punched in the first few numbers of the detonation code. He stopped cold, turned and gave Bolan an angry look.

"She's probably talking to Alberto's son," he said. "Goddamn little cock hound's always sniffing at my door."

Bolan shrugged his shoulders and gave Blancanales a nasty smile.

"Boy knows a sure thing," Bolan said. "What do you want?"

Guffaws sounded throughout the room. Even Guirrez's stony expression twitched before reverting back to steel. Blancanales let his phone hand fall at his side.

"Keep the trash talk to yourself, John," he said, gripping the phone, but pointing at Bolan with the index finger of the same hand. "Or I show these people my less diplomatic side. Don't forget who signs your paycheck."

"Sure, Hector," Bolan said to Blancanales. "Just having a little fun."

"Then make fun of yourself, not my daughter." Blancanales stepped closer to Bolan and distanced himself from the briefcases.

Bolan held up both hands, palms visible. "Let it go."

"That bullshit can blow up in your face. Remember that."

"I'll remember," Bolan said.

Pretending to be angry, Blancanales stalked off and positioned himself away from the briefcase. Still clutching the phone, he put his hands on his hips and stared outside. He heard Bolan stand up from the couch and move a comfortable distance from the explosive luggage.

Blancanales rested his thumb on the correct button and waited for Mendoza to return. It was time to make one hell of a racket.

PRETENDING TO BE CHASTISED, Bolan scowled, ran a hand through his hair and moved away from his seat. Guirrez, Bolan noticed, watched the warrior's every move. It was unclear whether the security chief saw through the pair's ruse or just wanted to make sure they behaved themselves as they went to their respective corners and let their tempers cool.

Bolan sized up the situation. One man stood over the briefcases, next to a bar that separated the kitchen from the living room. Two others continued to stand near the dining-room table and the sliding glass door. The hardmen who had searched Bolan and Blancanales stood behind the Executioner. Mendoza was the only one not in the room. Bolan wanted the man there so he could make sure Mendoza didn't warn Vega as to the attack.

Once Blancanales triggered the explosives, things would happen fast. Bolan had hoped to make Guirrez his first target, but decided to bestow that honor upon the gunners directly behind him. Once the briefcase exploded, the thugs would scatter, the chances of Bolan or Blancanales catching a bullet would heighten, the number of variables would escalate.

At the same time, the Stony Man warriors needed to take Mendoza alive, at least long enough to discover Vega's whereabouts. Otherwise, the whole undercover operation was a wasted effort.

Bolan had no time for wasted efforts.

He heard heavy breathing, the sound of fabric rubbing against itself, and knew Mendoza was returning. Bolan turned to Blancanales and nodded, encouraging him to unleash the explosives.

Blancanales returned the nod. The phone gripped in his left hand, he pressed the final number, hit Send and dropped for cover. Tossing the phone, he covered his ears with his hands. Bolan did likewise as he hit the plush carpeted floor.

The others in the room weren't so lucky.

The briefcase burst into a storm of leather, cardboard and metal shards. Bits of money wafted like confetti amid the smoke. The man closest to the explosion screamed, grabbed his face and stumbled backward. Out of reflex, the other gunners ducked, shielded their faces and split into different directions. Stunned, Mendoza stood in the hallway, his eyes wide with surprise.

The shock factor provided Bolan and Blancanales a precious moment of surprise. Both men knew how to exploit it for all it was worth.

Bolan rose to his knees, fisting the Beretta in a two-handed grip and searching for a target. The guard closest to the Executioner before the explosion had recovered his wits and was likewise searching for a target. Bolan drilled him with several shots to the chest and neck, killing him instantly. Before the dead man hit the carpet, Bolan was moving the pistol, searching for another gunner to take down.

A slug whizzed past Bolan's head, just inches from his face. With the Beretta leading the way, Bolan twisted at the waist, searched for and found the shooter. He spotted Guirrez on his knees, a .357 Colt Python extended in a two-handed grip. The revolver roared twice more, slugs slinging toward Bolan.

A moment before Guirrez unleashed the shots, the soldier hurled himself to the side and out of the path of the twin .357 rounds. He triggered his own weapon as he moved. The impact of his body against the floor jarred his aim and caused the 9 mm rounds to punch into a couch.

The warrior stared over the Beretta, caught Guirrez in the pistol's sights. A submachine gun's rattle grabbed Bolan's attention. He jerked his head to the right and saw a line of slugs tearing across the carpet toward him like a spinning buzzsaw shredding a pine board.

He rolled away, contorting as best he could to avoid the deadly stream of bullets. Raising the Beretta, he hunted for his assailant and hoped he could find the shooter before a bullet found him.

BEFORE THE ROAR of the blast died, Blancanales had cleared the Glock from his shoulder holster. He was on his feet, moving in a crouch even as he drew the SIG-Sauer from under his jacket with his other hand. He planned to take out the two gunners next to the balcony first, then perhaps Guirrez if Bolan hadn't already gotten to him.

Then it was on to Mendoza.

Bolan's orders from the outset had been clear: take Mendoza alive. If necessary, injure or kill him in self-defense, but only as a last resort. Mendoza knew where to find Vega and Sampson. That made him important to the Stony Man warriors and gave him a bargaining chip he could offer in exchange for his life.

If indeed Mendoza was smart enough to barter. That variable didn't worry Blancanales. Considering the portly man's life span in a deadly industry, Pol figured Mendoza would be more than willing to share what he knew in exchange for drawing a few more breaths.

One of the guards had dropped his pistol and covered his ears during the blast. Seeing Blancanales approach, he fell to his knees and lunged for the pistol. Blancanales's SIG-Sauer spit two bullets into the man, who groaned and dropped facefirst onto the ground, his gun hand inches from a weapon he never would reach.

Blancanales turned and tracked the other gunner. The Glock roared twice, and .40-caliber slugs dug deep into his opponent's abdomen, knocking him against a wall. Blancanales hammered the man with a shot to the head, ensuring a quick, merciful death.

Seeing the gunplay, Mendoza turned and hurried back down the hallway into the bowels of the penthouse.

Crossing the room in quick strides, Blancanales shot another guard, then tailed Mendoza. Like Bolan, he didn't want the drug lieutenant contacting Vega, warning him of their approach. Blancanales stepped into the dark corridor, flattened himself against a wall so he didn't offer Mendoza a silhouette target.

He holstered the SIG-Sauer and checked out the lengthy hallway. He saw four closed doors, two on each side of the corridor. Thin shafts of light escaped from underneath the sills, but were devoured by the darkness. Blancanales tried a light switch, but found it didn't work. A scared and perhaps armed drug dealer hid in one of the rooms. Blancanales also faced potential ambush from behind if Guirrez or the other gunners saw him chasing their boss.

Blancanales opened the first door, then pasted himself against a wall as he waited for retaliatory fire. When nothing happened, he went in low and found what apparently was an office. The room was outfitted with a big desk, a personal computer and other office equipment. Mendoza, however, was nowhere to be found. To his relief, Blancanales saw that in his haste, Vega's lieutenant had dropped his phone and stepped on it during his retreat.

Blancanales moved diagonally across the hall, tried to twist another doorknob and found it locked. Someone rustled inside the room. Blancanales retreated a few steps and weighed whether he could break down the door and successfully capture Mendoza without one of them getting killed in the process. Probably not, he decided.

Involuntarily his heartbeat and breathing quickened. He tightened his grip on the Glock to compensate for the slick residue greasing his palms.

Blancanales kicked in the door, whirled from the opening and flattened himself against a wall as the first rounds blazed through the spot he occupied moments ago. At first, Mendoza shot fast and wild, but he quickly began shooting smarter. Methodically the rounds hewed a horizontal arc first through wood framing, then drywall, pounding out a collision course for Blancanales's kidneys and lower spine.

His chances of taking Mendoza alive were beginning to lessen.

If he could take the guy at all.

PUSHED SNUG against an overstuffed chair, Bolan triggered the Beretta even as the sub gunner fired at him. A 9 mm slug drilled into the man's skull, knocking him dead before he hit the floor. The SMG jettisoned a last spray, which smacked into the floor near Bolan as the gunner's dead finger tightened on the trigger.

Cautiously Bolan got to his feet and spotted Guirrez heading into the hallway. Bolan didn't see Blancanales and assumed his partner had already made his way into the corridor. Apparently catching Bolan's motion from the corner of his eye, Guirrez turned and aimed the Python at his adversary's midsection. The Executioner's Beretta spoke twice and drilled two slugs into the security chief. Guirrez slammed helplessly into the wall as the slugs tore through vital organs. He was dead before his knees crumpled under him and he fell facefirst onto the floor.

Bolan scanned the dead shooters, making sure their threat had been alleviated. He turned his attention toward Pol and Mendoza.

Rapid gunshots from the hallway told him Blancanales's pursuit had degenerated into a firefight. On the run, Bolan emptied the Beretta and rammed home a fresh clip. He entered the hallway and stopped. Blancanales turned toward his friend, grimaced and motioned for Bolan to stay back.

His back to the Executioner, Blancanales was retreating from the doorway of the last room on the left as Mendoza fired through framing and drywall and into the hallway. As the dozen or so bullet holes ventilating the walls attested, Mendoza was scared and shooting double-time to keep his pursuers at bay.

Then came a sudden silence shattered by profanity as Mendoza's handgun cycled dry.

Taking his cue, Blancanales cautiously entered the room, the Glock leading the way. Bolan followed him in, twisting around the doorjamb, targeting Mendoza with the Beretta. The drug lieutenant sat on the floor and regarded the two men with wide, scared eyes. He clutched the autoloading pistol, jacket locked back and empty and patted himself wildly for a fresh clip with his other hand.

Blancanales approached the panicked man, the Glock pointing at Mendoza's head. He abandoned the search for fresh ammunition, dropped the empty pistol to the floor and whimpered.

"Looks like you've exhausted your options, Ed," Blancanales said. "I don't suppose you'd be willing to cut a deal with us?"

The look in Mendoza's eyes answered a resounding yes.

17

Bethesda, Maryland

By the time Ray Pitt returned home, he was tired, hungry and ready to sleep for a week. All he wanted was to hug his wife, Sandy, talk to his daughter Maureen. With that done, he would zone out in front of the television, fill his belly with vodka martinis and tortilla chips, sink his bare feet into the carpet and relax until he drifted off to sleep.

He wanted a normal night at home, but he knew that was the last thing he would get.

By all indications, it would be an evening of work. Agent Glynn was en route from Georgia to deliver an in-person report on Vega's plans. The public-information officer had completed a press release about the shooting, and was pushing the director to approve it. The President had sent word through an adviser that he wanted to talk to Pitt before the day ended. The purpose of the call was cryptic—something about beefing up security. Whenever Pitt checked his e-mail account via his laptop, he found it jammed with messages.

Nevertheless, Pitt could practically taste the martini as he neared the front door. Two agents—one in front, one in back—escorted the director as he crossed the sidewalk to the front porch. Sandy appeared in the doorway as he neared the home. The look on her face told him a leisurely drink and a moment to unwind were mere pipe dreams.

His wife stepped forward and embraced Pitt. She buried her head into his chest, pressed her body against his as he stroked her back with his right hand. Moist, warm tears soaked through his shirt. She shuddered as she released the pent-up anxiety wrought by the past few hours. A familiar specter of guilt surfaced in Pitt's heart. He knew she was scared. Hell, seeing his house, his family's safe haven, crawling with DEA agents scared him, too.

Pitt worried little for his own safety, but had fretted over his family's well-being ever since the incident in Orlando. He made a mental note to visit his study and arm himself with the Charter Arms Bulldog revolver he kept locked in a gun cabinet. He still had the borrowed Glock given to him after the shooting. But he had carried the Bulldog—without authorization, of course—as a rookie detective in Washington, D.C., and found comfort in it, like a visit from an old friend.

If anyone dared come for Pitt and his family, he wouldn't cower while his agents took bullets for him. Pitt led by example. And if Vega planned some sort of reprisal, the DEA director would fight tooth and nail to protect those he loved.

First, though, he would hear out his wife. Considering the hell she'd been through in the past few hours, he owed her that much.

Sandy pulled away from him. She took a step back and appraised him with chestnut-colored eyes. The slight crow's-feet at the corners of her eyes deepened and brows twisted in concern. Her lips trembled slightly as though she was ready to cry.

"Thank God you're okay," she said. Her effort to squelch the tears looked obvious and excruciating. "I've been so scared."

Pitt squeezed her biceps reassuringly and gave her a half-hearted smile.

"You know how I am when I'm interrupted in the bathroom," he said. "Guy never stood a chance."

The joke fell flat, a fact to which Sandy's face attested. His wife of thirty years had been mad ever since Pitt had forsaken retirement and accepted another law-enforcement job. Most of the time, she hid it well, letting off steam with an occasional backhanded comment, but otherwise outwardly accepting his decision. The intensity in her face told him those days were over, that the ultimatum would come soon enough. Retire, get a safer job with better hours, less travel, less stress. Or call in the lawyers and enter a world of separate homes and separate lives.

They released each other and walked inside. "Ray, we need to talk," she said.

Shit. Here it comes.

"Honey, can it wait?" Pitt said. He nodded over her shoulder at the agents behind him. Though both appeared engrossed in other pursuits, Pitt knew neither would ignore the boss getting a good dressing-down by his wife. Hell, truth be told, he'd probably eavesdrop, too, if the roles were reversed. "This isn't the time or the place."

"This is precisely the time and place," Sandy said, her face changing from vulnerable to stern in a heartbeat. "We need to talk about that man."

Puzzled, Pitt cocked his head slightly and furrowed his own brow.

"What the hell are you talking about? What man?"

"I believe the lady's talking about me," a voice called from the kitchen.

A grim-looking blond guy fitted with a bulletproof vest and a shoulder holster entered the room. An Ingram submachine gun hung from a shoulder strap. He seemed amused at Pitt's confusion.

"Who the hell are you?" Pitt asked.

"I'm Special Agent Irons. Justice Department," Lyons said.

He approached Pitt, stopped inches away from him, but did not extend a hand. Instead, he crossed his arms over his chest and stared at the DEA director.

"I'm here to single-handedly save your ass," Lyons said. "You don't like it, call the President. He ordered me here. Until I hear otherwise, you're stuck with me."

Pitt recognized the challenge and rose to it. "What if I say otherwise?"

"Then you're wasting your breath. Now, get the hell away from the front door, avoid the windows and have your people close the damn shades if they haven't already. Put your wife and daughter where they're safe. Start acting smart and you might live through the night."

"We can't seal off the house," Pitt said. "I've got an agent coming here to walk me through some information."

"Then the agent stays here all night because I don't want people coming and going as they please," Lyons said. "And I wasn't making a request. Move. We're putting your ass under wraps until the Vega situation is handled."

"What do you mean?" Pitt asked. "We're the ones handling this situation."

The blond guy flashed a wicked grin. "That, my friend, is what you think. Vega is being handled, but by forces beyond your control."

The bastard was talking in riddles, the trademark of a covert operator. Pitt had no patience for games of death and deception.

"Son, you'd better tell me what the hell you're talking about," the DEA director said, "or else we're going to have trouble."

Another wicked grin, but this time the eyes turned steely. "Your kind of trouble, Ray, I can handle."

With that, Lyons turned in the other direction and left the room.

Pitt ordered him to stop, but the guy kept walking as if he had turned deaf. Engulfed in anger, Pitt released his hold on his wife and spent the next few minutes barking orders at his agents, making sure last-minute measures to protect his family were being taken.

Satisfied, he ascended the stairs and headed for his study. It was time to call the President and get the skinny on this Agent Irons. Once he finished talking with the President, he would load and holster the Bulldog, mix that drink he'd been promising himself, take a private moment to enjoy a cigarette and fortify himself before returning to the hellground he used to call home.

Then, if forced into a corner, he'd show the mouthy blond bastard who really was in charge of the situation. Along with anyone else who dared stand between him and his family's safety.

Atlanta, Georgia

FACED WITH THE PROSPECT of a bullet to the head, Mendoza was only too happy to share what he knew with Bolan and Blancanales. He uttered the perfunctory protests, swore undying allegiance to his boss, then folded like a deck chair after Bolan pressed the Beretta's hot muzzle against his temple. The Executioner had seen it so many times. Thugs were cowards; cowards caved when faced with adversity. Bolan always had capitalized on their predictability.

Mendoza supplied them with a crudely drawn map and hand-scrawled directions pointing them toward the drug lab. With Mendoza in tow, they escaped from the eighteenth floor using a service elevator, then left the building by joining a wave of scared business executives and others flooding through the revolving doors into the streets, fleeing the upstairs shooting spree.

Minutes later, they were in the Mercedes and returning to the air base. Bolan planned to turn over Mendoza to the base authorities for safekeeping. He, Blancanales and Grimaldi would head for the drug lab via chopper, put down Vega and Sampson for good. Bolan had endured enough skirmishes on his latest campaign.

It was time for the final battle.

Bethesda, Maryland

CARL LYONS STOOD in the kitchen propped against the stove, seething over the DEA director's reaction to him. He was trying to save this jerk and his family, and Pitt repaid him with power games. The professional bureaucrat had gotten himself into a mess from which he had neither the brains nor the balls to extricate himself. Still, he wanted to exert control.

This was not writing a budget or pitching Congress on a new program.

This was war. It required a warrior's touch.

That suited Carl Lyons just fine.

Hearing footsteps, Lyons turned and saw a bulky agent with ash-blond hair approaching him. The guy had been among those witnessing Lyons's terse exchange with Pitt. The agent stopped nearly two feet from the blond warrior and extended an arm. In his hand, he clutched a headset and a slip of paper. Lyons snatched the hardware, fitted the headset over his scalp. He gripped the piece of paper between two fingers and stared at the DEA man.

"It's set on a tac channel especially for this op," the agent said. "You can check in with any of us anytime. I listed the agents and their numbers on that paper so you know who the hell you're talking to."

Lyons regarded the guy suspiciously. "Why you doing this?" he asked. "Aren't you afraid you'll piss off your boss?"

"Pitt's a good guy and a good director," the agent said. "He's a decent family man. A lot of us in the field respect him. But he's a fighter, not a warrior. You know what I mean?"

The agent paused and stared at Lyons, who, with an impatient nod, encouraged him to continue. Lyons knew precisely what the guy meant. Some people had guts, could think on their feet, walk away from a one-on-one encounter. But they didn't have the skills necessary to wreak wholesale havoc on predators.

"You're a warrior," the agent said. "I fought in Desert Storm. I know one when I see one. Every guy here supports Pitt. Right now that means supporting you. So you got our loyalty. Use it wisely."

Lyons gave another curt nod. It was the closest thing to a thank-you he could muster.

"That doesn't mean," the agent continued, "that we like you. But we'll follow your orders."

Lyons allowed himself a grin. "That seems to be the general feeling people have for me."

The agent grinned and gave him a thumbs-up. "I figured as much. I'm Tompkins. You need anything, you let me know."

"I'll do that," Lyons said.

As the guy departed from the kitchen, he studied the slip of paper and familiarized himself with the small roster of agents at his disposal. Including himself, there were six guys—seven if Pitt was counted, which he did so only grudgingly—against one of America's most powerful drug organizations.

Seemed like fair odds to him.

The President and the DEA, of course, had wanted to put Pitt and his family under lock and key until Vega was killed. From what Brognola had told Lyons during a quick briefing, Pitt would have none of that. Sending Lyons to him had been the next-best option.

The doorbell chimed. Lyons assumed it was the DEA agent Pitt had mentioned earlier. After all, assassins rarely announced their arrival with the doorbell. Probably nothing to even concern himself with.

Still, he drew the Python and started for the living room. Just in case.

18

Roswell, Georgia

Dressed in a combat blacksuits, their faces streaked with camou cosmetics, Bolan and Blancanales descended like vengeful shadows upon the sentries guarding the drug lab's exterior. Bolan killed his man with the twist of a garrote; Blancanales took down his target by snapping the man's neck powerfully.

It had taken them twenty minutes of trekking through backyards and tree lines to reach the drug lab's outer perimeter. Grimaldi had set down the helicopter on an empty street in a nearby housing development. Filled with recently turned dirt and the wooden skeletons of unfinished homes, the burgeoning neighborhood provided ample bare land upon which to touch down without drawing attention. Hidden in a nearby cluster of trees and unkempt grass, the Stony Man warriors had observed the guards for several minutes before attacking them.

It was the third pair of guards Bolan and Blancanales had encountered.

The Executioner shoved aside his guard's still twitching corpse and inspected the lone steel door at the building's rear. A box outfitted with a red light and a green light and bisected by a thin vertical trough secured the door. Kneeling, Bolan fished a keychain carrying five plastic cards from the pocket of one of the guards and swiped the different cards through the reader while Blancanales covered them both with his M16A1/M-203 combo.

After three tries, Bolan swiped the right card. The red light winked out and a green light pulsed approvingly at them. A bolt clicked back.

Bolan eased open the door and the two men entered. They found themselves in a cavern of concrete floors and steel girders illuminated by the dim glow of a single row of overhead lights while other rows remained dark. Two tractor trailers and three forklifts, all empty and idle, covered the floor. Throughout the bay, Bolan noticed sawhorses, paint buckets and tools, which indicated the building still awaited application of final cosmetic touches.

Bolan had a rough layout of the building etched in his mind. While leaving Easton Tower, he had given the drug lab's address to Grimaldi to pass on to Stony Man's cybernetic team. Kurtzman, with the help of fellow computer wunderkind Akira Tokaido, had tapped into the county's computers and taken whatever information they could on the structure. Bolan knew that other than the exterior and some basic dimensions, the plans would reflect reality only where it suited Vega and Sampson, but every nugget of information helped.

Slipping the MP-5 SD-3 from his back, the Executioner clicked off the safety and set the gun for autofire. He and Blancanales clung to the walls, enveloping themselves in the obsidian blanket of shadows. They moved slowly, deliberately, to avoid detection. Bolan noted cameras posted in different corners of the room. Whether the surveillance hardware was operating was unclear, but Bolan planned to operate as if he and Pol already had been seen. Moorings for an exterior camera had been secured above and to the left of the just-used rear door, but a camera hadn't yet been mounted. The bay extended up two stories, and a series of windows stared out over the massive room from the second floor.

Pulling open a steel door, Blancanales stepped into a dark room as Bolan brought up the rear, watching to ensure no one planned to hit them from behind. Bolan smelled fresh paint and new carpet. An air conditioner's hum filled his ears. Remnants of a distant light peeking under another door across from them and the murmur of voices told the warriors to expect the journey's third leg to be much bloodier than the preceding ones.

THE GUY HAD BALLS—Ahern would give him that much.

Belasko and his friend had downed the exterior guards—both of them Sampson's mercenaries—broken into the building and, wittingly or not, bypassed two electric eyes Ahern had earlier placed in the loading bay. They had killed four other guards along the way. All of them were Vega's men, and Ahern considered the loss a small one.

The former soldier had been quick to chastise the Roswell team when upon inspection he discovered the cameras weren't operating and the security system was something a teenage burglar could bypass in his sleep. Anticipating Belasko's arrival, Ahern and his men had scrambled to install security hardware with supplies purchased in Atlanta by Ahern's men with Sampson's money.

Given another day, Ahern could have had the cameras up and running, too. But Belasko had accelerated the timetable, and Ahern no longer needed to worry about it. The enemy had presented himself.

Ahern and his three-man contingent crossed the loading bay with brisk, light steps. When he had gotten word of the intrusion, Ahern had gathered his people, circled the building and reentered through the same door used moments earlier by Belasko and his comrade. The rogue soldier knew Belasko had only one entrance into the bowels of the building. And as long as he kept moving forward, he played exactly into Ahern's hands.

As Belasko bulled his way inward, he would run into a horde of Vega's people and, consequently, a gunfight. If he and the other man tried to retreat, they'd find Ahern and his men ready to chop them down with autofire.

Ahern planned to lie back and let Belasko shoot it out with

the drug lord's gunmen. After the hail of bullets died down, Ahern and his men had orders to finish off anyone left standing. If the two intruders had already died, so be it. Shooting Vega's men paid the same as killing Belasko, financially if not emotionally. Sampson planned to sever his partnership with Vega, and Ahern was only too happy to help Sampson make that happen.

But he hoped to find Belasko among the living.

Ahern wanted the guy for himself.

THE STONY MAN WARRIORS crossed the small room connecting the truck bay with the rest of the building. They stopped for a moment and dissected the murmurs emanating from the adjoining room. The rare snatches of conversation Bolan could decipher sounded like bullshit, a mixture of posturing, gossiping and griping. None of it passed as legitimate intel. Bottom line—the gunners lounging in the next room had outlived their usefulness.

Bolan clicked on a flashlight, muted its glare with a palm and communicated with Blancanales through a series of hand signals. He would go in first, Blancanales second. Pol replied with a hand signal of his own.

Guns at the ready, they passed into a huge room. Bolan recalled from the drawings that it had been designed as a call center, ostensibly for handling food orders. The builders had erected three rows of steel desks for the sake of appearances, but hadn't bothered to include telephones and computers. A steel door topped with a lighted Exit sign was across the room, blocked by five gunmen. One man sat on the first bank of desks, propped up by one leg as the other leg swung lazily. Three others gathered around another desk, while a fifth stood next to the windows, peering through the shades.

Bolan had little cover as he moved in. Legs pumping, he advanced upon the seated gunners. Triggering the H&K and sweeping it across the table, Bolan unleashed a fusillade of bullets into his opponents. Slugs hammered into one gunner's torso, knocking him back and twisting him around as he took the shots. He hit the ground, dead. Gunners two and three exploded from their seats, grabbed for weapons and moved in separate directions.

Clutching an Ingram, a man to Bolan's right sprinted from the table, triggering his machine pistol as he did. The Executioner stepped from the firing line and tapped out a burst from the H&K. The hastily placed shots went low, cutting the sprinter's legs out from under him and knocking him to the ground. Provided with a more stationary target, Bolan followed up his initial attack by slamming a killing burst into the man.

Two pistol shots burned past Bolan's head.

The warrior turned, fired at the approximate point from which the shots would have originated and found himself hitting empty air. Driven by instinct, he dived forward. As he hit the floor, he heard a pistol crack again and watched as bullets cleaved the air over top of him. Rolling onto his back, Bolan spotted the gunner, drew down and drilled a quick burst into the man's chest.

Rising from the floor in a crouch, Bolan turned to check on Blancanales. The M-16/M-203 combo hugged tight against himself, Blancanales had taken down one gunner and was firing upon another when Bolan sighted him. Before the soldier could join the fray, he heard the thump of 5.56 mm tumblers smacking into flesh, followed by groans from the stricken man.

The M-16's smoking muzzle pointed skyward, Blancanales gave Bolan a questioning look, nodded toward an enclosed stairwell across the room. The Executioner nodded.

Blancanales had just entered the stairwell when a chattering subgun diverted Bolan's attention. Bullets shredded the flooring around Bolan, careened into furniture. Slugs ricocheted from hard surfaces, zinged around and through Bolan's legs like a swarm of angry hornets. He raced for cover. Blancanales hesitated in the stairwell door, started to return to help his friend fight their latest attackers.

"Go!" Bolan shouted.

Blancanales frowned, laid down a sweep of cover fire for Bolan, then disappeared through the door. The Executioner knew one of them needed to keep searching for Vega and Sampson. The other had the equally undesirable task of staying downstairs to vanquish the remaining assailants.

Bolan heard gunfire crackle in the stairwell. Silently wishing his friend the best, Bolan refocused and continued on his path, switching his mind back to target-acquisition mode.

Reaching the steel desks at a dead run, the warrior placed his left hand on the nearest flat surface, pushed himself up and over the furniture with a powerful thrust of his legs. Locking his legs at the ankles, he swung them as one and let the momentum carry him effortlessly over the desktop. Shots blazed past Bolan, threw him off balance and fouled his landing. He collided with the concrete slab floor, grinding his teeth together to stifle a pained yelp as he hit the unyielding surface. Forcing the pain from his mind, the warrior shot up from behind the desk and triggered the H&K. The machine pistol bucked in his hands, spewing flames and littering the floor with hot brass.

The 9 mm rounds buzzed across the room, hungrily seeking out the four foot soldiers fanning throughout the big communications center. The other three gunners continued forward, each firing upon Bolan.

Yanking a stun grenade from his combat harness, Bolan pulled the pin and tossed the bomb at the advancing soldiers. Bolan steeled himself for the blast's disorienting effects. As the din died down, the warrior ejected the H&K's clip, recharged the weapon with a fresh magazine and propelled himself along the floor on his elbows. As he emerged from cover in a crawl, he found two of the three soldiers disoriented but struggling to make a quick recovery. Well-trained soldiers and police could shake off the sensory overload caused by the grenades. Luckily Bolan's toss had landed the device dead center between the two men, making the effects harder to overcome.

The H&K coughed, and Bolan took out both men with head shots. Bypassing the bullet-stopping Kevlar, Bolan also killed the third man with a shot to the head.

That left three dead, begging the question: what the hell happened to the fourth?

RIVULETS OF SWEAT passed down Richard Ahern's face as he crouched in the small room next to the call center. When he had seen the grenade arc over the desktops, Ahern sought cover in nearby quarters and waited for the danger to pass. Other men needed to be sacrificed first, Ahern reasoned, so he could remain alive to protect Sampson from the crazy Feds tearing up the drug lab.

When Ahern realized the hastily tossed object hadn't been an antipersonnel grenade, he felt his breath return. His mind slowed and he regained his power to reason, something he had momentarily lost during the heat of battle. Muffled gunshots and cries from the other room told him Belasko had taken out all three of his men.

That left him alone to stop Belasko from reaching Victor Sampson.

Shouldering his assault rifle, Ahern curled around the door frame, sighted down the barrel and caught sight of Belasko as he lay on the floor, a smoking machine pistol clutched in his hand. Ahern rattled off a quick burst that gouged the carpeted floor in front of Belasko. Swiveling the SMG with one hand, the big intruder returned fire, forcing Ahern to seek cover. As he folded in on himself, a line of slugs ripped through the wall above his head, covering him in bits of drywall and debris. When the shots ceased, he pulled back around the door frame, assault rifle blazing, and unloaded in Belasko's general direction.

The rounds hit empty ground. His adversary was gone.

Ahern wondered whether he had underestimated Belasko, then purged the thought.

His heart rate accelerated, his head lightened. After years of hunting humans, Ahern found one who could fight back. The notion exhilarated and scared him. Raw survival instincts ignited Ahern's every cell. The overload caused him to experience the closest thing to joy that he had felt in years. It was like the charge he experienced when he sniped someone, but magnified a hundredfold.

He'd be sure to thank Belasko for providing him the high.

Right after he burned the son of a bitch down.

Ahern swung his weapon around the door frame and hosed down the room with autofire.

BLANCANALES SWEPT his assault rifle in a tight horizontal line as it bucked in his hands and filled the stairwell with 5.56 mm stingers. The M-16's thunder took down two armed men, both of whom had appeared at the top of the stairs as Blancanales ascended the first three steps. One was clad in boxer shorts and a sleeveless T-shirt, the other in sweats. Both had the rumpled look of people jarred from bed. As Blancanales finished his ascent, stepping over the bodies that filled the stairwell, he wondered how many more gunners would await him when he reached the top.

He didn't have to entertain the question long.

As he negotiated the corner, Blancanales found another man crouched behind a bed, his arms extended across the mattress, a revolver clutched in a two-handed grip. Thrusting himself to one side, Blancanales squeezed the M16A1's trigger. The stream of slugs ripped into the man's chest and neck, causing him to jerk wildly before the light left his eyes.

In the same instant, Blancanales felt a mule kick to the ribs as a bullet fired from the dead man's gun slammed into his protective vest. The impact whirled him against the wall, and he was vaguely aware of the M-16 clattering down the steps. Sucking for wind, wincing against the pain, he leaned against the wall for support and fought to keep from blacking out.

He operated on autopilot, his fingertips scrambled for the Glock, found and freed it. He allowed himself a longing look at the M16A1 which rested at the bottom of the stairs, before approaching footsteps made him move. Blancanales entered the barracks, struggling to ignore the protests of pain from his ribs.

He took in his surroundings on the run. A single bedside lamp, probably switched on when the first shots sounded downstairs, washed one corner of the room in a whitish cast while shadows stubbornly congregated around the sphere of light's fringes and enveloped the rest of the room.

Footfalls sounded in the hall, quieted as they neared the barracks. Blancanales bent slightly at the knees, drew down on the door with his Glock. As he did, a thug dressed in baggy jeans, a maroon T-shirt and black leather sneakers came through the door. The guy cradled an Ithaca Model 37 stakeout shotgun with a shortened barrel and pistol grip. Taking in his surroundings, his gaze settled first on his downed comrades before he visually scoured the room for the killer.

Decked out in black and hidden behind a row of upright lockers, Blancanales blended with the shadows. He escaped the man's notice during the first pass, but chalked up his good fortune to carelessness borne of fear.

He expected his luck would change any second.

"Shit," the man called over his shoulder. "We got three guys down. I don't see the shooter. Get in here."

Two more gunners, one brandishing a pair of 10 mm Colt pistols, the other armed with a Kalashnikov AK-47, stepped into the room. None wore bulletproof gear.

Blancanales slowed his breath, let it come in quiet, shallow gulps and considered his situation. Certainly the thunder of gunfire had reached Vega and Sampson, warning them of approaching danger. And the longer it took Blancanales to find them, the better their chances of escaping. Or mounting an effective counteroffensive. At the same time, the rattle of weapons downstairs told him his comrade remained under fire.

Stepping from behind the locker and extending his arms, Blancanales sighted down the barrel and squeezed the trigger. The .40-caliber slug burst open Mr. Shotgun's head. Even as the gunner fell dead to the floor, Blancanales swiveled his arms, found a new target and squeezed the trigger. The next burst of rounds ripped into the head and throat of the man with the AK-47. As he died in a hail of bullets, the second man's fingers reflexively depressed the assault rifle's trigger. A burst of 7.62 mm rounds pounded against the ground.

The third gunner raised both pistols and popped several shots in Blancanales's direction. As the twin Colts roared, the man stepped backward, trying to gain some combat stretch between himself and his adversary.

The man apparently was going for quantity and not quality. The shots flew wide of the Stony Man commando. When the gunner finally seemed to draw a bead on Blancanales's chest, his legs collided with the bed, ending his retreat. The gun exploded twice more as the shooter went down, but the rounds went wild, slamming into the ceiling as the man fell backward.

The fallen man tried to right himself, but Blancanales had him dead to rights and finished the confrontation with two shots to the chest.

As he exited the room, Blancanales paused long enough to pick up the AK-47 and strap it across his back. Then, holstering his pistol, he grabbed the Ithaca, figuring it might serve him well in a close-quarters battle. Stripping the gunners of shotgun shells and rifle clips, he slipped the items into pockets of his combat suit and resumed his search for Sampson and Vega.

Stepping into the second floor's main corridor, he found it empty. Certainly others had heard the hellfire ripping through the barracks and apparently decided to fortify themselves, wait for the battle to reach them. Recalling the hastily studied plans, Blancanales tried to orient himself and craft an educated guess as to which of several rooms would most likely house the drug lab. There, he guessed, he would find Sampson and Vega, most likely fortified by an army of hardmen. Besides the barracks, a room situated two doors down the lengthy corridor and to the right ranked as the single biggest enclosed space within the building. Spacious and secreted deep inside the sprawling warehouse complex, it seemed the most likely spot for a drug lab.

Bethesda, Maryland

IF THE WOMAN HADN'T BEEN so damn attractive, Carl Lyons probably would have ignored her entirely. A redhead who had introduced herself to Sandy Pitt as Madeline Glynn sat on the living-room couch next to Pitt's wife and across from his daughter. The three women made uncomfortable small talk, with Sandy Pitt questioning Glynn about her flight from Florida and her overnight accommodations.

Lyons noticed Glynn occasionally brushed a lock of hair from her face and stole a furtive glance toward the stairs. He assumed she was looking for her boss. Dressed in jeans and a T-shirt, she had offered a self-conscious apology about her attire to Sandy and Maureen Pitt, explaining in vague detail that it had been a hectic couple of days but offering little other explanation for her casual attire.

From what Brognola had shared, calling Striker's Orlando campaign "hectic" was like calling World War II a minor disagreement.

Glynn turned her eyes toward Lyons when he entered the room. She started to stand and extend a hand, as if to introduce herself.

Lyons halted her with an upturned palm. "Don't get up."

Glynn shot him a surprised look, but dropped back into the seat. Sandy Pitt touched her knee reassuringly.

"Don't mind him," Sandy Pitt said. "He's an asshole."

Lyons ignored the crack.

"I'm in charge of security here," he said. "Stay out of my way unless you can add something of value. Your boss should be down in a few minutes. In the meantime, what do you know that can help me?"

Obviously irritated with Lyons, Glynn shared what she had learned about Vega and Sampson in vague, clipped sentences.

When she finished, Lyons said, "Tell me something I don't know." He ignored the stormy look that passed over her face and decided to check on the exterior guards.

Inserting his fingers between the slats of the blinds, he separated them with a scissorslike motion of his fingers, peered through the window. He looked out just in time to witness a DEA agent's death.

Apparently hearing a noise, an agent standing on the driveway turned toward the sound and caught a bullet in the throat. As he crumpled to the ground, Lyons heard brief rasps from a bloodied throat sound through the headset before it went dead silent. A moment later, the headset again came to life as agents began talking, trying to discern what had happened.

Even as he turned to the other agents in the living room, Lyons heard muffled cries from other agents passing through the headset. "Shit. Multiple officers down. Get those two women to safety. Check on Pitt. Haul ass. Go."

Tompkins and another agent jumped at Lyons's orders. Tompkins fisted a pistol from a waist holster clipped to his belt in a cross-draw style. The burly DEA agent gripped Sandy Pitt's arm, checked to make sure another agent had snagged Maureen Pitt, and the two men ushered their charges upstairs.

Glynn stood, a Glock in her hand.

"Lady, you move when and where I tell you," Lyons said.

Without a second glance, she shot him the middle finger of her left hand. She ducked into a crouch and started for the front door. Lyons holstered the Python and pulled his Ingram sub-gun to the front, swiveling it around on its strap. If Glynn was covering the front, Lyons figured, he could check the back. Chances were they could expect hitters from all sides.

If the DEA agents did their jobs—and they damn well better—they would stay upstairs and baby-sit the Pitts until Lyons sounded the all clear.

Provided he lived long enough to do so.

In the next room, bullets pounded against a sliding glass door, shattered it and scattered glass wildly through the back of the house. Lyons tightened his grip on his machine pistol and headed toward the gunfire, knowing in the back of his mind a saner person would run the other way.

Roswell, Georgia

PINNED BEHIND THE BANK of desks, Bolan unhooked a stun grenade from his combat harness and cupped it in his left hand, the pin still intact. He heard his attacker call out to him.

"Come out, Belasko," the man said. "You can't hide forever. I know you heard the gunfire upstairs. Your buddy's dead. Give up or join him."

He punctuated the statement by raking the room with gunfire.

Bolan grimaced, squelched a primal urge to vault the desk and begin spraying the man with his MP-5.

The warrior realized the trash talk was designed to crack his psyche. He also knew his opponent would have to turn it up several notches if he wanted to reduce Bolan to a quivering mass ready to surrender. Over the years, masters of torture and psychological warfare had attempted to trample his spirit, force him to give up. All had failed; most had died at his hands. This latest nameless, faceless predator was walking a well-trampled trail doused in blood and, blinded by arrogance, apparently believed he would arrive at a different destination from all those who had come before him.

Bolan guessed otherwise.

The man continued the tirade. "Can you hear me, you fucking coward? Come out!"

His voice cracked with tension. More gunfire exploded.

Bolan flinched involuntarily as the rounds flew wide and to the left before advancing toward him in a steady, mindless pulse. Armor-piercing slugs punctured the metal and wood furnishings that provided Bolan's cover. The soldier hugged the floor as the onslaught drew nearer.

The gunfire ceased with a startling silence. Bolan heard a pause, then rustling and clicking noises that accompanied a reload or clearing of a jam. Arming the grenade, Bolan raised himself from cover and hurled the canister into the adjoining room.

Even as the device thumped in the other room, the warrior was closing in on his opponent, relying on his training to work through the senses-dulling effects of the grenade. Bolan expected to find his opponent either disoriented or, if he had training similar to Bolan's own, he might be waiting in ambush for the warrior.

The Executioner found neither. The bastard had fled.

Bolan weighed whether to pursue him. Letting the enemy gunner run free added an unwanted variable to the battle. Bolan's first reaction was to give chase. It galled him to leave business unfinished, especially when this bit of business quite literally could return to stab him or someone else in the back.

Reluctantly Bolan decided to let the man go. Already the warrior had lost precious time fighting this man when he could have been pursuing Sampson and Vega. In the meantime, Blancanales had been forced to secure the second floor and chase down the mission's primary targets alone. It was time, Bolan decided, to join the main fray.

Less than a minute later, he was ascending the stairs in search of a new killzone.

Concern stabbed through Bolan as he passed what he believed to be Blancanales's rifle resting at the foot of the steps. On the second floor, he scanned the devastation as he wound his way through the collection of beds, white pine nightstands and stackable plastic organizers stuffed with clothes that lay about the barracks. He eyed his surroundings, searching for signs of his comrade. He found nothing but bodies and shell casings.

Bolan continued into the hallway, the subgun's muzzle running point for him. Turning right, he started down the hallway, and froze. Blancanales stood at the other end of the corridor, a shotgun gripped in one hand and a door handle in the other. Roughly twenty feet behind Blancanales, a man stood aiming a pistol at his back, ready to fire without warning.

The Executioner fired a short burst, the bullets striking Blancanales's attacker between the shoulder blades, severing the man's spine and killing him instantly.

At the sound of the gunfire, Blancanales turned his torso and shotgun as one, like a tank turret, saw Bolan and the dead gunner. He hurried to join Bolan, each watching over the other's shoulder for attackers as they conversed in whispers.

"I think that's the lab," Blancanales said. "The door's locked. If you cover my back, I can blow it with some C-4."

Blancanales went to work, molding C-4 around the handle and the dead bolt above it. He did likewise with the two sets of hinges holding the door in place. He armed the malleable explosive with a detonator, gave Bolan a thumbs-up, and the two men retreated and hunkered down several yards away. When Blancanales detonated the explosives, the blast buckled the door inward, launching it into the laboratory.

Both men were on their feet and headed for the lab. Blancanales came through the smoky portal low, followed by Bolan, who laid down cover fire of short bursts as he hurried through the door. Once inside, Bolan dropped to a knee and began looking for a target. Lab techs in white coats cringed against walls, behind computers and underneath tables while various hardmen positioned throughout the room fired upon the warriors. A bank of computer-controlled tablet presses, chemical mixers and loading carousels filled one side of the room. Vega and Sampson were positioned at opposite ends of the room. Each clutched a pistol and also fired at the intruders.

Bolan picked off two men with quick bursts, then continued moving, the H&K coughing 9 mm rounds as he ran. A burst of autofire blazed from behind, passing just inches from the warrior. Bolan dived forward and hit the floor belly first. The impact jarred the subgun from his fingers. Bolan grabbed for the Desert Eagle, freed it from its holster even as he rolled on to his back.

As he brought up the big .44 pistol, he cocked it to reduce its trigger pull. The Executioner sighted down on the hardman who was firing in Bolan's general direction. Two more men armed with SMGs were approaching, ready to join their comrade in the firefight.

Still on his back, the Desert Eagle clutched in both hands, Bolan triggered the big pistol five times. Two slugs hit the first shooter and ripped open his chest and abdomen. The force spun the man around and knocked him into one of his fellow gunners. The still living man barely had time to knock away his dead comrade before a .44 boattail pulverized his throat. The Desert Eagle's fourth round went wild, while a fifth hit the third gunner in the torso. The impact caused the man to fold in on himself as the force drove his body backward.

Pulling himself upright, Bolan nearly collided with a man with stringy blond hair, bald crown and worn jeans who was fleeing the room. The guy gripped a pistol, but nearly screamed when he encountered Bolan. His white arm and gun hand began an upward swing he never would finish. Seeing the pistol muzzle's ascent, Bolan fired the Desert Eagle twice, ending the skinny man's escape—and his life—forever.

To his right, Bolan heard the Ithaca roar twice in rapid succession. The Executioner turned and watched as two gunners, their torsos shredded by shotgun blasts, fell to the ground. In a single fluid motion, Blancanales racked another shell, spun and blasted open the midsection of a hardman who was drawing down on him with a revolver. Bolan's friend was racking a final shell as Bolan turned away and looked for the next threat.

A growl to his right caught his attention, and he brought up the Israeli-made Desert Eagle in a two-handed grip. Just as he did, a big man, probably two inches taller than Bolan's own six foot three and twenty-five pounds heavier, tackled him. Bolan felt his attacker's shoulder push into his abdomen as the man struck him with all his weight. The impact knocked the soldier to the ground and nearly caused him to lose his second weapon of the day.

The big man grabbed the wrist of the Executioner's gun hand and slammed it hard against the floor. At the same time, he drove a big fist into Bolan's face, causing an explosion of white light to flash behind the Executioner's eyes. The weight on his chest forced him to gasp through his mouth for air. Blood trickled from his nose into his mouth. His assailant's hand dripped crimson as he brought it back for another strike. Bolan saw a figure run past him. When the runner spoke, he immediately recognized the voice as Vega's.

"Kill the motherfucker," the drug lord snarled.

Then he was gone.

Bolan saw the fist plummet toward his face like an elevator car with a snapped cable. Bolan felt his left eye begin to swell shut almost immediately, and he wondered whether the last blow had cracked his eye socket. With one arm gripped by his assailant and the other pinned underneath the man's big body, Bolan knew reaching a second weapon was impossible. He pushed up his right arm anyway, curled his wrist and tried to point the Desert Eagle's muzzle at the man.

Eyes narrowed, cheeks flushed with rage, the guy drew back

his fist, ready to deliver another blow to his opponent's head. Then a black cylinder swooped down from above the two combatants and cracked Bolan's assailant in the face, tipping him to the side. A vicious side kick to the head helped push the guy the rest of the way to the floor. As Bolan's assailant rolled onto his back, a shotgun blast delivered by Blancanales left him DOA.

Blancanales knelt beside his friend. "That's the last of them. You okay?"

Bolan rolled painfully to his feet. He touched his eye with his left hand, then immediately withdrew his fingers. Even slight pressure sent currents of pain coursing from the eye socket into his brain. His right elbow was stiffening and swelling. He shook his head to clear the disorientation.

"I said, are you okay?" Blancanales persisted.

"Fine," Bolan lied. "You get Sampson yet?"

Blancanales shook his head. "He followed Vega out the door. I think they split up after that."

"You take Sampson," Bolan said. "I want Vega."

Blancanales nodded and departed. Spotting his submachine gun, Bolan reloaded the Desert Eagle and holstered it, then picked up the H&K from the floor. Leaning against a lab table, he ejected the partially spent clip, stuck in a new one and chambered a round. Lab techs continued to cower, along with a young man dressed in a shirt and tie. A thick sweep of hair fell across the left side of his face, and tears rolled from his eyes.

"You one of Sampson's men?" Bolan barked at a man dressed in a navy-blue suit and glasses.

The man nodded, tried to form words with quivering lips, but instead uttered an unintelligible squeak.

"What's your name?" Bolan asked.

"Thomas. Bill Thomas. I'm an executive vice president with Sampson Industries."

"So you have some authority?"

Thomas straightened some, but not enough to be threatening. "Yes, yes, I do."

"Good," Bolan said. "You make damn sure these lab techs

remain here. Got it? Anyone gets caught in the cross fire, I will hold you personally responsible. You won't like that."

Thomas hunched slightly, clutched his middle as though nursing a stomachache. "Of course I won't."

Bolan retraced his steps through the building and inventoried his wounds. His right arm felt stiff but unbroken. His left eye was swelling shut, eliminating that side's peripheral vision. His head was splitting like a cantaloupe slammed in a car door. Still, he counted himself lucky that Vega had bolted rather than taken a moment and shot Bolan while he was helpless. That, Bolan vowed, would prove to be Vega's undoing.

This round had gone to the drug lord. The final round would go to the Executioner.

19

Bethesda, Maryland

A fusillade of bullets ripped through the sliding glass door that led from the backyard into the family room, which then opened into the dining room and kitchen. Slugs flew into walls, couches and chairs, knocked framed family pictures to the floor. The gunners were destroying Pitt's home, and it stood to reason they planned no less for the DEA director himself.

But first they had to get through Lyons.

A trio of gunners followed shortly behind the bursts of bullets tearing through the house. The intruders fired intermittently at shadows, moving with a bulldozer's subtlety. Each invader wore black clothing and a black mask, which covered all facial features except eyes and mouths. The distinctive curves of one member of the hit team told Lyons he faced a coed band of killers.

Their methods surprised him. Obviously they wanted to make a big noise, distract and intimidate their victims before killing them, then get the hell out of the house in a hurry. But they were also sure to draw police attention.

With the Ingram spitting flames and shell casings, Lyons fired the machine pistol into the pack of killers. Bullets punched through the midsections, pelvic areas and upper thighs of two invaders. He pummeled the third invader with a burst to the chest. His opponents down, Lyons sprinted into the family room to finish off the shooters and check the backyard for more trouble. Two of them—a man and a woman—continued to breathe. Glassy eyes peering through eye slits in the mask tipped him that they were slipping into shock. The man who had taken several shots to the chest was dead.

Slipping the Ingram to his left hand, Lyons snatched the Colt Python from its rigging and plowed a .357 slug into the man and woman, thereby eliminating any further threat to himself, Glynn or other innocents. He holstered the Python and passed through what remained of the patio door.

Cool, moist air was the first thing to hit his face.

A rifle butt against the jaw was the second.

Catching the attack with his peripheral vision, Lyons saved his own life by rolling with the impact. Even with a glancing blow, though, the Able Team leader reeled, tried to will collapsing legs to steel themselves and unfocused eyes to sharpen. Unable to get his bearings, he clutched the Ingram and fired a wild spray. He heard the slugs strike concrete and brick, not flesh.

As his vision cleared, Lyons saw his black-clad assailant shoulder the rifle and aim at center mass. At that distance a rifle slug easily would pierce his Kevlar vest. Lyons had less than a second to discern this, knowing in his heart rather than his head he was about to die.

Lyons pointed the machine pistol at his enemy even as the man's finger tightened on the trigger.

Neither got a chance to fire.

A weapon fired repeatedly from above and behind Lyons. Bullets struck the hardman in the face, throat and chest, whipsawing his body crazily.

Though he knew before he looked, Lyons turned to see to

whom he owed his life. Pitt stood in the window of his study, a .44 revolver clasped in both hands, his eyes and gun seeking another target. Lyons gave him a thumbs-up, but Pitt didn't return it. Lyons doubted the guy was nursing a grudge so much as unwilling to take either hand from his handgun.

Tompkins appeared in the window frame next to Pitt, placed a hand on his chest and gently moved the DEA director from view, inserting himself between the boss and the open window.

Okay, so maybe I was wrong about the guy, Lyons admitted to himself grudgingly. Maybe he's got more ass then I credited him for. Probably should thank him when all this is over.

Sounds of battle from within the house caught Lyons's attention. He heard guns thunder, glass shatter. Without hesitation, he entered the house, reloading the Ingram on the run. He attuned his combat senses for signs of danger, letting his stinging jaw remind him of what happened when he didn't pay attention.

GLYNN HESITATED for a moment when she heard gunfire roar upstairs and in the backyard. Chances were some as yet unseen evil was plowing through the door, cutting its way toward Pitt, his wife and their daughter. At the same time, it was evident the Justice Department agent in back was taking fire, possibly in need of assistance. Admittedly the guy was an asshole, but personalities weren't a factor in a firefight. It was a matter of duty to help a fellow officer in trouble.

The question was, which officer needed help first?

Two men swinging a battering ram knocked the front door from its moorings, while two more burst into the house and raked the first floor with autofire.

The officer most in need of help, she decided, was her.

Positioning herself behind a heavy oak armoire filled with china and crystal, Glynn raised the Glock and fired several shots into the cluster of black-clad hardmen forcing their way into the house. One of her shots ran through a shooter's arm and swung him around, causing him to fire wildly as he spun. Two others dropped the battering ram, fisted pistols and sprinted in different directions.

The man approaching the stairs became Glynn's first priority. Drawing down on him, she squeezed off four shots. At least two slugs hit the man's torso. Kevlar plating halted their progress and saved his life. Still, the force spun him and knocked him to the ground. Rolling onto his back, the man raised head and hand and prepared to return fire. Before he could, though, Glynn's Glock boomed, punching a bullet into his nose. She was looking for her next target before the dead man's skull smacked against the floor.

Fleetingly, she wished there had been time for her to outfit herself with communications headgear and a protective vest before all hell had broken loose. She wanted to talk with those huddled upstairs, tell them to use the precious seconds they had to fortify their position.

Gunshots brought her back into the moment.

Streams of bullets splintered wood, shattered glass and smashed fine china, eroding the already flimsy cover offered by the cabinet. Glynn ducked down farther, twisted around the cabinet and returned fire as best she could.

Intuition told her that without help she was living on borrowed time.

The Glock's jacket locked back.

She burrowed in behind the cabinet, ejected the pistol's clip and opened an ammo pouch located on the left side of the shoulder rig, opposite the holster. As she withdrew the fresh clip, a hot pain lanced through her left shoulder, causing her to drop the ammo. A slug drilled through the cabinet, ripping into her shoulder. The slug tore muscles and nerves, shattered bone as it tried to pass through her body. Grinding her teeth against the pain, Glynn willed the arm to pick up the small box of ammunition that lay just inches from her left hand.

The arm and hand remained paralyzed at her side. Her other hand clutched an empty pistol. Just as she figured she was good as dead, blasts from a submachine gun told her otherwise.

The Justice Department agent entered the house, his jaw swollen, his hair sweat-soaked and matted against his head. Gripping the Ingram in both hands, he unloaded streams of lead into the final gunners, filled the room with a blazing figure eight of 9 mm rounds. The slugs struck arms, necks, chests and heads as he fired upon Glynn's attackers.

He didn't ease off the trigger until both men lay on the ground, dead. Even when he let up, it seemed he did so only grudgingly.

Ejecting the clip, he slammed a fresh one into the Ingram's butt, then jacked a round into the chamber.

"Any more upstairs?" he asked without looking at her.

She shook her head, the motion sending waves of pain through her shoulder. The agent disappeared for few moments, probably checking for more intruders. Glynn heard more gunshots outside before he returned.

"Escape vehicle," Lyons said when he returned.

He dropped to his knees beside her and with surprising gentleness rolled her onto her back, inspecting her wound. "You're losing a lot of blood," he said. She strained to hear him, process and understand his words as though a great distance separated them. "But you'll live. Just shut up and stay still."

She did just that even though the screaming pain in her shoulder made it difficult to do so.

Relaxing became easier when blood loss and shock plunged her into merciful blackness.

Roswell, Georgia

AS HE REALIZED he was sealed in the stairwell, Victor Sampson felt his hands begin to shake and his heart pound. A warm moisture spread across the front of his pants as he wet himself. The last action caused self-loathing to surge from the depths of his soul. With excruciating effort, he pushed down the panic and self-hate and concentrated on escaping the building.

After the laboratory debacle, he had slipped down a stairwell at the front of the building. The stairs led into the first-floor lobby. At the bottom, Sampson discovered the steel door was shut. He had lost his plastic security cards. Or had he handed them to his trusted assistant, Richard Ahern, for safekeeping before the bastard disappeared?

He couldn't remember now. Not that it mattered.

Longingly he stared through the rectangular window of re-inforced glass fitted just above the knob and wished he were on the other side of the door. The lobby and the front door mocked him, dangling the promise of freedom in his face. Through the big glass windows of the building's front, he saw midnight-blue skies and the lush lawn illuminated by halogen spotlights.

Sampson hadn't been outside in hours. He wondered what it was like. Was it cool? Were crickets chirping? Would he ever again know freedom?

From above, he heard the whisper of footsteps. He turned and saw the stocky commando descending the steps toward him, the shotgun leading the way.

Blood pounded in Sampson's ears. His throat throbbed. Lips and teeth quivered involuntarily.

He hated the fear. Hated himself. Fleetingly he imagined what the scandal would mean for the Sampson family name. As scared as he was, there was only one way to redeem himself and that was to kill this man and escape, forget the whole thing ever happened.

"This can go one of two ways," he heard the commando say-ing as he approached Sampson.

Probably so. And Sampson planned to make it go his way. It was a desperate, almost pitiful ploy, but it might work.

He raised the .380 pistol, but too late. Shotgun blasts echoed through the stairwell, their brutal payload destroying his torso. Mercifully he would never know how undignified his bloody corpse looked, bloodied and balled up at the bottom of the stairs.

BOLAN BOLTED into the woods outside the warehouse-drug lab. His gait was steady, his breath came and went in even pulls as he jogged quietly, trailing Vega into the trees and underbrush that surrounded the building. Bolan gripped the H&K subgun as he ran. His left eye throbbed each time his feet struck the ground.

Training his ears, Bolan heard heavy footfalls and strained

breathing ahead. The warrior picked up the pace, tuning his senses into his surroundings as he moved deeper into the brush. A third set of footsteps, a snapping twig to Bolan's right caught his attention. A dark shape hurtled from the bushes toward him.

Bolan sidestepped the attacker, but as the man passed, a blade sliced through the flesh of the Executioner's forearm and caused him to drop the SMG.

The man whirled and faced his adversary. He clutched the knife, now smeared with Bolan's blood, and was drawing a pistol from his hip holster. The soldier had noticed a fallen M-16 as he had exited the building, guessed that the man had ditched his weapon in haste because of a jam or other mechanical problem. He hadn't stopped long enough to inspect the assault rifle and verify his theory.

Part of Bolan had expected to encounter the guy again before the night was over. Hell, he had hoped so. The Executioner didn't want a crazed, desperate hardman running loose near a residential area. It was a ready-made hostage situation, and he would have felt guilty if an innocent family had gotten caught in the maelstrom of his war, if innocent blood had been shed because he let a dangerous man go.

The gun. Bolan needed to neutralize the gun and the knife.

There wasn't enough time and space for the warrior to draw one of his own weapons without catching a bullet before he cleared leather. Bolan needed to gain control of the man's pistol hand immediately.

He stepped into his opponent, gripped the wrist of the man's shooting hand before it cleared the holster, forced it to stay down. He pulled the man forward, knocking him off balance. Simultaneously he delivered a back fist that pulped the man's nose, knocked his back and exposed his throat. Bolan followed through with an elbow strike to the throat.

The result was instantaneous. The man dropped his weapons, reeling until he fell against a tree. Slowly he slid down along its rough surface until he settled on his buttocks, groaning and gasping for air. Bolan's leg thundered forward in a side kick. The outer edge of his foot connected with the man's throat, crushing his windpipe. For a moment, Bolan's opponent sucked desperately for air before his hands settled into his lap. His head tipped to one side at an odd angle. Dead eyes caught Bolan's own.

The conflict took only moments, but it allowed Vega to gain a greater lead over Bolan, who, after picking up the H&K on the run, was moving double time to find the drug lord.

THOUGH A SLENDER MAN, Emilio Vega wasn't an athlete, a fact to which his body attested as he propelled himself through the forest. His lungs burned and his throat felt raw as he wheezed for breath. The trail, probably worn into the forest floor by neighborhood children, met his footsteps with unforgiving hardness.

As a younger man, Vega hadn't participated in organized sports, but always had been in good enough shape to do his job whether it entailed running from cops, clambering down a fire escape after a hit or going toe-to-toe with a mouthy pusher. Financially the years had been kind to him. But the comforts of wealth and the complacency of having a veritable army at his disposal had enticed him into a more sedentary existence.

It was a safe bet either of those two bastards who had just destroyed the prototype lab was in better shape than him. Judging by their hardware, they were also better armed, almost certainly better trained than he was. They carried submachine guns and assault rifles; he had a pistol.

Vega was outgunned and outmanned, but he'd be damned if he'd surrender. He hadn't survived this long to give up when he found himself alone.

The drug lord eyed each side of the trail. Trees, brush and weeds protected both sides, offered ample cover.

If he couldn't outrun the SOBs, he could at least outfox them. Staying on the trail, taking the most obvious path was a no-win idea. He pushed himself through the brush, settling into the cool grass, cursing softly as low-lying branches scratched at his hands, neck and face.

He checked the load on his pistol and settled in. Anything,

he decided, that came down that path was dead meat, whether friend or foe.

He tried to regain his breath, knowing the huffing would give him away. Slowly he laid himself on the ground, stretching his legs behind him, tangling them with the underbrush. As he listened for footfalls, he recalled his retreat from the drug lab. Seeing so many of his men dead or dying had caused him to panic, to flee. The flight response felt foreign and shameful to him. Vega thrived on scaring others, watching them cry, hyperventilate, piss themselves, whatever, as they begged for life. During his career, he had held the power of life and death over hundreds of people, countless more if you counted those who had used and often died from the drugs he sold.

Until the past forty-eight hours, he couldn't remember the last time someone had held the power of life and death over him. Now it had happened with alarming frequency, and he hated every minute of it. So he had bolted, left Estevez to fight his fight for him. If it had cost the big bodyguard his life, so what? That's what he paid the bastard for, wasn't it? Estevez was a bare-knuckle brawler, a thug.

I'm no thug, Vega thought. I'm a businessman. Businessmen use brains and strategy to win. I'm smarter than this crazy bastard who's been chasing me for the last couple of days. Running isn't the answer.

So he waited in the underbrush, feeling the ground pressing moist and cold through his shirt. Sweat from exertion rolled down his forehead, wetted his eyes. As he rested, his breath slowed.

Slowed, that was, until he heard the soft scrape of a footstep against soil. As he gripped the gun, the drug lord's breath again accelerated. He peered ahead, waiting for the Feds to descend upon him. Trying to convince himself he wasn't scared, Vega scanned the area around him, saw nothing but the black skeletons of trees. He smelled his own sweat and the stench of a dead animal rotting somewhere nearby. Occasionally he heard a raccoon, possum or other small animal scurry somewhere in the brush.

Vega shivered, knowing he wasn't alone. It wasn't the small animals he feared. At least one of the black-clad Feds was out there, pursuing him, ready to end his life. Crawling sensations registered all over his body, as if one thousand unseen eyes watched him. The hairs on the back of his neck rose against his shirt collar, and gooseflesh rippled along his arms and back.

He stood to walk away from this entire debacle with both hands empty. Two children and countless associates dead. Houses and cars seized, bank accounts frozen, a hobbled organization unable to defend its territories against hostile takeovers.

Emilio Vega back at the same place he started: penniless. At least, he hoped, he could make those responsible for his plight suffer. Make them pay restitution with their blood.

As BOLAN FORGED AHEAD, he slowed his pace, engaging all his senses rather than blindly pursuing his quarry. The sounds he needed—footsteps, breaking branches, strained breath—had disappeared. That meant one of two things—either Vega had outdistanced Bolan and perhaps had gotten away, or he lay in wait somewhere, ready to ambush the warrior as he happened along the trail.

Bolan called upon his senses, his training and experience as a jungle fighter. He stepped off the trail, blended with surrounding trees and foliage, melded with his surroundings. Crouching, he slipped from tree to tree, making their shadows his own. Through his crepe-soled shoes, he sensed as much as felt each rock and stick, stepping from them before they snapped under his weight and betrayed his position.

His forearm throbbed from the knife wound. His elbow still hurt from the encounter with the big hardman. He had taken a moment to dress the knife wound before blood loss drained too much of his energy. The knife had bit deep, and Bolan doubtless would need medical attention, something well beyond a field dressing, when events concluded here. As it was, he tried to ignore the pain while paying attention for any signs that he had lost too much blood.

His nose rather than his ears alerted him to his prey. The smell of perspiration mixed with cologne was faint but strong enough to tip Bolan to Vega's presence. The smell told him the man was near, but gave little indication of his precise whereabouts. In the deep brush, Bolan knew he could thrash several yards in any direction before he came upon the drug lord.

He crouched and waited for telltale sounds to betray the drug kingpin's position. At this point, if Vega bolted, Bolan was close enough to give chase easily. He had the seconds he needed to pinpoint the drug lord's position. At present, seconds were as valuable as hours and he planned to make use of them.

Straining to cut through the chirp of crickets, the rattle of branches as breezes passed through them, Bolan dissected the various noises, pulled them apart and categorized them, listened for those distinctly human.

It didn't take long. For all their intellectual superiority, humans made for easy, predictable prey.

A slight rustle of fabric gave Bolan a general direction. Homing in, plunging ahead, he picked up other sounds—breathing, crunching of small sticks as a body readjusted itself against packed dirt.

He closed in, sighted Vega. Almost lazily he pointed the H&K's muzzle in the drug lord's direction.

"It's over, Emilio," Bolan said.

Vega started, reflexively hunched his shoulders, brought in his arms for protection before gathering his wits. He rolled onto his side and swung up his gun arm. Bolan caressed the H&K's trigger, watching dispassionately as the slugs riddled Vega.

Pulling himself erect, Bolan went to the drug lord, pushed him onto his back with a toe. Sure that Vega was dead, Bolan began the return trip to the drug lab. He would let the authorities retrieve the body, let Brognola stroke egos with the Florida and Georgia police, the DEA and anyone else who wanted to complain about this latest black op.

For the first time since he had met with Brognola at Stony Man Farm and heard of Vega's plan, the muscles of Bolan's shoulders and back loosened as his latest battle came to an end.

Epilogue

Stony Man Farm, Virginia

"So they offered me a job, Hal," Lyons stated. It was the following afternoon and Lyons, Brognola, Bolan and Blancanales were in the farmhouse basement seated around a large table in the facility's War Room. The three warriors had reconvened at the ultrasecret facility late the previous night, disappeared into their bedrooms to grab some sleep, promising Brognola they would meet the following afternoon for a debriefing. Mission controller Barbara Price joined them a few minutes later.

"Pitt offered you a job?" Brognola said as he chewed an unlit cigar. "Why the hell would he do that?"

Lyons shrugged. "Man knows class, Hal. I was incredible in Maryland, a fighting machine unleashed."

"Especially when you took a gun butt to the face, eh, Carl?" Blancanales said.

Lyons ignored him. "Admit it, Hal. I kicked some ass. We all did."

Brognola nodded. "You always do. I suppose this is where I beg you to stay, right, Carl?"

"With Carl, begging's optional," Blancanales said, smiling. "A good stroke to the ego might help with job retention."

Few people could get away speaking like that to Lyons. Blancanales could; the two men, along with Hermann "Gadgets" Schwarz, formed Able Team.

"I think you guys all are great," Brognola said. "You know that."

Bolan felt impatient with banter.

"How's Agent Glynn doing?" he asked. Price, the slim, honey-blond mission controller, gave him a dark look, which he ignored. "And Detective Waters," he added.

"I talked to Pitt this morning," Brognola said. "Glynn remains hospitalized in Maryland. Her wounds aren't life threatening, but it might be a while before she regains full use of her arm. Pitt said she might even have to leave the agency on disability."

"Too bad," Bolan said.

Brognola nodded. "Pitt assured me he won't leave her hanging. She helped save his life. He'll take care of her."

"Guy didn't do shit for me," Lyons groused.

Brognola continued. "Waters is expected back at work soon. The head wound probably hurts like hell, but he's okay. Guess he's going to get a commendation for saving Pitt's life. Should look good in his personnel file."

"I didn't get any damn commendation," Lyons said.

Brognola swiveled his chair, leveled his gaze at Lyons. "What the hell's eating you, Carl?"

Lyons's own gaze didn't waver. "We put our lives on the line out there. I took a hit to the head, Mack got his arm sliced, Pol damn near got killed in a stairwell. Nobody even knows who the hell we are. Sometimes it just gets to me, okay?"

"You don't feel appreciated," Blancanales said. It wasn't a question.

"Hell, no, I don't."

"How about a vacation, Carl," Brognola suggested. "You go

to Miami for a couple of days. Let off some steam. Would you feel appreciated then?"

"Appreciated and hung over," Blancanales muttered.

Lyons straightened in his chair. A glimmer of a smile flitted across his face. Bolan knew visions of hard drinking and womanizing filled Lyons's head. "Four days."

"All right," Brognola said. "On one condition."

"What's that?"

"You come back with a sweeter disposition."

"Hell, Hal," Lyons said, "I can't promise that."

"Think about it."

"What happened with Sampson Industries?" Bolan asked. "Any more cleanup work needed there?"

Brognola shook his head. "Nothing the IRS, the DEA or the FBI can't handle," he said. "Sampson wisely kept his business separate from his partnership with Vega. He has no living heirs, so the shares probably will transfer to someone else or be sold on the open market, depending on what arrangements he made. My guess is the company will continue on in some form or fashion. The *New York Times* and the *Wall Street Journal* are having a hell of a field day with it, though."

"It's a scandal," Bolan said, "and a damn shame. None of it ever had to come to this. Sampson let greed and revenge cloud his judgment and it cost him his life. Same for Vega. He could have walked away a year ago and retired somewhere with his millions. He had to keep pushing for more."

"The police seized all the equipment at the drug lab, gutted the building," Brognola said. "The lab techs are being investigated for their roles in synthesizing the drug. My guess is the Feds will charge them with something."

Brognola looked at Bolan. "What about you, Striker? Medics say you need to let that arm heal for a few days before hitting the road again."

Before Bolan could speak, Price interjected. "He's staying here. He needs time to heal. He's too stubborn to take it for himself."

Bolan stayed quiet. She was right; his battered body craved rest. Besides, the look in Price's eyes told him if he wanted to take issue with her, he would find himself in a fight he couldn't win.

Stony Man is deployed against an armed
invasion on American soil...

THE THIRD PROTOCOL

As the violence in the Holy Land reaches critical mass,
the Arab world readies to involve itself militarily in the
conflict between Israel and the Palestinians. Only Stony Man
and the Oval Office understand the true horror behind the
bloodshed: a decades-old conspiracy and a plan involving
highly trained, well-equipped, well-funded moles, planted
in every Arab nation, now activated for the final act—
nuking the Middle East into oblivion.

STONY MAN

*Available in
June 2003
at your favorite
retail outlet.*

Or order your copy now by sending your name, address, zip or postal code, along with
a check or money order (please do not send cash) for $6.50 for each book ordered
($7.99 in Canada), plus 75¢ postage and handling ($1.00 in Canada), payable to Gold
Eagle Books, to:

In the U.S.
Gold Eagle Books
3010 Walden Avenue
P.O. Box 9077
Buffalo, NY 14269-9077

In Canada
Gold Eagle Books
P.O. Box 636
Fort Erie, Ontario
L2A 5X3

GOLD EAGLE®

Please specify book title with your order.
Canadian residents add applicable federal and provincial taxes.

GSM65